BECOMING ANDY HUNSINGER

Jere' M. Fishback

Published by
NineStar Press
PO Box 91792
Albuquerque, New Mexico, 87199
www.ninestarpress.com

Warning: This book contains scenes of dubious consent and mentions of suicide.

Print ISBN # 978-1-947139-62-6
Cover by Natasha Snow
Edited by Jason Bradley

It's 1976, and Anita Bryant's homophobic "Save Our Children" crusade rages through Florida. When Andy Hunsinger, a closeted gay college student, joins in a demonstration protesting Bryant's appearance in Tallahassee, his straight boy image is shattered when he is "outed" by a TV news reporter. In the months following, Andy discovers just what it means to be openly gay in a society that condemns love between two men and wonders if his friendship with Travis, a devout Christian who's fighting his own sexual urges, can develop into something deeper.

Dedication

This book is dedicated to the founders of Florida State University's Alliance for Gay Awareness. I remember each of you as though I saw you yesterday: Dave, Tony, Wayne, Dwight, Dan, Julie, and Ollie Lee in his colorful jumpsuits.

Being yourself back then was never easy, but we stood up for each other and I believe we changed things for the better.

I truly do.

"It takes courage to grow up and become who you really are."

E. E. Cummings

One

ON MY SEVENTH birthday, my parents gave me a Dr. Seuss book, *The Cat in the Hat.*

I still have the book; it rests on the shelf above my desk, along with other Seuss works I've collected. Inside *The Cat in the Hat*'s cover, my mother wrote an inscription, using her precise penmanship.

"Happy Birthday, Andy. As you grow older, you'll realize many truths dwell within these pages. Much love, Mom and Dad."

Mom was right, of course. She most always was. My favorite line is this one:

"Be who you are and say what you feel because those who mind don't matter and those who matter don't mind."

LORETTA MCPHAIL WAS a notorious Tallahassee slumlord. On a steamy afternoon, in August 1976, she spoke to me in her North Florida drawl: part magnolia, part crosscut saw.

"The rent's one twenty-five. I'll need first, last, and a security deposit, no exceptions."

McPhail wore a short-sleeved shirtwaist dress, spectator pumps, and a straw hat with a green plastic windowpane sewn into the brim. Her skin was as pale as cake flour. A gray moustache grew on her wrinkled upper lip, and age spots peppered the backs of her hands. Her eyeglasses had lenses so thick her gaze looked buggy.

I'd heard McPhail held title to more than fifty properties in town, all of them cited multiple times for violation of local building codes. She owned rooming houses, single-family homes, and small apartment buildings, mostly in neighborhoods surrounding Florida State University's campus. Like me, her tenants sought cheap rent; they didn't care if the roof leaked or the furnace didn't work.

The Franklin Street apartment I viewed with McPhail wasn't much: a living room and kitchen, divided by a three-quarter wall; a bedroom with windows looking into the rear and side yards; and a bathroom with a wall-mounted sink, a shower stall, and a toilet with a broken seat. In each room, the plaster ceilings bore water marks. The carpet was a leopard skin of suspicious-looking stains, and the whole place stank of mildew and cat pee.

McPhail's building was a two-storied, red-brick four-plex with casement windows that opened like book covers, a Panhandle style of architecture popular in the 1950s. Shingles on the pitched roof curled at their edges. Live oaks and longleaf pines shaded the crabgrass lawn, and skeletal azaleas clung to the building's exterior.

In the kitchen, I peeked inside a rust-pitted Frigidaire. The previous tenant had left gifts: a half-empty ketchup bottle, another of pickle relish. A carton of orange juice with an expiration date three months past sat beside a tub of margarine.

Out in the stairwell, piano music tinkled—a jazzy number I didn't recognize.

McPhail clucked her tongue and shook her head. "I've told Fergal— and I mean several times—to close his door when he plays, but he never does. I'm not sure *why* I put up with that boy."

McPhail pulled a pack of Marlboros from a pocket in the skirt of her dress. After tapping out two cigarettes, she jammed them between her lips. She lit both with a brushed-chrome Zippo, then gave me one.

I puffed and tapped a toe, letting my gaze travel about the kitchen. I studied the chipped porcelain sink, scratched Formica countertops, and drippy faucet. Blackened food caked the range's burner pans. The linoleum floor's confetti motif had long ago disappeared in high-traffic areas. Okay, the place was a dump. But the rent was cheap, and campus was less than a mile away. I could ride my bike to classes *and* to my part-time job as caddy at the Capital City Country Club.

Still, I hesitated.

The past two years, I'd lived in my fraternity house with forty brothers. I took my meals there, too. If I rented McPhail's apartment, I'd have to cook for myself. What would I eat? Where would I shop for food?

Other questions flooded my brain. Where would I wash my clothes? And how did a guy open a utilities account? The apartment wasn't furnished. Where would I purchase a bed? What about a dinette and living room furniture?

And how much did such things cost? It all seemed so *complicated.* Still...

Lack of privacy at the fraternity house would pose a problem for me this year. Over summer break—back home in Pensacola—I'd experienced my first sexual encounter with another male, a lanky serviceman named Jeff Dellinger, age twenty-four. Jeff was a second lieutenant from Eglin Air Force Base. I met him at a sand volleyball game behind a Pensacola Beach hotel, and he seemed friendly. I liked his dark hair, slim physique, and ready smile, but wasn't expecting anything personal to happen between us.

After all, I was a "straight boy," right?

We bought each other beers at the tiki bar, and then Jeff invited me up to his hotel room. Once we reached the room, Jeff prepared two vodka tonics. My drink struck like snake venom, and then my brain fuzzed. Jeff opened a bureau drawer; he produced a lethal-looking pistol fashioned from black metal. The pistol had a matte finish and a checked grip.

"Ever seen one of these?" Jeff asked.

I shook my head.

"It's an M1911—official air-force issue. I've fired it dozens of times."

Jeff raised the gun to shoulder height. He closed one eye, focused his other on the pistol's barrel sight. "Shooting's almost...sensual." Then he looked at me. "It's like sex, if you know what I mean."

I shrugged, not knowing what to say.

Jeff handed the pistol to me. It weighed more than I'd expected, between two and three pounds. I turned it this way and that, admiring its sleek contours. The grip felt cold against my palm and a shiver ran through me. I'd never fired a handgun, never thought to.

"Is it loaded?" I asked.

Jeff bobbed his chin. "One bullet's in the firing chamber, seven more in the magazine; it's a semiautomatic."

After I handed Jeff the gun, he returned it to his bureau's drawer while I sipped my drink, feeling woozier by the minute. Jeff sat next to me, on the room's double bed. His knee nudged mine, our shoulders touched, and I smelled his coconut-scented sunscreen.

Jeff laid a hand on my thigh. Then he squeezed. "You don't mind, do you?"

I looked down at his hand while my heart thumped. *Go on, chickenshit. He wants you.*

I gazed into Jeff's dark eyes. "It's fine."

Moments later, my swim trunks lay in a corner and Jeff knelt in front of me, slurping away. Currents of pleasure crept through my limbs, and then I felt a buzzing between my legs. When I came, I thought I'd pass out. I closed my eyes and drew a deep breath. Then I watched fireworks explode inside my head.

Jesus, this feels good. Why haven't I done this before?

Thereafter, we rendezvoused several times during summer, always at the same hotel.

"I get a military discount here," Jeff explained.

I quickly learned the basics of male/male sex from Jeff, and each session proved better than the one before. During these meetings, Jeff introduced me to anal intercourse, something I'd never dreamed I would do.

The first few times, Jeff took a passive role. But then he asked me to surrender my cherry, and I acceded. Jeff's initial penetration felt painful, but soon I relaxed, and I discovered a side of myself I hadn't known existed. A fullness and warmth crept through my body as Jeff thrust inside me. The whole thing felt so...natural.

Whenever I lay in bed with Jeff, after sex, I always rested my head on his chest, and while I listened to his heartbeat I felt like a guy released from jail. I *knew* I was queer then—there was no doubt about it—and the realization made me feel a bit foolish, like I was the last guy at the party let in on the joke. I was a faggot, a fudge-packer, a butt pirate. My attempts at dating women had been a ruse—I'd only done it to fit in with my fraternity brothers—and what a waste of time it had been for all concerned.

Like most guys, I'd masturbated chronically since my early teens, and now I knew why visions of naked men crept into my thoughts whenever I did so. Now I knew why my friends' girlie magazines had never held my interest. No *wonder* showering with my PE classmates in high school had thrilled me so.

It all seems stupid in retrospect. How could I not know I was gay? But in 1976, most guys weren't in touch with their inner selves. I don't know why, but we weren't. Feelings weren't a topic of male conversation. Emotional needs took a backseat to more "important" matters: achievement, sports, and politics—"normal" concerns, if you will.

My summer with Jeff changed all that, for me at least. In the sexual sense, I had found my mother lode. I belonged in the arms of a man—I would settle for nothing else—and I was fine with it. But now fall had arrived, and I would live in Tallahassee again. I couldn't drive to Fort Walton Beach every weekend. That would mean a three-hour drive on monotonous Highway 90, passing by cow pastures and slash pine forests, just to meet up with Jeff. And how much sense did that make? I needed a boyfriend who lived nearby, and assuming I found one, I would face a few problems.

If I remained at the Lambda Chi house I'd share a room with a fraternity brother, so I'd have no privacy. Plus, the guys at Lambda Chi wouldn't understand if I dated another male, no way.

Wasn't it time I had my own place?

Now, in her run-down rental apartment, McPhail blew a stream of blue smoke. After the cloud rose to the kitchen's cobwebbed ceiling, she looked at me with her insect eyes.

"Well?" she said.

I studied my shoes and licked my lips. *Go on: do it.*

I swung my gaze to my future landlady.

Two

ON A SATURDAY evening, I arrived at the four-plex with a sofa tied to the roof of my Chevy Vega. Two ladder-back chairs occupied the backseat, along with a portable TV.

Already, I'd learned how to buy used furniture.

"Avoid Salvation Army and thrift shops," my friend Biff Schultz had told me. "Their stuff's overpriced. Buy the Friday *Democrat*, check the classifieds for garage sales. You'll find stuff cheap if you shop around, and sometimes folks will *give* you stuff if you show up toward the end of the day."

Biff had been my dorm mate our freshman year. At the time, he dressed preppy like me, but even then he displayed an irreverent streak. When I asked him to join me in pledging Lambda Chi, he looked at me like I was crazy.

"I don't have to *buy* friends, and I don't need my ass paddled, either. Go ahead and join if you want, but I have no interest."

Now, Biff was a dope-smoking nonconformist. He shared a house with two other guys, both pre-med majors like Biff. They often hosted weekend parties, and the odor of burning marijuana pervaded the rooms of their home.

I envied the freedoms Biff enjoyed. Sometimes he attended classes barefoot and shirtless. Weekends, he camped in Ocala National Forest with his housemates, or he canoed nearby rivers with his girlfriend. Also, Biff was a dedicated nudist. At home he paraded around in his birthday suit; his cock wagged and his balls swung to and fro. He'd lie on his stomach, on a blanket in his fenced backyard, displaying his beefy butt while he studied a biology text.

"Clothes are a pain in the ass," he told me. "Who needs them?"

I guess Biff's nudity didn't bother his roomies—they hardly seemed to notice—but it took me a while to adjust to his immodest ways. I found it hard to ignore his muscled butt cheeks and stogie wiener; they made me think indecent thoughts.

Aye-yi-yi.

Two weeks had passed since I'd moved into my apartment. Already, I had collected a Barcalounger, a floor lamp, a bookcase, a rocking chair, a card table with folding legs, and two aluminum chairs. I slept on a comfortable queen-size bed. All these items had cost me less than fifty dollars total.

My folks gave me flatware, linens, and kitchen utensils. My grandma gave me her old set of Melmac dinnerware, along with a Betty Crocker cookbook, published in 1952. I opened accounts with the electric and telephone companies, and also joined a food co-op. In exchange for working at the co-op four hours per week, I could buy provisions there at a discount.

My apartment was not air-conditioned, but my folks had given me a box fan. I placed the fan on my bedroom's windowsill; it kept me cool at night. The place was no Taj Mahal, but it was mine. Finally, I had my independence and privacy. *I* set the rules in my apartment.

Now, as I pulled into our little gravel parking area, a couple my age tossed a Frisbee back and forth in our rear yard. The guy was Fergal, the piano player who lived downstairs. The girl I'd never seen. They were both barefooted, and Fergal wore only blue jeans. Sunlight reflected in marmalade ringlets cascading down his neck. The girl wore cut-off denim shorts and a halter top. Her dark hair grew past her shoulders.

I'd spoken to Fergal once or twice while toting furniture up the stairwell. His door was usually open, and he'd wave. We had exchanged names—he'd told me he was Australian and a music major at FSU—but I didn't know much more about him than that.

Now, while I loosened the rope encircling the sofa, he approached. I was six foot one, and he was nearly as tall as me, with a slender frame and emerald eyes. A riot of copper-colored freckles danced across his nose and cheeks.

His gaze traveled to the sofa, and then he spoke to me in his Aussie accent.

"Been shopping again, mate?"

I nodded while untying a slipknot.

"This thing's a beast," I said. "Could you help me with it?"

We grunted while maneuvering the sofa up the stairwell. Fergal's stringy muscles flexed while sweat beaded on his forehead. His chest heaved and his mane of curls bounced here and there as we labored. After we'd positioned the sofa against my living room wall, I offered him a cold beer.

"Thanks," he said between breaths, "but I must go 'cause Gina's serving me dinner at her place. Some other time, eh?"

When we descended the stairs, Fergal in the lead, his ass cheeks twitched in his jeans and his shoulder muscles rolled under his freckled skin. A tingle arose in my undershorts, and I licked my lips while I pondered how it might feel to touch Fergal intimately.

Then I shook my head.

Easy, Andy, he may be friendly, but you don't hit on straight boys.

IN THE MID-1970S, FSU operated on the quarter system: fall, winter, spring, and summer terms. Fall term began the Tuesday after Labor Day. By then I'd painted all the rooms in my apartment. I had scrubbed the bathroom and even replaced the toilet seat.

One weekend, my folks visited. They stayed down the street, at the Travel Lodge. My dad hung Venetian blinds at my windows while Mom stocked the kitchen cupboards with things she thought necessary: salt and pepper shakers, a sack of sugar and another of flour, boxes of macaroni and cheese, and Hamburger Helper. She gave me bottles of garlic salt, oregano, black peppercorns, and dried rosemary leaves.

My folks brought an ice chest from Pensacola, too. They filled my freezer with packages of ground beef, chicken legs, pork chops, catfish fillets, and boxes of frozen vegetables.

"You'll need to cook healthy food," Mom said in her sternest junior-high English teacher voice. "No eating at burger joints."

Each day, I spent a half hour with my grandma's cookbook; I studied culinary techniques: sautéing, searing, steaming, frying, and so forth. At the co-op, I bought cooking oil, vinegar, breadcrumbs, spaghetti noodles, and jars of pasta sauce. I visited a discount department store to buy a set of measuring spoons, a spatula, a steam basket, a measuring cup, and a colander. I learned how to fry chicken and catfish, and how to steam fresh vegetables like yellow squash, zucchini, and broccoli.

Cooking became a game for me, a challenge like a jigsaw puzzle. The hardest part was getting everything ready to eat at the same time. Initially, I had problems with overcooking or undercooking certain dishes. But after a few weeks, I developed a better sense for when a recipe was ready for the table.

A month into my tenancy, Mom phoned. "How are things?"

"Not bad; keeping house isn't so difficult."

"Oh, *really*?"

I chuckled before I answered. "Yeah, Mom, I'm the new Betty Crocker of Franklin Street."

After I hung up the phone, my gaze traveled about the barren walls of my silent apartment, and then I shook my head. Maybe I *was* becoming an accomplished cook, but what good were my newly acquired skills if I ate my meals alone? Wasn't it time I found myself a boyfriend?

Who would he be? And where would I find him?

Three

EVERY SATURDAY AND Sunday morning, I rose at six thirty, showered, shaved, and then slipped into a pique polo shirt with a Capital City Country Club logo embroidered on the chest. I put on khaki slacks and a pair of golf shoes. After a hasty breakfast, I pedaled my bike to the club, making sure I arrived for the earliest tee times. I caddied for rich people, ones like I'd never met before: state cabinet officers, Florida Supreme Court justices, high-flying lobbyists, and the city's most successful lawyers, doctors, and bankers.

I had landed the caddying job through a family connection, three years before.

The clubhouse pro, Byron "Bucky" Buchholtz, had served with my dad during WWII, copiloting Flying Fortresses over Germany. Dad and Bucky had been shot down twice—both times narrowly escaping capture by the enemy—and they'd remained friends ever since. Each fall, they took a trip together, to Montana or Wyoming, where they hunted elk and deer, or fly-fished for steelhead trout.

Bucky was a "man's man," a dedicated bachelor, and sports fanatic.

"Your mother excepted," he told me once, "I can't abide the company of women. They talk and talk, but never have anything worthwhile to say."

Half a head shorter than me, Bucky had wavy, prematurely gray hair and a deep suntan. He kept his waist trim through a program of rigorous calisthenics. He liked bawdy jokes, barbecue, and bourbon with branch water.

Every year, he spent the four-day Thanksgiving weekend with us in Pensacola, and every year he asked my dad to play a round of golf.

Dad always refused.

"It's no fun playing with you," Dad would tell Bucky. "You're competitive as hell, and too damned good to play with a duffer like me."

So I played a round with Bucky—sometimes two if the weather was good—at Pensacola Country Club, an elegant facility my dad could never have afforded to join on his Department of Transportation engineer's salary. Bucky enjoyed membership privileges at PCC, due to his job at Capital City. We played alongside Pensacola's elite—"fat asses," Bucky called them—a group of businessmen, lawyers, and retired colonels, the kind of guys who mixed plaids and stripes when dressing for the links.

I was never much of an athlete, but my dad taught me and my brother the basics of golf at an early age. The three of us played public courses all over northwest Florida: Crestview, De Funiak Springs, Fort Walton Beach, and the university course at Tallahassee. By the time I reached high school, I'd developed a smooth swing and reasonable consistency on the greens. My handicap drifted between eighteen and twenty-two.

Bucky, of course, was a scratch golfer—I wasn't in his league—but I offered him companionship on the golf course whenever he visited Pensacola. When we played, I only spoke when spoken to, and then I always addressed Bucky as "sir." He taught me tricks while we walked the links: foot positioning, club selection, compensation for wind, sloping lies, and wet turf. He discussed reading of greens. When I shanked a putt, muffed a pitch, or hit a lousy chip shot, he'd explain what I had done wrong—in detail.

"When you hit from the rough, open your club face a bit. Otherwise, the grass will pull your shot left."

Or "Right now, you're pitching onto a green with a wicked slope. Use your fifty-two-degree wedge. Loft the ball so it plops onto the green and doesn't roll."

Or "Stop trying to kill the ball."

Or "Don't swing with your arms. Let your body do the work; put your hips into your shot."

Once, when I was sixteen, I lit a cigarette on a tee box at PCC. As soon as I took a drag, Bucky snatched the cigarette from my lips. Then he tossed it into the branches of a gardenia bush.

"Andy, those things are garbage. They damage your health and foul the air; they have no place on a golf course."

Bucky lived on Cherokee Drive, east of the Capital City course. He shared a neat cinder-block house with his brother, Eddie and Eddie's walleyed wife, Flo.

Flo cooked meals, did laundry, and kept the house clean.

A shell-shocked Korean War veteran, Eddie spent his days puttering in his yard. He fertilized azaleas, pruned camellias, raked pine needles and oak leaves, and mowed the clover-green grass. Some days he'd sit on a lawn chair in the home's one-car garage, watching traffic pass on Cherokee Drive and staring at the cars like they were Mardi Gras floats. I don't know what sort of financial arrangement Bucky had with Eddie and Flo, but the situation seemed to work for all concerned.

When Bucky learned I would attend FSU, he phoned me in Pensacola, just before my freshman year began.

"You should caddy for me at the club. The money's good—you'll earn more on a weekend than you could flipping burgers or bagging groceries in two weeks—and you'll meet influential people in this town, those who count."

The job was a godsend. My work didn't interfere with my university classes or my study hours. As Bucky had said, the money was great. Rising early on weekends kept me from partying too hard on Friday and Saturday nights, so I didn't use drugs too often or binge-drink like most guys in the dormitory did.

My buddy Biff Schultz teased me about the job—he called my employer "Capitalist City"—and he often gave me shit about my golf attire.

"Look at Mr. Country Club. I love your outfit—the saddle shoes and all. How big's that corncob you've got stuffed up your ass?"

The Capital City course was a beauty designed by A.W. Tillinghast. Towering live oaks, long leaf pines, and magnolias framed the emerald fairways. The greens were as smooth and soft as cut-pile carpet. The clubhouse offered Tallahassee's best prime rib dinner, and the lounge served martinis so potent they could have felled a rhino. Membership typically required a three-year wait, as slots only became available when an existing member either died or quit.

The only black person I ever saw at Capital City was Rufus, an elderly man who served as the attendant in the oak-paneled men's locker room. Dressed in a white waiter's jacket, tux pants, and patent leather shoes, Rufus passed out towels and offered cologne spritzes. He made sure the porcelain sinks shone. Word had it Rufus was close to eighty years old, but his memory was sharp. He knew the name of every club member— every staffer as well—and he always addressed me as "Mr. Andrew."

By custom, six boys caddied at the club on weekends, and when my senior year at FSU began, four guys I worked with attended a private academy; they were high school age and sons of prominent club members. One kid's father was a Tallahassee city commissioner; another's dad was a former lieutenant governor. These boys were local patricians—way out of my league—and I didn't try becoming part of their world. But one caddy, a boy named Jerry Justus, I befriended when I returned to school, in the fall of 1976.

Jerry's dad was head greenskeeper at the club; he wore Dickies work clothes and lace-up boots, and I'd never once heard him raise his voice. He mowed fairways, spread fertilizer, and trimmed camellia bushes, often while whistling tunes I didn't recognize.

"Do me a favor," Jerry's dad once told me. "Whenever you pull the pin, try not to step on the edge of the cup. It's tough enough keeping the edges level, and I'll catch hell from members if the greens are less than perfect."

Jerry was a senior at Lincoln High School. About six feet tall, with broad shoulders and big hands, he parted his chestnut hair on the side. His huge, cola-colored eyes and square chin lent him a sexy aura, but Jerry suffered from stuttering. He couldn't complete a sentence without halting once or twice, and he rarely spoke, unless someone spoke to him first.

The other caddies shunned Jerry; I think they considered him socially inferior because he attended public school.

One caddy, Dustin Ausley, a slender kid with a cleft chin, freckles, and a mouthful of white teeth, liked to pick on Jerry. Dustin would mimic Jerry's stuttering—right in front of him—and the other caddies would giggle. When this happened, Jerry's cheeks would color; he'd shake his head and feign laughter himself. But I felt certain he inwardly seethed at this sort of taunting.

Who wouldn't?

I always made it a point to engage Jerry in conversation during lulls at work. We talked while hitting balls at the driving range, or while we played gin rummy in the caddies' tent. I liked his baritone voice and syrupy drawl.

Jerry fished for freshwater bass, his favorite activity. "You d-d-don't talk much w-w-when you fish," he told me.

In his wallet, he carried several snapshots of bass he'd caught in lakes surrounding Tallahassee. Each photo featured a grinning Jerry dressed in a flannel shirt, blue jeans, and a ball cap. He would hold his fishing rod in one hand and a glittering bass in the other, always with his fingers thrust inside the fish's crimson gills. In the background, cypress knees and cattails sprang from dark and placid waters. Some of Jerry's catches were huge—as long as a man's lower leg—and I could not imagine how he'd coaxed them out of water with his spindly rod.

"Do you eat the fish you catch?" I once asked him.

Jerry shook his head. "I c-c-could if I wanted, but I don't like k-k-killing things. After I catch a b-b-bass, I always release it."

Jerry's golfing performance was a mixed bag. His short game was wickedly precise, but chaos reigned when Jerry stepped into a tee box or when he swung an iron on the fairways.

"He's a Jekyll and Hyde," Bucky told me. "Any shot less than one hundred yards, he'll nail. But longer than that...look out. I never know where it's gonna go."

Once Jerry told me, "My dad stuck a p-p-putter in my hands when I was three. He thinks golf is my t-t-ticket to wealth, but I c-c-could care less about the g-g-game. I'd rather f-f-fish."

Jerry could pitch from twenty yards out and place the ball a foot or two from the cup, consistently. Once, I watched him pitch from the rough, sixty yards out, where his ball rested in a thatch of pine needles. Using a lob wedge, he popped the ball over a mature laurel oak. His shot landed on the green, and then the ball rolled right into the cup.

Jerry's putting was deadly, too. I rarely saw him two-putt, even on the larger, more sloping greens at the club. He possessed an uncanny ability to read greens and then to adjust his strokes to suit the terrain, something I couldn't seem to manage no matter how much I practiced.

Jerry's long game was another matter. He couldn't control his drives from the tee box. His shots often hooked or sliced. Bucky tried working with Jerry on this problem; they spent hours together at the club's driving range, trying to straighten out Jerry's swing, without success. The same held true when it came to Jerry's second shots on par fours and fives. Whenever he used a fairway wood or a three iron, his balls never flew where he wanted them to go.

Once, late on a Saturday afternoon when the course was empty, Jerry and I played nine holes, just before sundown, using clubs we'd borrowed from Capital City's rental closet. The second hole had a huge water hazard to the right of the fairway—a lake with mallard ducks swimming in it—and Jerry drove three consecutive shots from the tee box into the water.

The ducks squawked and flapped their wings in protest.

Jerry's lost balls were new Titleists he'd just bought at the pro shop.

"G-g-g-goddammit," Jerry cried, "I hate this f-f-fucking game."

This was the first time I'd ever heard him curse. The sound of his voice echoed in the pines while he glared at the wooden-headed driver in his hands. His face grew brick red. He strode from the tee box to a nearby live oak and then beat his driver against the tree's trunk until the club's shaft snapped in two.

Jerry looked at me and grinned like a kid on Christmas morning.

I shook my head. "You'd better hope Bucky doesn't find out you did that."

"I don't care if he does," Jerry said. "I'll pay for the club if I have to."

I made a face. "Why destroy a perfectly good driver? What's the point?"

"It feels good," Jerry said. "That's the point. Now, lend me your driver."

I drew back while knitting my eyebrows. "Only if you promise you won't break it."

Jerry's fourth drive landed two hundred yards from the tee box, in the middle of the fairway, and nowhere near the water hazard.

I whistled. "You should do that more often," I said.

Jerry gazed at me and waggled his eyebrows.

By the time we finished our nine holes, the sun had already dipped below the horizon. I had shot a forty-seven and Jerry a thirty-nine, not counting the three balls he lost to the water hazard. I told Jerry goodbye, and then I pedaled my bike home in twilight. The glow from headlights of oncoming cars made me squint, and I shivered in the cool fall air. In my mind, I replayed the round I'd played with Jerry. I analyzed where I'd made mistakes at each hole, and I almost reached home before I realized something I hadn't thought of earlier.

Jerry had ceased stuttering—quite entirely—for the duration of our round, right after he'd smashed his borrowed driver to pieces against the live oak.

I WAS A good caddy: attentive, polite, and unobtrusive. I quickly developed regular customers who requested my services, including Florida's Insurance Commissioner, Raymond Conner, a lean man from Ocala with tailored golf slacks, a smooth swing, and a treasure trove of racist jokes he liked to share with me when others couldn't overhear.

"Hey, Andy, do you know why God invented orgasm?"

"No, sir."

"So the niggers'll know when to stop fucking." Or...

"Andy, do you know why the Jews spent forty years in the desert?"

"Not really, Mr. Conner."

"Somebody dropped a nickel."

And so on...

I didn't like Conner's coarse humor—I found his jokes offensive—but wasn't in a position to complain about it. When he made his wisecracks, I'd pucker one side of my face while feigning a snicker and shaking my head. How could a guy in his lofty position be so insensitive?

I also caddied for Circuit Judge Doyle Davis, a courtly silver-haired native of Leon County and a Harvard Law graduate. Every Sunday morning at 9:00 a.m. sharp, he played in foursomes with lawyers who sometimes appeared before him during the workweek. The lawyers never discussed the cases they had before Judge Davis—that would have been ethically verboten—but they discussed other pending suits: medical malpractice claims, product liability cases, murder, or rape prosecutions.

I found these conversations fascinating. It seemed to me these men held the fates of their clients in their hands; they were demigods of a sort. And yet, these lawyers were also mortals with ordinary problems in their own personal lives, ones they sometimes discussed while golfing: wives who drank, kids with drug addictions, bad investments, and medical difficulties.

The intricacies of legal matters these men discussed intrigued me. Sometimes, while listening to them, I asked myself, could I practice law? If so, how would I perform in the courtroom? Would I flub my speeches before juries? Could I handle the pressure these guys dealt with every day?

The club paid me a minimum hourly wage required by law—not much, really—but the tips I received were stellar. Each day, after I finished work, I pedaled home with a wad of cash in my pocket, money

I needn't declare on my income tax return. My earnings covered my rent, my food bill, and even my school books.

My folks paid my tuition—that was all.

Some Saturdays, Bucky treated me to dinner at the clubhouse. I kept a pair of penny loafers at the club. Bucky would lend me a sports jacket from the pro shop, and then we'd dine alongside Tallahassee's elite.

"Order whatever you want," Bucky always told me.

I might devour a one-pound pork chop or a New York strip, accompanied by sides of au gratin potatoes and onion rings. Maybe I'd order an ice cream sundae or banana cream pie for dessert. All the members knew Bucky. While we dined, he spent much time exchanging greetings with folks passing by our table. Members sometimes greeted me as well—they patted my shoulder or mussed my hair—and their attentions made me feel light-headed.

Still...

"Don't ever forget," Bucky told me once, "we're only hired help. We are not members and never will be. Don't mistake their friendliness for social acceptance; they're a breed apart from us. They know it, and we have to remember our place, always. Understand, Andy?"

Four

BEFORE I'D MOVED to my apartment, I spent most evenings with my fraternity brothers. We played card games like Spades or Hearts, or board games like Risk and Stratego while drinking beer and smoking cigarillos. We threw keg parties. On weekends, the house teemed with sorority girls.

But I never saw my fraternity brothers now. I had placed myself on "inactive status" with Lambda Chi, meaning I didn't have to pay social dues. I avoided the house and rarely heard from the guys there. To be honest, I was through with Greek life. I wasn't part of my fraternity's day-to-day rhythm, and now, in retrospect, the whole thing seemed a bit immature.

I wasn't a kid anymore, was I?

In 1976, gay bars didn't exist in Tallahassee. But one establishment, the Pastime Tavern on Tennessee Street, offered a gathering spot for gay men, both students and townies. The size of five tennis courts, the Pastime had a U-shaped bar and a dozen pool tables in the rear. A woman known as Miss Kitty ran the place. She sold half-gallon pitchers of Budweiser for three dollars and bags of peanuts roasted in the shell for a quarter. Cigarette smoke in the bar grew so thick you couldn't see across the room. The men's toilet stank like an outhouse. Ammonia pucks resting in the urinals did little to lessen the rankness. The sink was rust-stained, and my shoe soles always stuck to the linoleum floor. The paper dispenser in the toilet stall rarely held paper. Above a battered condom machine someone had scrawled an observation with a felt-tipped pen.

"This gum chews mighty tough."

I spent considerable time at the Pastime my senior year at FSU, and never once saw a fraternity jersey there. The place catered to nonconformists of every stripe: hippies, bikers, musicians, local artisans, and so forth. Gay boys gathered on the left side of the bar; they occupied stools or sat at tables with brimming ashtrays. They smoked cigarettes and sipped from beer glasses. Broken peanut shells littered the concrete floor around them.

The gays drank and talked while scrutinizing one another. Cruising for sex was a subtle process at the Pastime: guys didn't touch one another; they only exchanged glances or conversed in lowered voices. Then, around midnight, young men paired up. They left together, and I always felt jealous, seeing them depart.

My first visits to the Pastime were uneventful. I'd grab a stool on the left end of the bar and then watch the goings-on. My sexual tastes ran toward slim guys with dark hair and eyes, young men who reminded me of Jeff Dellinger.

Some of these types frequented the Pastime, but whenever our gazes met they always looked away—a sure sign of rejection.

A few guys hit on me. A man in his thirties named Bob, with thinning blond hair and a sissy's lisp, bought me a beer. Then he asked me home, but I declined. A chubby guy my age, who I recognized from campus, struck up conversation with me on a Friday night. He brushed my thigh with his fingertips, but when he suggested we leave the bar together, I let him know it wouldn't happen.

I was desperate, but not *that* needy.

As time passed, I began to wonder if I'd ever meet a guy I found attractive—one who might also want me—but I had no success finding anyone.

Maybe my experience with Jeff was dumb luck.

Each Friday and Saturday night, I returned home from the Pastime, to my empty apartment, and then I lay on my mattress, staring at the ceiling.

Is this how it's always going to be?

Sometimes I second-guessed myself; I wondered if maybe I had made a mistake in leaving the fraternity house. Maybe I wasn't suited for the gay subculture. Was there something about me that gay men—guys my age, anyway—found unappealing? Was it so obvious I was a needy youth with little knowledge about the homosexual world and its rituals?

Nonetheless, I kept visiting the Pastime; I figured *something* would eventually happen.

And finally something did.

On a Saturday in early October, just before midnight, a guy my age took a stool next to mine at the bar. I'd seen him at the Pastime before, talking with various people, sometimes leaving with one guy or another. He was a bit taller than me and his black and wavy hair grew to his shoulders. He wore bib overalls and high-top Converse sneakers, but no shirt. A red bandana drooped from his right rear pocket. After he'd ordered a beer, he swung his gaze toward me, and then he spoke in a raspy baritone flavored by a southern Georgia drawl.

"You're always alone when I see you here. How come?"

My cheeks steamed. What should I tell him? "I'm new at this," I said.

He crinkled his forehead. "You're new at drinking beer?"

I shook my head. "At meeting guys."

A smile crept onto his lips. "Cruising's an art I haven't figured out. Some nights I win, other times I can't catch a break, know what I mean?"

I nodded but didn't say anything.

"I'm Aaron."

I told him my name, and then we shook. His hand was warm and moist. Just touching him that way, in a public place, had my pulse racing. For a moment, I felt like a schoolgirl at a dance; I couldn't think of anything more to say. Aaron sipped from his beer and smacked his lips. Dark hairs peeked at me from his armpits. His biceps looked like baseballs, and his big hands were large-knuckled. After turning toward me, he rested his feet on the stringers of his barstool. Then he gazed at me with a puzzled expression on his face.

"You're as pale as a ghost," he said. "Your hands are trembling, too. Why?"

I lowered my gaze. What an *idiot* I was. "I'm nervous," I said.

"Don't be," Aaron said. "There's nothing to be scared of."

I took a swig from my beer. Then I watched bubbles rise in my glass while my pulse raced.

"Andy?"

I looked at Aaron.

"I'll leave you alone if you want. I can—"

Say something; you're losing him.

"I don't *want* you to leave me alone. It's just..."

"What?"

"I don't know how to invite you to my place."

Aaron snickered. "I think you just did."

AARON'S GAZE TRAVELED about my living room. By now, the room was fully furnished, and rock band posters decorated the walls: the Rolling Stones, the Who, and Yes, among others. Aaron pointed to a framed copy of Max Ehrmann's *Desiderata* I'd hung over the sofa.

"I like what he says about love and not being cynical about it. Does that make me a romantic?"

I crinkled my forehead. Aaron's remark took me by surprise. Love and romance weren't topics Jeff and I had ever discussed; our relationship was purely about sex. We never went to a movie or dined at a restaurant together. We never held hands or kissed. After all, we were two men, and men didn't fall in love with each other, right?

I gestured toward the Ehrmann poster. "I read it each morning before leaving here, to prepare myself for the day."

I brought us two beers, and after we sat on the sofa, we rested our feet on a coffee table I'd found beside a dumpster. My belly did flip-flops; I couldn't believe Aaron was in my apartment and seated so close to me. I could actually feel his body heat and smell his skin. What, if anything, would happen during the next hour?

"I share a house with three friends," Aaron told me. "I have my own room, but my roommates don't know I'm gay. I can't bring guys home."

I nodded.

"It must be nice," he said, "having your privacy."

I explained about the Lambda Chi house, and how I'd moved to McPhail's building so I could live as I pleased. "It's taken some adjustment. Most evenings, I spend alone."

Aaron placed his beer bottle on the coffee table. After turning to me, he reached for my cheek and stroked it with a thumb. Right away, my heart thumped.

Aaron's dark eyes gazed into mine. "You're good-looking, Andy. Do you like me?"

I nodded.

"Can I kiss you?" Aaron asked.

Holy shit.

"I'd like that," I said.

Aaron brought his hand to the back of my neck. He pulled my face to his, and then our mouths touched. He pried my lips apart, our tongues rubbed, and our chin stubble made a scratchy noise. The kiss lasted a minute or so before Aaron broke away. He wiped his shiny lips with the back of his hand. Then, after reaching for his beer, he took a swallow.

"I like the way you kiss," he said.

I told him about Jeff and the things we'd done in bed. I spoke of the girls I'd dated, too. "But you're the first male I've kissed. Jeff's not the romantic type, and he's the only man I've ever had sex with."

Aaron crinkled the corners of his eyes. "I'd like to change that, if *you* would."

My pulse drummed inside my head. Was this how it worked? Was finding a boyfriend really so easy? I led Aaron to my bedroom. After I lit a candle on the bureau, I killed the ceiling fixture, and then our shadows appeared on a wall: two silhouettes removing clothing. Aaron kicked off his shoes and peeled off his socks. He unclipped the shoulder straps on his overalls, and they fell to his ankles. His genitals bulged in his olive-colored cotton briefs. When he slipped his thumbs into his briefs' waistband, I spoke up.

"Let me take those off."

Aaron looked at me with his eyebrows gathered, and then a smile crossed his face.

"Is that a bit of kink you have, Andy?"

I nodded. "Jeff always let me."

Aaron's hands dropped to his hips. "Be my guest."

After kneeling before Aaron, I ran my hands up the backs of his legs. Dark hair carpeted his calves and thighs; the hairs looked like raindrops streaming toward his ankles. I squeezed his butt cheeks; they felt firm and rounded. Already, he had stiffened.

"Go on," Aaron said.

I shucked his briefs south. Then I took him into my mouth. His crotch smelled musky, and I salivated at his scent. How I'd missed intimacy with another male.

Moments later, my boxers lay crumpled in a corner and Aaron lay beside me in my bed. We kissed like a pair of love-starved kids, caressing each other's private places. Waves of pleasure slithered through my limbs. We both sweated in the warm October night; our scents mingled in the still air. For a moment, I considered switching on the box fan on my windowsill, but...

No.

I *liked* sweating with Aaron. I enjoyed the smacking sounds our flesh made wherever our bodies touched, and the sour scent wafting from Aaron's armpits made me crazy with lust. Outside, our neighborhood's resident whippoorwill sang his nightly tune.

Woo-who-hoo, woo-who-hoo.

A car passed on Franklin Street; headlights swept my bedroom walls with their milky glare. I felt completely removed from the world I normally lived in, as if Aaron and I had traveled to some distant and magical location, where no one but the two of us dwelled.

At Aaron's request, I took him on his back, with his legs draped over my shoulders, the way Jeff had taught me.

When I eased partway inside him, Aaron clenched his teeth, and then a blue vein popped out on his forehead.

"Jesus, Andy, you're big."

"Are you okay?"

His chest rose and fell. "I think so, but give me a minute."

I stayed inside him, keeping still and listening to him breathe. The warmth of his gut and the scent of his skin seemed like exotic gifts.

"It's been a while," he said, "and the last guy wasn't..."

"What?"

"As *large* as you; I'm surprised your friend Jeff let you leave Pensacola."

I chuckled. "I can pull out if you want."

Aaron shook his head. "Go on."

I thrust my hips while Aaron grunted and we both sweated. Candlelight made our skin glow and our hair gleam, as if we'd just emerged from the sea. More than ever, I felt far removed from the mundane world I normally dwelled in. My heart chugged and chills ran up my spine. I shook my head in amazement while I thrust.

This is where I belong. This is what I need.

I wanted our lovemaking to last forever, but of course it didn't.

Aaron came first; he let out a wail I hoped the neighbors wouldn't hear. His irises rolled up inside his head, and then his chest heaved. I came moments later; I heard a crackling in my ears. When I closed my eyes, I saw fireworks, like my first time with Jeff. I felt my orgasm in my scalp, in the cleft of my buttocks, and even in the soles of my feet. I cried out Aaron's name, more than once. If the neighbors hadn't heard Aaron's wail, they most certainly heard my shouting. I'm sure I sounded like a lunatic.

I stayed inside Aaron while catching my breath. Neither of us spoke. We listened to the whippoorwill's tune as our pulses slowed. Sweat trickled from my armpits and scalp. My hips and thighs stuck to Aaron's butt as though our skins were glued together. I ran my fingers through his damp hair; I savored its thickness while I shook my head in amazement.

How had I survived three years of college without this? I'd been a fool, but no longer.

No longer, Andy.

NEXT MORNING, I woke to find Aaron's arm draped across my belly and his cheek resting on my sternum. I inhaled the scent of his hair; it smelled like freshly mown grass. Fixing my gaze on the ceiling, I listened to his soft breathing while I marveled at the moment's intimacy.

Back in Pensacola, I had never spent the night at Jeff's motel unit. He'd never invited me, and I'd never thought to ask. My relationship with Jeff was all about sex, nothing else. We weren't even friends, really.

Would things differ with Aaron and me? Did I want them to?

Five

"I'M NOT A political person," a blond boy with a lisp said.

Tom, a grad student from the Education Department, responded. "Living your life as an openly gay man *is* a political act."

The blond boy shrugged. "I joined this group to make friends, not to wave a placard. Besides, I'm a Republican and we don't *do* protests."

The Gay Rap Group, as it was known, met every Sunday night. The group had no elected leaders, no procedural rules, and no agenda. A chunky boy with ice-blue eyes, wavy brown hair, and a silky voice "facilitated" our meetings. His name was David Pettyfield; he majored in psychology at FSU. At each meeting, after everyone sat down, David began things.

"Does anyone have a suggestion for a discussion topic?"

Then guys would talk.

We discussed everything: coming out to parents and friends, promiscuity, STDs, the best sexual lubricant, the better pickup bars in North Florida—you name it. The group was a hodgepodge of students, university staff, and Tallahassee townies. A few members were in their forties, and one kid, Eddie, was a senior at Leon High School.

This particular January evening, a group of twenty guys occupied a circle of chairs in a classroom on FSU's campus. Tallahassee winters were cold—temperatures often dropped below freezing—and the building's heating system wasn't turned on. Most of us wore sweaters or jackets. When guys spoke, their breaths steamed in the frigid air. This was the fourth meeting I'd attended, and I had never heard politics mentioned.

Now that would change.

Anita Bryant, a gospel singer and anti-gay activist, had come to Tallahassee to offer her homophobic ideology for consideration by the Florida Legislature. Bryant, a former Disney Mouseketeer, was now Florida's "Orange Juice Queen." She appeared in television ads, sang jingles on the radio. She wore dowdy clothes even my mom wouldn't be seen in, and she coiffed her brunette hair in a teased-up and lacquered "flip" style. Still, for as long as I could remember, Anita had seemed like a big sister to me.

Not anymore.

Bryant had already succeeded in repealing Dade County's gay rights ordinance through her religion-drenched "Save Our Children" campaign. And now she wanted a state law banning adoption of children by gay men and lesbians. Her "crusade" had drawn nationwide media attention. You couldn't open a newspaper or turn on your television without confronting Bryant's likeness and her smug, self-righteous grin.

"Homosexuals don't reproduce," Bryant said during her Dade County campaign. "They recruit new members for their subculture by preying upon innocent young people; they even adopt them, legally. We can't allow this to continue."

Now, in Tallahassee, the very next day, Bryant would appear before a Senate committee to urge passage of the adoption ban.

While I shivered in the Rap Group circle, a hefty, bearded guy named Earl spoke up.

"My boyfriend's a server at Fontana's Restaurant. Anita has a lunch reservation there tomorrow; I suggest we organize a protest."

Eddie, the high school kid, chimed in. "I have a cousin who works at WCTV. We can tip them off, maybe get a little airtime."

The discussion raged for over an hour.

"If my parents saw me protest on TV, they'd disown me."

"We've *got* to make our voices heard. This is personal; she's attacking us."

So on and so forth.

I kept my mouth shut, not knowing what to say. I thought of Vietnam War protests I'd seen as a teenager, on TV. I recalled the tear gas, the sirens, and the riot police with their helmets and nightsticks. Protests were something for radicals with beards and bullhorns, right?

The meeting ended without consensus.

"I'll be there tomorrow, with a poster," Tom the grad student said. "Those of you with *balls* are welcome to join me."

After our meeting, certain members of the Rap Group visited the Pastime, to drink beer, socialize, and, of course, cruise. We did this every week. We'd grab a circular table on the left side of the bar and then settle in. Miss Kitty called us her "Sunday Boys." She always greeted us with a smile and a free pitcher of beer to prime our pump. Then we spent a couple of hours there, drinking many more pitchers and talking away.

This particular night, the political discussion continued.

Should one join the Bryant protest? Was participation inviting trouble?

"The woman's a bully. We have to fight back."

"What good can come of it? No one will pay attention."

"What if the cops arrest us? What then?"

David Pettyfield sipped from a glass of beer. After brushing his bangs from his eyes, he looked at me with a furrowed brow.

"Andy, you didn't voice an opinion at the meeting. Why?"

I lit a Marlboro, exhaled a stream of smoke. "My boyfriend's deep in the closet. I don't think he wants me waving a sign on Monroe Street tomorrow."

Boyfriend? Is that what Aaron is now?

For over three months, we had spent much of our free time together. Aaron slept at my place most every Friday and Saturday night. Each Wednesday evening, we dined at an all-you-can-eat seafood place on Tennessee Street. Our sex was frequent and explosive, made all the more special by the fact we showed true affection toward each other, without reserve. Often, after washing up following our lovemaking, we climbed back under the covers, and then we talked for an hour or so, about our childhoods, our families, and the loneliness of our high school days, when sex between boys was *verboten*. Conversation flowed easily between us, and we didn't hold back.

My brother Jake excepted, I hadn't ever been closer to another guy.

One Saturday, I left work at Capital City early. Aaron and I drove to Alligator Point, an isolated beach on the Gulf of Mexico where slash pines grew to the edge of a narrow crescent of sugar-like sand. After we swam in the balmy Gulf, we doused ourselves with fresh water from a gallon milk jug, and then we made love in my car.

How sweet it had been.

Now, seated in the Pastime, with cigarette smoke swirling about my head, I recalled the sour scent of Aaron's armpits during our sex session at Alligator Point. I remembered his sighs, the crackling of vinyl upholstery, and the creaky springs in my Vega's backseat.

I thought of a brilliant afternoon in December, when Aaron and I had visited a crafts fair on the FSU campus. We searched for Christmas gifts for our parents. The sky was cloudless and the sun shone as brightly as a newly struck coin. We both wore sweaters and blue jeans; the cool air felt refreshing on my skin. Among the limbs of live oaks, Spanish moss beards hung as limp as dishrags.

We walked side by side, amidst the throng, pausing at booths to examine the various offerings: weavings, wood carvings, ceramics, and so forth. We didn't hold hands or put our arms around each other, of course. But still, it felt special to be in public with Aaron. We had made love, earlier that day, and the memory of our mutual passion still lingered inside my head.

Aaron was a quiet person, satisfied to pass an hour without saying a word to me, and I came to appreciate his silences. We might spend a few hours walking through Maclay Gardens and then share a picnic lunch without speaking two dozen words. Simply having a companion seemed quite enough for both of us. And though we hadn't declared a commitment to each other, Aaron had not shared a bed with another man since he'd first come to my place.

I hadn't strayed, either; I didn't care to. Aaron was all I needed.

Aaron worked at the Department of Revenue, in the collections department—a nine-to-five desk job. He'd earned an associate's degree from Tallahassee Community College. His family was fifth-generation Georgian; they lived in Thomasville, a forty-five-minute drive from Tallahassee. Every Sunday morning, Aaron drove up to Thomasville, attended church with his immediate family, and then shared a midday meal with his extended family, at his grandparents' home.

"My granddaddy's a preacher at First Baptist," Aaron told me, "and Daddy's a deacon. They wouldn't understand the gay thing, nor would Mama. I'll *never* come out to them."

"One day, I'll tell my parents," I said in response. "I don't want to hide that part of me."

Now, at the table in the Pastime, I told myself, *I guess Aaron is my boyfriend.*

My gaze traveled from face to face at the table. These were not the sort of guys I'd befriended at the Lambda Chi house. They wore clothes from discount stores. They didn't play sports, and some were outright girlish. But they had the courage to be themselves.

Did I?

I looked at David, and then my voice cracked like a teenager's when I spoke.

"What time should I be at Fontana's?"

"YOU'RE CRAZY. YOU know that, don't you?"

Over the telephone later that night, Aaron's voice sounded panicky.

"It's just a small protest," I said. "And besides, someone has to stand up to this woman. Who does she think she is, anyway?"

"Look," Aaron said, "it's one thing to visit the Pastime; it's a mixed bar. But to stand on the street with a pack of queers and wave a sign is different. You might as well have the word 'gay' tattooed on your forehead."

"I don't really—"

"I'm serious. What if your fraternity brothers find out?"

"They don't run my life."

"What about *me*? Don't you care about my feelings?"

I chewed my lips while twisting my wall-mounted phone's spiral cord around my finger. The more Aaron objected to my involvement in the protest, the more my attendance seemed an imperative. My dad had once told me, "The only way to deal with a bully is to stand up to him." And Anita Bryant was a bully, wasn't she? Why *wouldn't* Aaron see the need for my participation?

"I'm not asking *you* to be there," I said.

"That's not the point. I visit your apartment all the time. People see us together whenever we're out. If you're branded gay, then I'll be, too. I could lose my job."

I let out my breath.

"I'm sorry," I said, "but this is something I have to do."

I ONCE READ a statement about leaving the closet. It said, in part: "For anyone who still has yet to come out, you don't need me to tell you it gets better afterward. But the closet does things to you that people aren't meant to go through. The constant introspection and overanalyzing and the fear: it stops. It goes away and doesn't come back.

"Remember that telling people isn't so much a clarification for them, but a fight for you and your life. No matter how much it feels like your environment is dictating to you, remember this: you can give your environment the finger and change it however you like."

I think *that* pretty well describes the feelings stirring within me in the winter of 1977.

I STOOD ON a Tallahassee sidewalk, in front of Fontana's, an Italian place with red canvas awnings and a plate-glass storefront, a favored dining spot for legislators. The January day was cool, but sunny and still. Perhaps two dozen gay men, mostly members of the Rap Group, had assembled there. Many held placards. One read, "Anita Bryant Sucks Oranges." Several guys wore sunglasses, not because of the brightness, but to obscure their identities. Me? I clutched a headless mop handle with a poster I'd stapled to it. The poster said, "Squeeze a Fruit for Anita."

Two squad cars sat at the curb, each occupied by two cops. A television camera crew waited nearby. Across the street, a gaggle of onlookers, probably state employees on lunch break, gathered to watch the show. A reporter from the *Democrat* interviewed Eddie, the boy from Leon High.

"Shouldn't you be in school?" the reporter asked.

"Some things are more important than school," Eddie replied.

I affected a calm demeanor, but my knees trembled and my hands shook.

"Here she comes," someone hollered.

A silver Lincoln Continental approached. Sunlight glanced off the Lincoln's massive chrome bumpers and grille. The four cops left their vehicles. They put on their hats, hitched their pants; they adjusted the nightsticks hanging from their gun belts. One cop, a guy with a beer gut, approached our group. He spoke in a drawl as thick as Loretta McPhail's.

"Do you *gentlemen* have a leader?"

Someone pushed David Pettyfield in the officer's direction.

David looked around him, and then he raised a hand. "I guess that's me."

"We don't want any trouble," the cop said. He pointed to an oak tree, about fifty feet from Fontana's front door. "You fellows step over there, and don't come any closer. This lady's going to have her meal in peace."

We all moved back, including the news people. Then Bryant emerged from the Lincoln. I suppose I'd expected her to resemble Satan, with horns and a tail. Instead, she looked like a Junior Leaguer attending a fundraiser for the Children's Hospital. She wore a white wool suit, stockings, and white high heels. Her neatly coifed chestnut hair reflected sunlight. While two cops spoke to her, I noticed the top of her head was barely level with their shoulders.

After all three turned their gazes toward our group, Bryant frowned like she'd stepped in dog shit.

"Ms. Bryant," Eddie called out, "will you speak with us a moment?"

A pained expression crossed Bryant's face. "I can't," she cried. "People are waiting for me inside."

David Pettyfield stood right next to me. After cupping his hands at either side of his mouth, he hollered at Bryant, "Gay rights now. Gay rights now."

Our group raised our signs, and we all took up the chant.

"Gay rights now. Gay rights now."

I'm sure people heard us two blocks away. Lights from the television crew cast a glare. The two cops hustled Bryant along the sidewalk, each holding one of her elbows. Her heels clunked on the concrete while her hair bounced against her shoulders. She looked terrified, as though we might physically attack her.

And then she was gone.

A TV camera focused on me. The brightness of the camera crew's light made me squint; the glare was brighter than the overhead sun.

A reporter from the TV station approached; he said, "What's your name, son?" and thrust a microphone in my face.

"U-m-m, I'm Andy."

"Why are you here?"

"To stick up for me and my friends."

"You are gay?"

Go on…

"Yes," I said.

"Do you think what Anita Bryant's doing is wrong?"

I nodded. "She doesn't understand what it's like to be different. She thinks anyone who's not exactly like her is a bad person, but I disagree."

"Do you really think you'll make a difference by waving a sign?"

I patted my chin with my fingertips, and then I looked into the camera lens.

"Maybe," I said.

HOURS AFTER THE Bryant demonstration, my phone rang nonstop.

Biff, my former dorm mate, called.

"I'm proud of you, man. Your balls are bigger than a bowling alley's. How come you never told me?"

The chapter president at Lambda Chi phoned. It seemed an "emergency meeting" at the fraternity house had just concluded.

"Your membership's revoked, Andy. Don't set foot on our property, ever again."

David Pettyfield called.

"The *Democrat* wants to do a feature story on us; they want an interview. How about it?"

"Let me think on it," I said. "I'll let you know tomorrow."

When Bucky Buchholtz phoned, his tone sounded grave. "Do your folks know about this?"

"Not yet," I said, "but I plan to tell them soon."

"Look, there *will* be talk at the club; Tallahassee's a conservative place. I suggest you take two weeks off. Let this situation simmer down, okay?"

And then the call from Aaron came, the one I'd dreaded ever since the TV camera had focused on me.

"I can't believe this: you've destroyed our future together."

"Aaron—"

"I'm serious, Andy. I can't be seen with you again." Before I could say anything more, Aaron hung up.

Shit.

I placed the phone receiver on its cradle, and then I sat on my sofa. I stared at the carpet, feeling as if someone had just punched me in the stomach. A tremble ran through me and my vision blurred. How could Aaron have dumped me, just like that?

What have I done? What a fool I am.

A knock sounded at my door, and I swung my gaze. Who could it be? I opened the door just a crack, half expecting I'd find some homophobe with a baseball bat, but instead it was Fergal. He wore blue jeans and a black watch sweater. His marmalade curls reflected light from the foyer's overhead fixture. In one hand, he clutched a box of Ritz crackers.

"You busy?" he asked.

I shook my head, afraid if I answered verbally my voice would break.

"If it's okay," Fergal said, "I'll take you up on that beer you once offered."

I fetched two cans, and then we sat side-by-side on my sofa. Fergal rested his stocking feet on the coffee table. He sat close enough I smelled his skin, a piney aroma I found appealing, even in my misery.

Fergal's gaze traveled about the room. "It looks good in here—real homey."

I nodded, but didn't say anything.

Fergal nudged my shoulder with a finger. "You're awfully pale, Andy. Are you sick?"

Ahh, shit....

I couldn't help myself; the day's events had overwhelmed me. My face crumpled, and then I let out a wail. I wept like a kid whose dog has just been run over by a car.

Fergal wrapped an arm about my shoulders. "What is it, mate? Tell me."

I wept so hard I could barely breathe. In between wails, I told Fergal, "I've fucked up everything. My life is ruined."

Fergal pulled me to him; my head rested against his shoulder.

"Shhh," he said, "it can't be all *that* bad."

"It *is* that bad. I'm an idiot."

Fergal brought me a paper towel from my kitchen. "Blow your nose, then tell me what happened."

After I honked into the towel a few times, I wiped my dripping eyes. My voice quivering, I told Fergal about the Bryant demonstration, and then about the calls I'd received, including the one from Aaron.

"I never should have gone today; I never should have joined the Rap Group. I thought of attending law school, but now I probably won't get in. My boss at the country club's upset, too."

Another wave of tears burst forth. My shoulders shook like a sapling in a gale.

Fergal patted my back. "Come on, mate, I think you're making this a bigger problem than it is. In Melbourne, anyway, if you're gay, it's not an issue. Things can't be all that different here."

Fergal sipped from his beer. "Your boyfriend...what's his name?"

"Aaron."

"He'll change his mind when he cools off, I've no doubt."

I shook my head. "You don't know him."

Fergal shrugged. "I'm always getting into rows with Gina, over this or that. We both sulk a few days, and then we're back together."

While I sipped from my beer, I pondered the fact I had just come out as queer to Fergal, and yet he didn't seem shocked or put off by my revelation, not at all. It was like I'd told him I was vegetarian.

Still, my thoughts churned.

Should I feel bad about my banishment by Lambda Chi? If the guys at the house couldn't handle my sexuality, maybe *they* had the problem, not me. And maybe they'd never been my friends in the first place. Perhaps they only liked the false Andy Hunsinger, the image I'd created in order to please them and the rest of the world.

And what if Aaron wouldn't change his mind? What if I never saw him again? Where would I find another boyfriend like him? But if I wanted him back in my life, I'd have to atone for my behavior: go back in the closet and stay there. Did I really want to hide who I was from the world? After I wiped my upper lip with the back of my wrist, I looked at Fergal and squared my shoulders.

"Are we still friends?" I asked.

Fergal held my gaze. A grin crossed his freckled face, and then he mussed my hair like I was ten years old.

"We certainly are, mate. Now, have a bloody biscuit and drink your beer."

MY PARTICIPATION IN the Anita Bryant protest shattered my straight-boy facade—instantly and permanently—and since that day, I haven't hidden my sexual orientation from anyone. I have lived as an openly gay man, an unapologetic faggot who loves as he sees fit.

Six

FALLOUT FROM MY television appearance was neither as bad as I'd expected, nor as harmless as Fergal had predicted.

The day afterward, at the conclusion of economics class, my professor asked me to remain after the dismissal bell.

Balding and bespectacled, Dr. Wiskowitz had a beak for a nose and a belly like Santa Claus. When the room had emptied, he sat in a desk next to mine, and the desk creaked under his hefty weight. He spoke to me in a voice barely louder than a whisper.

"Andy, I saw you on television yesterday."

Heat rushed to my cheeks, and then I lowered my gaze.

Wiskowitz squeezed my shoulder, ever-so-gently, almost a caress.

"Thank you for your courage. You have no idea how much yesterday meant to so many people in this town—among them me."

During change of classes, someone had taped a scrap of paper on my back. I don't know how long I wore the note before a girl tore it off and gave it to me. My tormentor had scrawled the word "faggot" on the paper scrap, using a felt-tipped pen.

Great.

I shared a European history class with two Lambda Chi brothers—normally, we sat together and chatted before class began—but when I entered the room, they both turned away from me, as if I weren't there. I sat in another part of the room instead, and thereafter neither boy spoke to me ever again.

Three days passed before I called Aaron.

"It's Friday night," I told him. "Meet me at the Pastime; we can talk. I miss you."

Aaron waited a few seconds before he spoke.

"I told you, we can't be out in public together. People from Thomasville go to school here, kids from my high school. If one of them saw us..."

"What?"

"They might tell my folks, and I can't risk that."

"Come to my place, then."

Aaron let out his breath.

"Not tonight," he said, "maybe some other time."

Aaron's tone of voice let me know, not subtly, there'd never *be* another time.

Okay, I told myself, *let it go. At least you tried.*

Two nights later, I attended another Rap Group session.

Six new people participated, two of them women, one a petite lesbian named Julie. She spoke in a husky voice.

"If you guys have the courage to demonstrate on the street, then I should have the guts to join your group on Sundays. You *do* allow women, don't you?"

It seemed I wasn't the only one thanked, or harassed, during the preceding week. Eddie, the Leon High student, had been shoved and spat upon in a school hallway.

Another boy, an FSU freshman named Blake, played clarinet in the Seminole marching band. Someone had spray-painted "cocksucker" on his dorm room door, and now he spoke in a shaky voice.

"I don't know if the graffiti was a one-time thing or if it's just the beginning. I keep asking myself if taking part in the demonstration was a mistake. I don't know how to fist fight. What if I get beat up?"

After I spoke of my talk with Dr. Wiskowitz, David Pettyfield nodded while he rearranged his limbs. "Half a dozen people thanked me: students, a professor, and the assistant manager at the fried chicken place I work at. I think we're onto something here."

"Like what?" someone asked.

David's gaze traveled from face to face in the chilly room. "We need to formalize our group, create an official student organization recognized by the university. We need office space in the student union."

"It'll never happen," said Kit, a Chinese-American boy from Orlando.

David closed his eyelids. After he re-opened them, his gaze drilled into Kit's.

"We can try," he said.

AFTER A TWO-WEEK hiatus, I returned to Capital City on a brilliant but frigid Saturday morning. A cold front had swept into town, and my breath steamed in the chilly air when I pedaled my bike to work. The sun shone in a cloudless sky. At the club, dew glistened on the putting green. Men struck balls on the driving range, making sounds like pistol shots. They wore sweaters and wool slacks to ward off the cold.

Inside the clubhouse, I found Bucky Buchholtz in his office, a comfortable space with a view of the first tee and beyond. Trophies gleamed on the shelves behind Bucky's desk, and framed photos of Bucky, standing next to golfing greats like Jack Nicklaus and Sam Snead, decorated the forest green walls. Steam rose from a paper coffee cup resting on Bucky's desk. When I knocked on the doorjamb, Bucky looked up from a clipboard. His face clouded, and when he spoke, his voice sounded flat.

"Come in, Andy, and close the door behind you."

Uh-oh.

I took a chair before Bucky's desk. Then I studied my hands in my lap.

Bucky cleared his throat. "How've you been?" he asked.

I shrugged and didn't say anything.

"You know, your dad and I have been best friends for thirty years. I'd do anything for him."

I nodded.

"The same holds true for you, Andy. Jake and you are like sons to me; I mean that."

I looked up, and then my voice cracked like an eighth-grader's when I spoke.

"Are you going to fire me, Bucky?"

Bucky's eyes narrowed. "Shit no, but I'm going say things that'll hurt you, and I don't like it—not one bit."

I kept quiet while my brain churned.

Bucky rose; he turned to a window facing east. Sunlight revealed the deep creases in his face. He stuck one hand in his pants, jingled his pocket change.

"I don't understand this whole *gay* thing you're involved in. I mean, I was in the service, I saw all kinds of things you wouldn't believe. The fact you like boys is...your business. You're still Drake Hunsinger's kid— I won't ever forget that—and you're a damned fine caddy to boot."

"Thanks, Bucky."

He looked at me from over his shoulder. "Just the same, we have problems."

I crinkled my brow. "Like what?"

"You know how this place is: news travels fast. The day after I saw you on TV, half a dozen people asked me about the situation. I've heard unkind words, stuff you wouldn't believe. And you've lost one of your best regulars, Ray Connor. He told me, 'I don't want that little cocksucker anywhere near me.'"

Tears welled up in my eyes. "Jesus, Bucky..."

Bucky returned to his swivel chair. After he rested his elbows on his desktop, he formed a steeple with his fingers. Then his gaze met mine.

"There's more: two club directors have asked me to dismiss you from service. I told them no, but they still want you fired. The monthly board meeting's two weeks from now, on a Wednesday. Your employment's on the agenda."

My stomach did a flip-flop. "Should I quit?"

Bucky lowered his gaze. "That's a decision only you can make. I'm behind you if you want to stay, but the final decision's not mine."

I rearranged my limbs. "How many board members are there?"

Bucky held up seven fingers.

"Do any have open minds?"

"Some, I'd say, would listen to reason. They're not all prigs, if that's what you mean. But if you don't speak up for yourself—if you don't fight back—you'll lose your job. It's that simple."

I stared out a window and rubbed my chin with a knuckle. I pictured myself in the club's oak-paneled board room, just down the hall. I'd face seven Tallahassee bigwigs who would lose nothing if they fired a faggot. And they'd gain nothing by retaining me in service. Did I have the balls to show up for the meeting? Would they let me speak if I did? If I spoke, would they listen to my side of things?

You've gone this far, Hunsinger. There's no turning back, now.

I looked back at Bucky. "What time's the meeting on Wednesday?"

A smile crept across Bucky's face. "Seven p.m. If you'd like, I'll speak on your behalf."

At the caddy tent, Dustin Ausley sat on a folding camp chair; he chatted with two other caddies while Jerry Justus stood nearby, cleaning a member's golf clubs with a rag. Like me, all the boys wore sweaters with the Capital City logo on the chests, and golf slacks. When I approached the group, the chatter died. Dustin and the two other rich kids stared at me like I was an alien from outer space.

Jerry looked up from his work. "H-h-hi, Andy. H-h-how are you?"

I rubbed my hands together, to warm them. "Good. How about you?"

Jerry gazed at the club in his hand. "I'm okay, I g-g- guess."

I seized a clipboard hanging from a nail driven into a tent support. Then I studied each caddy's assignments for the day. I would assist two nonmember golfers who visited from a private club in Atlanta, and I crinkled my forehead in puzzlement. Normally, I caddied exclusively for Capital City members.

Not today.

Dustin Ausley would caddy for Raymond Connor.

Connor's golf partner was Robert Du Bose, president of the Florida Senate, a gruff-talking redneck from Okaloosa County with a reputation as a boozer *and* a womanizer.

Jerry would caddy for Du Bose.

I glanced at Dustin. "I hope you like racist jokes. You'll hear a bunch from Connor today."

Dustin lowered his gaze and shrugged. "I hear he tips well."

"It's true," I said.

Dustin looked up at me with his eyebrows arched. "Is it also true you're a fag, Andy? Do you like dicks instead of chicks?"

My face grew warm while the other two rich kids snickered. I kept my gaze fixed on Dustin. Then I said, "If you're asking if I'm gay, yeah, I am. Is that a problem for you?"

Dustin shrugged again. "It's a problem for *some* people, I guess."

"Those people," I said, "I really don't care about."

I turned on my heel. Then I walked to a thermos provided by the club's kitchen. While I poured coffee into a foam cup, someone behind me made kissing noises. More snickering erupted and the tops of my ears burned. I turned to face Dustin, ready to say something—what I wasn't sure—but Jerry Justus intervened. He stuck a golf club in Dustin's face.

"Cut it out," he cried. "Leave Andy alone."

Dustin looked at Jerry, and then Dustin's lips spread into a smile.

"W-w-what's the m-m-matter, Justus? Y-y-you don't like m-m-me teasing your boyfriend? I *know* you g-g-guys are close."

The two other rich kids giggled.

Jerry dropped the golf club. He *lunged* at Dustin, tackling him and tipping Dustin's camp chair backward. Dustin's head hit the tent's earthen floor. After Jerry shoved the chair aside, he sat on Dustin's belly. Then he slapped Dustin's cheeks, three or four times.

"Take that back, you stuck-up bastard. Take it back, or I'll beat the crap out of you. I swear to God I will."

Dustin tried struggling loose, but Jerry pinned Dustin's wrists to the ground. Then Jerry spat on Dustin's face.

"Take it back, you rich punk."

Bucky Buchholtz appeared from nowhere. After grabbing Jerry's shirt collar, he pulled Jerry off Dustin.

"Stop it—both of you—right now."

Jerry pointed at Dustin, who remained on the ground. "He called Andy a fag."

Dustin wiped Jerry's spit from his nose and cheek. His face glowed as red as a stop sign.

"Is that true, Ausley?" Bucky said.

"It's true," I said.

Bucky glared at Dustin first. Then his gaze traveled from face to face. "This is a country club, boys, not a high school locker room. Each of you will conduct himself like a gentleman at all times, no exceptions. Understand, Ausley?"

Dustin rose; he brushed dirt and debris from his clothing, but he didn't say anything.

Bucky placed his hands on his hips. "I want an answer, Ausley— *now*—or you're finished as a caddy at Capital City."

Dustin drew a breath while his gaze traveled here and there. "Yes, sir, I understand."

Bucky pointed at me. "Ausley, apologize to Hunsinger, right now."

Dustin worked his jaw from side to side. Looking at me, he spoke in a tone that actually sounded sincere.

"Sorry, Andy."

"The two of you shake hands," Bucky said.

I shook with Dustin, firmly, and then Bucky glanced at his wristwatch.

"The morning's first tee time is ten minutes from now; we haven't time for nonsense. Let's get to work."

Bucky strode toward his office while Dustin headed for the men's locker room to wash his face. The other two rich kids studied the clipboard, not saying a word, while I followed Jerry toward the first tee.

"Thanks," I said, "for sticking up for me."

Jerry gazed at me and nodded. Then he spoke without hesitation.

"You're my friend, Andy. If one of those little pricks tries that again, I'll break his fucking jaw; I mean it. Who do they think they are, anyway?"

I couldn't help myself; I had to laugh.

Jerry scowled. "What's so funny?"

"Do you realize your stuttering stops whenever you blow your stack?"

Jerry nodded; he looked at me as though I'd stated an obvious fact.

"I don't understand," I said. "How come?"

Jerry picked up a fallen pine tree limb, a small branch lying near the tee box. He swished the limb back and forth a few times. Then he tossed it into a stand of camellia shrubs.

"My doctor thinks I stutter 'cause I'm angry inside."

"Are you?"

Jerry shrugged. "I guess so."

"What are you angry about?"

Jerry shook his head.

"That's the problem," he said. "I'm angry 'cause I stutter."

Seven

I WASN'T MUCH of an athlete. Yes, I'd played Little League as a boy, and I golfed. But I had never lettered in a sport during high school; I never exercised routinely. So when Biff Schultz asked me to join him for a run at the university track, I didn't know what to say.

"You won't believe the high you'll experience, after running a few miles," Biff told me over the phone. "My roomies and I do it every day."

"I smoke cigarettes," I said. "I'd probably have a heart attack."

"Nonsense; meet us at five thirty, and wear a wristwatch to set your pace. Believe me, you won't be sorry you came."

After digging through my closet, I found a pair of tennis sneakers. I wore those, a sweatshirt, and a pair of gym shorts with my high school's mascot emblazoned on one leg. While walking to my car, I shivered in the cool evening air. Goose bumps sprang up on my legs, and I shook my head, thinking of what lay in store for me in the coming hour.

This is crazy.

Still...

Biff had stuck with me, that awful day of the Bryant demonstration; he wasn't afraid to be seen with me, even though he knew I was queer. So, if he wanted me to run with him and his housemates, I would.

Located near Tennessee Street, FSU's track wasn't far from the Pastime Tavern. Slash pines ringed the track, serving as a windbreak. Dusk came early during Tallahassee winters, and field lights bathed the facility in their brilliant glow. I entered through a chain-link fence gate. On the track's west side, a press box crowned a dozen rows of metal bleachers. Rubbery Tartan turf surfaced the track, a garnet oval with gold lane striping.

Groups of male and female students jogged around the track. Girls' ponytails bounced, and guys' sweatshirts darkened in the armpits. A boy in an FSU track uniform leapt over a high-jump bar; he fell onto a huge blue mattress, looking more like a circus performer than an athlete. A gaggle of skinny high school boys, all wearing shorts and singlets, gathered about a middle-aged man who read to them from a clipboard.

This was my first visit to the track, ever, and I felt I'd entered alien territory.

Biff waved to me from the emerald infield. He and his housemates sat on the grass with their legs outstretched; they performed toe touches. I'd met Biff's pals a few times, at parties I attended. As mentioned before, both his friends were pre-med majors like Biff, but I knew little else about them.

Austin, a sinewy biracial guy from Kingston, Jamaica, had skin the color of creamed tea. His sandy-colored hair grew in ringlets to his shoulders. When I approached the trio, he flashed a smile at me. His big teeth reminded me of piano keys. He spoke in a lilting manner one often hears in the Caribbean.

"It's good to see you, Andy; or shall I call you 'Mr. Civil Disobedience' now?"

My face grew warm. Of *course* they knew about my TV appearance. Was there anyone in Tallahassee who didn't?

I shook Austin's hand. "Andy will do just fine."

Biff pointed to his other housemate. "You remember Travis, don't you?"

I nodded while gazing into Travis's blue-green eyes. His dark hair was parted on the side; it grew over his ears and all the way to his shoulders. His milky skin, turned-up nose, and long eyelashes gave him an androgynous look, but the deepness of his voice rivaled Bucky Buchholtz's. Travis's limbs were lanky and his hands were big. He and Biff had been classmates and best friends at Jacksonville's Robert E. Lee High School.

Travis spoke to me with a North Florida drawl while his gaze studied my face. "How's it going, Andy? It's good to see you again." When we shook, his firm grip felt warm and moist.

All three guys wore similar outfits: hooded sweatshirts, running shorts slit at the thigh, and odd-looking shoes—ones I'd never seen. The shoes' uppers appeared to be made of nylon material. A swoosh logo appeared on their sides. Grooves crosshatched the shoes' thick and rubbery soles. The heels on the shoes had padding a half-inch thick.

I pointed at Biff's feet. "Where'd you get those things?"

"We ordered them through a sporting goods shop. An Oregon company called Nike makes them."

"Are they comfortable?"

"You're damned straight they are," Biff said. Then Biff arched his eyebrows and slapped his forehead. "Oops. Sorry, Andy: when I said you were 'straight,' I didn't mean, you know..."

Everybody laughed, including me.

When I had shared a dorm room with Biff my freshman year, he had kept his auburn hair cut short like mine, but now it grew in waves to his broad shoulders. With his handlebar moustache and sideburns, he resembled a gunslinger from the Wild West. All he needed was a horse, a pair of leather chaps, and a Colt .45 to complete the look. Brainy but unaffected, Biff planned to enroll at the medical school at University of Florida in Gainesville, where his dad had attended twenty-five years before. To my knowledge, Biff had never earned less than an A in any class he took during his years at Florida State.

My gaze swung back to Travis. After kneeling on the grass, he bent his upper body backward, until his shoulders touched the ground behind him. He stared into the darkening sky, blinking. His sweatshirt's hem had crept up his belly, and now his hairy navel winked at me. His genitals bulged in the crotch of his running shorts. Dark fuzz dusted his calves, but his thighs were as smooth as a boy's.

"We run three miles each session," Biff told me, "at an eight-minute pace. But you should start with just one mile, at maybe a ten-minute pace. When you're done, cool down by walking a lap in the outside lane."

After sitting on the infield grass, I followed Biff's lead. I joined the soles of my shoes before me. Then I grabbed my toes with both hands, to stretch my hamstrings. Already, my thighs burned.

Austin and Travis arranged themselves in another curious position: a yoga maneuver called the "plow pose." After lying on their backs, they raised their feet and legs above their heads. Then they lowered their toes to the ground behind them while steadying themselves with their arms outstretched in front of them. Both guys reminded me of contortionists at a carnival.

"Doesn't that hurt?" I asked.

"On the contrary," Austin said, "it stretches the back, preventing an injury or strain running might cause."

After shifting position, I tried the plow pose myself, but I couldn't bring my toes to the ground behind me. My back simply wouldn't stretch that far.

"It takes practice," Travis said. "Your body's not flexible enough right now."

All four of us walked to the chain-link fence. Gripping the fence with both hands, we each extended a leg behind us. Then we stretched the extended legs, applying pressure by pushing our upper body weight against the fence. After a minute, we changed legs and repeated the process. The backs of my thighs burned and twitched.

"Stretching's key to a good run," Biff said. "You should always feel loose when you hit the track."

When the three took off running, they reminded me of a team of horses, Travis in particular. He ran fluidly. He kept his arms low and his hips didn't move from side to side. He seemed to float above the track.

My first lap wasn't too bad. The track's flexible surface prevented the jarring I'd experienced while running on a basketball or tennis court, and I chugged along, occasionally glancing at my wristwatch to be sure I kept a ten-minute per mile pace. Then, halfway through my second lap, my lungs began to burn, and then my knees wobbled. My heart pounded so hard I thought it might burst from my chest. I had to walk a minute or so before I recommenced running.

During my final two laps, I tried to concentrate on my breathing and the pace of my strides, but with difficulty. No matter how much I tried, I couldn't gather enough air into my lungs. Toward the end, my vision blurred and my legs grew rubbery.

When I'd finished my fourth lap, I collapsed onto the infield grass. Chest heaving, I lay on my back and stared into the night sky.

This isn't fun; it's torture.

Once my heartbeat slowed and my breathing returned to normal, I sat up, just in time to see Biff, Austin, and Travis cruise past me. Biff waved and I waved back.

Biff's sweatshirt was dark in the armpits and in the small of his back, but he didn't look tired at all; neither did his companions. They ran at a smooth pace with their legs striding, their arms chugging, and I shook my head in wonderment.

How did they do it?

Following Biff's advice, I dragged myself to my feet, and then I walked another lap around the track while Biff and his housemates finished their run. Afterward, when we hit the drinking fountains by the bleachers, I sucked water like a camel.

"If you'll join us here, every day," Biff told me on the way to the parking lot, "your cardiovascular system will adjust pretty quickly. Soon, you'll run three miles with no problem."

I wasn't so sure about *that*, but while I drove home, I seemed more relaxed than I normally was. All the tension had drained from my body *and* my mind. I sat at a stoplight on Monroe Street, watching Spanish moss beards sway among limbs of a towering live oak, and I felt almost drugged, as though I'd injected morphine or some other opiate. My limbs were like Jell-O, but in a *good* way, and when the traffic light turned green, I had to pinch myself back into reality before I pressed my car's accelerator.

Maybe this is the "runner's high" Biff spoke of.

I motored toward my apartment, ever so slowly. I hummed a tune while thinking of how much my life had changed since I'd met Jeff in Pensacola, several months before.

What lay in store for me in the months ahead?

TWENTY-SIX STUDENTS from the Rap Group, including myself, signed an application for recognition of the Alliance for Gay Awareness (AGA) by the university.

We elected David Pettyfield as our president, and because I majored in communications, the group elected me editor of our soon-to-be-published monthly newsletter.

Regarding our petition, the Dean of Student Affairs said he didn't have a choice in the matter. The university's legal counsel had advised the dean he would violate our First Amendment and Equal Protection rights if he denied our request.

In March 1977, the dean declared AGA an accredited student organization, and then the university assigned us a cramped office space in the student union. We would enjoy access to a photocopy machine and we'd participate in campus events, just like fraternities, the Hispanic Society, and the glee club.

A columnist for the *Tallahassee Democrat* declared the Dean's decision "an appalling lack of judgment, an endorsement of deviant lifestyles."

The pastor at First Baptist Church on College Avenue told a news reporter, "The FSU campus is now officially Sodom and Gomorrah. Will homosexual orgies take place in the student union?"

David Pettyfield told the *Democrat*, "I don't know why people are so upset. We aren't demons; we're just a group of students who happen to be gay."

The AGA office wasn't much. We shared a room with the Physically Challenged Seminoles, a student group with members who moved about campus using walkers or wheelchairs. The university provided us a desk and chair, a file cabinet, and a telephone with local service only—no long distance. On the day we received our office key, we threw a party, complete with Hawaiian Punch and a tray of supermarket gingersnaps. Three-dozen people showed; they brought contributions of paper clips, pens and pencils, writing tablets, and a bulletin board. The owner of a local office supply store gave us stationery and a box of envelopes. Eddie's parents contributed a roll of postage stamps and a battered Olivetti typewriter.

A Rap Group member named Leonard made his living arranging displays for a local department store. Leonard contributed a male mannequin we named Bruce. Bruce wore a hula skirt and lei, along with a sailor's cap. Standing at the AGA's door, he held a sign. "Beware: you are entering a queer zone."

FSU's student government occupied a large office just down the hall. Buttoned-down political types passed by our door while the party took place; they sneaked glances in our direction when they did so. Curious expressions appeared on their faces, as though they'd witnessed a gruesome car wreck or an execution. Their gawking made me feel a bit strange, but still I felt a sense of pride in our accomplishment. We had our own territory now—we dwelled among the "normal" people—and so far no one had called us names or shot spitballs at us.

Being different wasn't so hard, was it?

A guy in a wheelchair—a Physically Challenged Seminole officer—welcomed us. While munching on a gingersnap, he gazed at Bruce and shook his head.

"This place is *really* a freak show now," he said, "but I kind of like it."

Eight

ON A WEDNESDAY evening, I met Bucky Buchholtz in his office at Capital City, a half hour before the club's March board meeting. I wore a blue blazer, khaki slacks, penny loafers, a button-down shirt, and a regimental necktie.

Bucky wore a tweed jacket, an open-necked golf shirt, and dress pants. He sipped from a glass of Jim Beam and ice.

We discussed the board members I'd face.

"Your enemies are Tom Bannister and Kelly McCrae," Bucky said. "Bannister's a third-generation Tallahassean, a deacon at First Baptist, and a teetotaler. He probably hasn't screwed his wife in twenty years. I'm sure he thinks subscribing to *Penthouse* magazine is a mortal sin.

"McCrae's Irish Catholic; he hobnobs with the bishop, never misses Sunday mass. His house looks like a shrine to Notre Dame's football program; it's even painted green and gold, no joke. A few years back, when McCrae visited Rome, he had an audience with the Pope. The guy probably has a rosary stuck up his ass."

I grimaced. "Any chance I can change their minds?"

Bucky shook his head. "But there are five others who may listen to you, and that includes Ben Longstreet, the board's chairman. He's the president of Lewis State Bank; his grandfather was a Civil War general. Most board members follow Ben's lead on controversial matters; they trust his judgment."

"How come?"

Bucky tapped a pencil against his desk pad. "Several years ago, a fellow named Stan Levy submitted an application for membership at Capital City. Levy was chief of staff at Tallahassee Memorial at the time, a highly respected surgeon. Levy's application sat on the club's waiting list for years; the board passed it over several times because Dr. Levy was a Jew.

"Levy grew fed up with the situation. He wrote a letter to the *Tallassee Democrat*, accusing Capital City of anti-Semitism, and rightfully so. The rabbi at Temple Israel organized a protest at the club's front gates, with picket signs and all. Hundreds of Jews showed up."

"What happened?" I asked.

"Ben Longstreet had just been elected to the board—this was long before you came to work here—and he made a formal motion at a board meeting, seeking approval of Levy's application. He said something like, 'We're acting like Ku Klux Klansmen; it's an *embarrassment.*'"

"Did Levy get admitted?"

Bucky chuckled deep in his throat. "His application *was* accepted—by a four-to-three vote—but then Levy withdrew his request for membership. He told the *Democrat*, 'They can keep their *goy* golf club. I'll play the municipal course instead.'"

"Are there other board members with an open mind?"

Bucky swiveled back and forth in his desk chair. He twirled a pencil in his fingers. "On this issue it's hard to say—board members don't talk about gay rights in the clubhouse lounge—but Kate Bonner's a firecracker; she's the first woman ever elected to the Capital City board. Trust me: she won't take shit from mossbacks like McRae and Bannister."

Bucky glanced at his wristwatch. Then he looked at me and raised his eyebrows. "Ready, Andy?"

I drew a deep breath. "Let's do it."

When I rose from my chair, my knees liquefied. My heart pounded so hard, I thought it might burst from my chest. For the umpteenth time, I thrust my hand into my pants pocket to be sure I'd brought notes I'd made: points I wished to make when addressing the board. I had spent three hours the night before, seated at my dining table, trying to think of what I should say.

Should I sound angry? Apologetic? I hadn't crafted a formal speech. I'd simply jotted down a few points I felt I should make.

I followed Bucky through a pair of swinging oaks doors, and then we entered the board room, a space perhaps the size of a tennis court, with a raised dais at one end. Recessed can lights in the ceiling cast their glow upon seven middle-aged people: one woman, six men. They sat behind a curved oak desk, in leather swivel chairs. The men wore business suits or sports jackets. The woman wore a silk blouse and pearls; she conversed with a stout man with a slick-bald head wearing aviator eyeglasses and a turtleneck sweater under his navy-blue blazer.

Framed photographs hung on the oak-paneled walls, portraits of every Capital City board chairman since the club's founding. Some of the guys in the older photos wore pince-nez eyeglasses; they sported bow ties. All were white, and looked like they'd never missed a meal. Most weren't smiling, as though golf at Capital City wasn't something to be taken lightly, as though the board performed critical work in the Tallahassee community.

A lectern stood before the dais. Perhaps twenty feet separated the two.

Behind the lectern, two dozen upholstered chairs faced the dais, as well, and several were already occupied. I recognized Jack Orsini, head chef in the clubhouse kitchen. Jerry Justus's dad was there, wearing the same clothes he always wore to work: a green Dickies work shirt, matching pants, and a pair of steel-toed work boots. He had removed the ball cap he normally wore; it rested in his lap. Mildred Farber, the club's banquet hostess was present, and so was the club's bookkeeper, Alice Makepeace, a spinster who wore her hair in a bun and *never* smiled or said hello when I passed her in the club's hallways.

Bucky and I took a seat, and then Bucky whispered in my ear. "See the guy sitting in the center chair up front?"

I nodded.

"That's Ben Longstreet, the board chairman."

Longstreet looked like Ward Cleaver from the *Leave it to Beaver* television show: cleft chin, salt-and-pepper hair, thick eyebrows, and dark eyes. His athletic build filled out his suit jacket nicely. Something told me Longstreet had never once experienced a sense of inadequacy, of not quite belonging in whatever societies he dwelled in.

"Which one's McCrae?" I asked.

"The guy on the far right," Bucky said, "in the checkered jacket."

McCrae's thinning hair was as white as table sugar, combed back from his freckled forehead. His florid and jowly face seemed to suggest he'd spent too little time in church and too many hours in pubs. I tried to imagine him shaking hands with the Pope at the Vatican, but couldn't. He looked like he belonged on a used car lot, selling junkers to rednecks.

McCrae conversed with a tall, thin fellow in a tailored business suit who wore bifocal eyeglasses. Right away, I knew the man in the suit was

Bannister. He looked like a guy who felt uncomfortable if he wasn't clutching a Bible to his chest, the type of guy you'd see gathering collection plates on Sunday morning, while an organ groaned and a soloist belted out "Nearer, My God, to Thee."

I'd never seen McRae or Bannister on the club's golf course in the four years I'd worked at Capital City, but I *did* recognize two other board members: Dr. Hardemann was a Tallahassee gynecologist I'd caddied for three or four times. A soft-spoken man, he owned one of the smoothest swings at Capital City—effortless and efficient. He could drive a ball two hundred and fifty yards from the tee, but when doing so, he looked like he'd hardly exerted himself. Hardemann was as thin as a greyhound with ice-blue eyes, a widow's peak, and acne scars on his cheeks. I'd never heard him speak a harsh or angry word—not even when his shot went awry—and that didn't happen too often.

The other guy I recognized was Bert Ready. I'd never met the guy; I'd only seen him on TV ads for his Ready Appliances retail outlets. He sold refrigerators, stoves, air conditioners, clothes washing machines, and so forth, in stores from Pensacola to Jacksonville. Bert always wore iridescent business suits when appearing in his ads. He'd tout whatever merchandise was presently on sale, speaking rapid fire, like a guy pumped up on amphetamine. At the end of every ad, he'd always point a finger at viewers. "You won't *find* a better price; not anywhere, not ever."

A sexy blonde woman with huge boobs and a bouffant hairdo always appeared with Ready in his ads. Her name was Jeanette, and she'd gush over the quality of the icemaker in her Frigidaire, or she'd rave about the turkey she had roasted in her Amana microwave oven.

"Bert's the guy with the buy," she always told her TV audience.

Once, when my brother, Jake, and I were boys, we watched a Ready Appliances TV ad with my mother, in our den in Pensacola. In the ad, Jeanette claimed she'd prepared an entire Thanksgiving feast exclusively on appliances she'd purchased from Ready. The food looked delicious: turkey, dressing, sweet potato casserole, fresh green beans, and even a red velvet layer cake.

My mother looked at Jeanette and shook her head. "I guarantee you that woman's never cooked a meal in her life. She probably doesn't know how to boil water."

"Do you think she's Bert's girlfriend?" Jake asked.

My father, also present, cleared his throat. "Or something like that."

Now, in the boardroom, Bert Ready looked more like a lawyer than the pop-eyed salesman I'd seen on TV. He wore a three-piece pinstriped suit with a white shirt and paisley necktie. A pair of tortoise-shell reading glasses rested on his nose. He fingered his lips while he studied a document he held in one hand.

The seventh board member, the slick-bald guy in the turtleneck sweater, I'd never seen before.

"That's Karl Katzenbach," Bucky told me, "head of the music department at FSU. I'm told his wife's the richest woman in Leon County."

I puckered one side of my face. "I don't get it. I've worked at Capital City four years. How come I've never seen most of these people on the golf course?"

Bucky snickered. "They don't *play* golf, Andy. They only belong to Capital City for the prestige, to establish themselves as part of Tallahassee's elite. Most wouldn't know a pitching wedge from a putter."

Ben Longstreet cleared his throat. Then he spoke in a smooth baritone. "Unless anyone objects, I'd like to call this meeting to order."

The room fell silent.

Longstreet looked right and left. "Do all board members have a copy of tonight's agenda?"

Up on the dais, six chins bobbed.

Longstreet said, "Under Robert's Rules, a reading of our last meeting's minutes can be waived. Do I hear a motion?"

Bert Ready raised a hand. "I move we waive reading of those minutes."

"All in favor?" Longstreet said.

All seven board members raised their hands, and then the meeting proceeded. Jack Orsini presented a proposed menu for the club's annual tournament banquet to be held in April. A budget for the meal was discussed.

"You'll save members six dollars a head if we go with Cornish game hens instead of beef tenderloin."

Bert Ready made a face. "Cornish game hens? I always feel I'm eating a parakeet when I'm served one."

People chuckled. And so it went.

Conditions of the fairways on the club's eighth and fifteenth holes were discussed with Mr. Justus, and with Bucky. Cost of repairs to the tractor used to gather practice balls at the club's driving range were discussed, as well as refurbishment of the restrooms between the ninth hole's green and the tenth hole's tee box.

"The walls are unpainted cinder block, and those toilets are ancient," Dr. Hardemann said in a voice so quiet I barely heard him. "The situation's unsanitary, in my view."

A children's golf clinic was discussed, and then replacement of the lifeguard stand at the club's swimming pool. I shook my head. The tension I'd felt earlier soon gave way to boredom. Why would anyone voluntarily serve on this board?

My thoughts wandered.

Three days hence, on Saturday morning, I would take the Law School Admissions Test. For the past few months, I had spent an hour each night, poring over a thick preparation manual I'd bought used at the campus bookstore.

The test, it seemed, did not gauge intelligence as much as aptitude for learning the law. It even included a section devoted to learning a "nonsense language." I had taken a practice exam, and I'd performed pretty well, but how would things go when I took the actual test?

My decision to seek a law degree hadn't been an easy one to make. This would mean three more years of school, three more years of subsistence-level living, three more years of cockroaches in McPhail's drafty apartment, three more years working as a caddy at Capital City, and three years of studying like I never had before.

Biff Schultz's older brother, Rex, was a third-year law student at University of Miami, and Biff had told me, "The first year, they worked him to death. He had no social life, spent all his time with his nose in books. In each class, his entire grade rode on a final exam. It's a ball-buster course of study."

And what about the fact I was gay? Would the Florida Bar grant me a license to practice law if they learned of this? If I became a lawyer, could I attract clients if I lived as an openly gay man?

"Ladies and gentlemen," Ben Longstreet said, "our next agenda item involves continued employment of Andrew Hunsinger as a Capital City caddy. Mr. McRae, I believe, has a motion he wishes to make?"

"I do," McCrae said in a scratchy tenor.

My scalp prickled. I straightened my spine and flexed my fingers.

"Here we go," Bucky whispered.

"Mr. Chairman," McRae said, "I move for Andrew Hunsinger's immediate dismissal from his caddying job at Capital City. It's come to my attention Mr. Hunsinger recently participated in a civil demonstration—a protest if you will—against Anita Bryant's 'Save Our Children' campaign."

Bert Ready made a face. "What's she saving our children from?"

Tom Bannister cleared his throat. "Mrs. Bryant spoke as a guest at First Baptist when she visited Tallahassee. She doesn't want our young people recruited by the homosexual community."

Ready shook his head. "Recruited for *what*?"

Bannister lowered his chin, but he kept his gaze fixed on Bert Ready. "For a *deviant* lifestyle, sir."

Kate Bonner knitted her eyebrows. Then she raised a hand. "I don't understand what this has to do with Mr. Hunsinger's job at Capital City."

Bannister turned to Kate Bonner. "He appeared on TV during this protest against Mrs. Bryant; he admitted to a reporter he is homosexual."

Dr. Katzenbach spoke with a lilt in his voice. "What's that got to do with the price of tea in China?"

"Karl," Kelly McCrae said, "he's a self-proclaimed sodomite. His continued employment reflects poorly on Capital City's reputation, and I—"

Bucky jumped to his feet; he pointed a finger at McCrae. "Just a minute here. I've known Andy all his life, I—"

Longstreet seized a gavel; he banged it on the desk top before him until the room grew quiet. "Let's have order here, folks. Everyone who wants to speak on this issue may do so, but we'll do so *one* at a time. Is that clear?"

No one responded.

Longstreet looked at Bucky. "You wish to address the board on this issue, Mr. Buchholtz?"

"I do."

"Go ahead."

Bucky strode to the lectern. Then he turned and looked at me. "Stand up, Andy. Let these folks see what a handsome young man you are."

My eyes itched when I rose. I looked each board member in the face. Then I sat down.

Bucky turned back to face the dais. "Like I said, I've known Andy all his life; his dad and I piloted bombers over Germany during World War Two. There's no finer family in Pensacola than the Hunsingers, I can tell you that. Andy's about to graduate from FSU. He's a bright boy, and a damned fine caddy too."

"Mr. Buchholtz," McRae said, "I'm told certain club members have refused Mr. Hunsinger's services because he's homosexual."

Bucky nodded. "A few have—it's true—and that's their choice. But should they dictate who we hire or fire? In my opinion, no."

Bannister cleared his throat. "*I*, for one, would not employ Mr. Hunsinger."

"Yeah, Tom," Bert Ready said, "but you don't play golf."

Bannister lowered his gaze; he didn't say anything.

"My grandson's thirteen," McRae said, "*he* plays golf here twice a week. I don't think he should be exposed—"

"Oh, for God's sake, Kelly," Kate Bonner said, shaking her head. "Do you really think Andy wants to 'recruit' your grandson?"

Longstreet banged his gavel again.

Dr. Hardemann raised a hand. "Mr. Chairman?"

"Yes, Doctor?"

"Perhaps Andy would like to address the board? I'm interested to hear what he has to say."

All seven board members turned their gazes to me.

"Mr. Hunsinger?" Ben Longstreet said.

Go on, have some balls. Do it.

My knees crackled when I left my seat. My voice broke like a teenager's when I spoke.

"I have a few things to say," I told Longstreet.

"Then come forward," Longstreet said.

Bucky sat down, and I took his place at the lectern.

My hand shook when I pulled my notes from my pants pocket. I chewed my lower lip while looking the notes over. The room was as quiet as an empty church. My heart thumped so hard I heard my pulse inside my head. I looked into Ben Longstreet's eyes, and then I spoke.

"I'm Andy Hunsinger, the *same* Andy Hunsinger I was before the Anita Bryant demonstration. I haven't changed. I was gay before; I'm still gay now. I caddied well before, I caddy well now. The only thing that's changed is that now you, and everyone else in Tallahassee, knows exactly who I am. I'm not hiding a thing from anyone."

I shifted my gaze to Katzenbach.

"My parents taught me honesty is important. And they taught me you can never be happy unless you are true to yourself. That's all I'm doing: being myself. I'm not a child molester; I'm not interested in having sex with a kid. But I don't like girls; I'm not attracted to them, never have been. That's just me, and I'm never going to change."

I kept on. I spoke of the AGA and our office in the student union. I talked about how I wanted to become a lawyer, and how I'd take the LSAT Saturday morning. I told the board I'd earned at three-point-seven GPA at FSU. I would graduate with honors in June, I said.

I swung my gaze to Bannister. "I'm not a 'deviant,' sir. I'm a human being who seeks love and companionship from another man. Does that make me unfit for employment by Capital City? I don't think so."

Bannister lowered his gaze.

I looked at Kelly McRae. "I know certain Capital City members no longer want me to caddy for them. I also know, from personal experience, these same people are intolerant of anyone who's not exactly like them. They represent the worst of this club, in my opinion."

Finally, I turned my gaze to Bert Ready. "I'm not ashamed of who I am. I'm proud I have the courage to be myself. And I'm proud of the work I've done at Capital City. I hope to continue caddying here while I attend law school. I hope you'll let me."

I picked up my notes, and then I returned to my seat.

Bucky patted my shoulder. "Good job, Andy. I'm proud of you."

Ben Longstreet looked right and left. "I wish to speak to the issue before us. It seems to me Mr. Hunsinger's a good caddy and a fine young man, as well. His private life, in my view, is *his* business, not this board's nor this club's. I'm concerned with Mr. Hunsinger's performance when he works here, not what he does on his own time, and in the privacy of his home."

Kelly McRae responded. "Ben, he *forfeited* his right to privacy by discussing his private life on the streets of our city."

Longstreet looked at McRae and raised his eyebrows. "How so, Kelly? By answering a reporter's question honestly? Would you have preferred he lied?"

McRae lowered his gaze and did not respond.

"Ladies and gentlemen," Longstreet said, "these are changing times. You heard what Mr. Hunsinger said: the university has officially recognized this student organization he belongs to. And I daresay most members of this board have befriended one or two homosexuals, be they men or women; I know *I* have."

Longstreet kept on. "I know Kelly and Tom believe the motion before us deserves to pass, but I disagree. I think their view is plain wrong."

"I call the question," Katzenbach said.

"Very well," Ben Longstreet said. "All in favor of Mr. McRae's motion?"

McRae and Bannister raised their hands, but no one else did.

I kept my job at Capital City.

Nine

I TOOK THE Law School Admissions Test in Ruby Diamond Auditorium, on the FSU campus, along with two hundred other aspirants. I filled in little circles with a number-two lead pencil while proctors roamed the hall, making sure no one cheated.

Chewing my pencil's eraser, I glanced here and there.

Was I as smart as the kids around me? Was I nuts, thinking I could become a lawyer? Was I capable of arguing cases in court? And would people even *hire* an openly gay lawyer?

Concentrate, Andy. Concentrate.

IN LATE MARCH, about eleven on a Thursday evening, a violent storm swept through Tallahassee, disrupting electrical service in our neighborhood. Rain drummed my windows, lightning flashed, and thunder shook the four-plex. Wind howled in the live oaks and pines. I didn't own a flashlight or even candles, so I sat in darkness on my sofa, listening to the storm roil.

Downstairs, Fergal's piano tinkled. He played a halting version of a tune I didn't recognize. He started, then stopped, then started again. The herky-jerky music sounded weird, but offered some measure of relief from the storm's howling. I peeked into the stairwell. Fergal's door was ajar; a caramel glow emanated from his apartment, and it cast a faint rhombus of light onto the stairwell floor. After fumbling my way into my kitchen in darkness, I seized two beers from my fridge. Then I descended the stairs to Fergal's, clutching the railing while treads beneath me squeaked.

Fergal sat at his upright piano with his back to the doorway. He wore only blue jeans; he was shirtless and barefooted and his marmalade hair reflected light from a brass candelabrum atop the piano. When I knocked, he started so violently I thought he might jump out of his skin. His voice cracked like a teenager's when he spoke.

"It's crazy outside, isn't it?"

Nodding, I held up the beers. "Care for one?"

We sat side by side on Fergal's battered sofa. I'd never been inside his apartment. The layout was identical to mine, but he'd furnished his place differently. A stuffed kangaroo head with huge glass eyes hung on one wall, looking spooky in the candlelight. A bookcase constructed with planks and concrete blocks held texts, framed photographs, and stacks of sheet music weighted down with glittering geodes. A footlocker served as a coffee table, and a wicker rocker with a cushioned seat occupied one corner. A dinette with two chairs stood against a wall by the kitchen. The candelabrum on the piano held only one candle, and its flame barely moved in the stillness of the room.

Temperatures in Tallahassee varied widely in March. On any given Monday, your breath might steam while you crossed campus under overcast skies. The cold and dampness passed right through your clothes and chilled your bones, and you needed an electric blanket to keep warm when you went to bed at night. But by Friday, perhaps, the sun would shine on the magnolia blossoms at Park Avenue. Mockingbirds would sing, dew would glisten on Landis Green, and a light flannel shirt was all you needed to be comfortable.

Now, although a storm raged beyond Fergal's windows, I felt reasonably warm in a T-shirt and jeans. I placed my bare feet on his footlocker, crossed my ankles. Then I sipped from my beer while listening to rain sheet off our building's eaves.

"Does it often storm like this here?" Fergal asked me.

I nodded. "At this time of year, you have cold air from Georgia clashing with warm air from down south. We get a few of these every spring, but this one's...especially bad."

Outside, lightning flashed again, illuminating our front yard like a high noon sun. Limbs on trees thrashed about like frenzied participants in a tribal dance. Thunder rumbled; it sounded like someone had dropped a bomb on Franklin Street. Our building shook and the windows rattled. In the kitchen, drinking glasses chattered and a drawer full of silverware hummed like a swarm of bees. The air was so charged with electricity, the hairs on the backs of my forearms stood up.

"Jesus *Christ*," Fergal cried. "Do you think we're safe?" Color had drained from Fergal's face. His eyes bugged, his breath whistled in his nose, and beads of sweat appeared on his upper lip. He trembled like a scared little boy.

"We'll be fine," I said.

After putting down his beer, Fergal rearranged himself on the sofa. He clasped his arms in his hands and rocked back and forth. Candlelight reflected in his eyes.

"I don't like lightning *or* thunder," he said. "They scare the hell out of me. I tried playing music just now—to calm myself—but I'm so frightened my fingers won't work properly."

"It's only a storm, Fergal."

He drew a breath, let it out. "I'm sorry if I'm acting like a pussy. It's just..."

"What?"

Fergal's gaze met mine. "Want to hear a story?"

I said, "Sure."

"My granny, on my mum's side, lives in Cairns, in northeast Queensland. Heard of it?"

I shook my head.

"It's a town on the Coral Sea, near the Great Barrier Reef. They'll sometimes get violent weather up there—as bad as this, or worse."

I sipped from my beer and didn't say anything.

"When I was little, we visited my granny for a week, my parents and I. This was during July, which is winter holiday time for schools in Melbourne. Granny's house was old, and I slept in an attic bedroom by myself; I think I was eight."

Fergal moistened his lips. "One night, after I'd gone to bed, the adults decided they'd stroll to a pub a few blocks away, to drink a pint or two. They left me alone, but I didn't even know they'd gone; I was fast asleep, you see."

After Fergal drank from his beer, he continued. "A storm came up, quite suddenly, a bad one with lots of thunder and lightning and high winds. It woke me up. The house shook and rain pounded on the roof, right over my head. I screamed for my mum and dad, but they weren't there."

Fergal grimaced. "I felt so scared I crapped in my PJs; it was awful."

"Look," I said, "I've lived around this kind of weather all my life. As long as you're indoors, you're safe."

He looked at me with an expression that said he didn't quite believe me.

"It's true," I said. "This building's made of brick; it's not going to fall apart. And the roof is sound. You have nothing to worry about."

Another lightning bolt flashed. We both glanced out Fergal's front windows, just in time to see a limb snap off a live oak. The limb fell into the four-plex's yard; it crushed a row of galvanized metal trash cans, making a sound like a car crash. Fergal leapt to his feet, his eyes grew as big as silver dollars. After darting across the room, he crawled under his dining table and covered his head with his arms.

"Jesus Christ, Andy. The world's coming to an end."

Do something before he hyperventilates.

"Fergal?"

"Yeah?"

"Come out from underneath the table. Come sit by me again."

Fergal didn't budge.

"Come on, it'll be okay."

Fergal's knees crackled when he rose. After shuffling back to the sofa, he plopped down beside me. I wrapped my arm about his shoulders and pulled him to me, so his cheek lay against my shoulder. He shook so hard the springs in the sofa creaked.

"We'll ride this out together," I said. "I won't let anything hurt you."

"What if Gina saw me like this? She'd think—"

"Gina would understand. Storms scare some people, just like snakes or plane flights. You can't help it."

Lightning flashed anew, and another thunder clap shook the four-plex. Fergal rubbed his knees together, and then a shiver ran through him.

"It's late and I'm tired," he said. "Will you do something for me?"

"What's that?"

Fergal's gaze turned to mine. "Spend the night with me?"

Huh?

Fergal's request caught me completely off guard, and I couldn't help myself; between my legs I felt a stiffening. I looked into Fergal's frightened face, trying to decide what I should say.

Careful, Andy. E-a-s-y…

"Are you sure you want me to do that?" I asked.

Fergal nodded. "I know it sounds a bit strange, but I'm afraid to be alone right now. I won't sleep a wink all night if you leave."

"All right," I said. "I'll stay if you'd like."

Fergal locked his front door. He seized the candelabrum, led me into his bedroom. There wasn't much in there: a double bed covered by a Navajo blanket, a bureau, a ladder-back chair, and a closet with bifold doors, just like mine. A poster of Jimi Hendrix was taped to one wall. I draped my jeans and shirt over the back of the chair while Fergal stowed his jeans in his closet. After we'd both visited the bathroom, Fergal blew out the candle, and then we crawled into his bed, a tight fit for two fully grown guys. We both lay on our backs. Fergal's hip, shoulder, and knee touched mine, and our leg hairs commingled. Lightning flashed and thunder rumbled.

Fergal pulled the covers up to his chin. He continued to tremble.

"Are you okay?" I asked.

"Andy, I'm scared shitless. Thanks for staying."

"I don't mind," I said.

Six weeks had passed since I'd last touched Aaron, and now, lying so close to Fergal, my pulse quickened. I smelled his skin and hair, felt his body heat, and heard his breathing. I thought of the day he'd helped me get my sofa upstairs, and how I admired his slim physique. Minutes before, when we'd sat in his living room, I honestly hadn't thought about sex with Fergal, despite the fact he was shirtless and my arm had rested about his bare shoulders. The storm's violence had been foremost in my mind, but now I pondered whether I should make a move on him.

He's Australian, I told myself, *bisexuality's probably common over there. And he's the one who invited you to bed; this was his idea. It may be the only chance you'll ever have to test the waters with him.*

But then I thought of Fergal huddling beneath his dining table, scared out of his wits, and I knew touching him sexually would be wrong. He'd been a friend to me, ever since I moved into the building. When I told him I was queer, the day of the Bryant demonstration, he accepted my revelation without a second's thought.

How could I forget his kindness?

Nothing Fergal had ever done or said suggested a sexual interest in me. He seemed to care for his girlfriend, and right now I occupied his bed only because he was frightened, not because he wanted me to touch him between his legs.

Show a little class, Hunsinger. Don't take advantage of the situation.

"Andy?"

"Hmm?"

"If I turn on my side, will you hold me?"

Ahh shit, Hunsinger. Be a friend.

"Of course," I said.

The sheets rustled while we rearranged ourselves. My knees met the backs of Fergal's. My hips pressed against his buttocks, and my chest met his shoulder blades. After I wrapped my arm around him, I held him close. His skin felt warm and soft. I buried the tip of my nose in his thick hair, and then I listened to his labored breathing. Gradually, the storm's intensity lessened. Lightning ceased flashing, and thunder became intermittent.

Fergal scratched the tip of his nose, and then he cleared his throat. "Good night, Andy; and thanks so much."

A smile crept across my lips.

"You're welcome, Fergal," I said. "You sleep tight, now."

A FEW DAYS after I'd spent the night at Fergal's, I sat at my dinette, filling out a stack of papers an inch thick; this was my application for admission to FSU's College of Law. The school wanted to know everything about me and my past. Had I ever been arrested? What extracurricular activities had I participated in during my undergraduate years? What were my parents' occupations? At what addresses had I resided while at FSU? What were the names and addresses of every school I'd attended since first grade? I had to call my mom for some of the older information. The law school even wanted to know if I suffered from any medical or psychological disorders.

Of course, I had to write a five-hundred-word essay explaining why I wanted to become a lawyer, and why I wished to attend law school at FSU. I must've written half a dozen drafts before I felt satisfied with the final version.

Days before, I'd received my LSAT results in the mail.

I had scored in the 87th percentile, better than I'd ever hoped for. Because my grades in my undergraduate studies were pretty good, I thought I stood a decent chance of getting admitted, but who knew? Competition for slots in next fall's first-year class was ferocious; less than half the applicants would be accepted, according to a letter from the law school's dean that accompanied my application package.

It took me several hours to complete the entire thing, and when I'd finally finished, I rubbed my eyes with the heels of my hands. My head ached and my brain felt numb. If just *applying* for law school was this time-consuming, how heavy would the workload be once classes started?

I stacked all the paperwork into a neat pile, and then I shoved everything inside a manila envelope the school had provided me. I climbed on my bike and headed for the post office, wondering as I pedaled whether I was kidding myself about my chances for admission. After all, I was a kid from a middle-class Pensacola suburb and a self-proclaimed gay boy who knew little about the law.

Did I stand a chance?

AFTER THE NIGHT I slept with Fergal, our friendship grew closer. His girlfriend, Gina, was performing an internship at an elementary school that quarter, and she couldn't devote the time to Fergal that she normally did. So I gave Fergal my companionship more frequently.

Often we prepared evening meals together, and then we studied at his place or mine. We tossed a Frisbee in our backyard or rode our bikes to a nearby park to kick a soccer ball back and forth. On a weekend when Capital City was closed for maintenance, we camped at St. George Island, on the Gulf Coast, in a beautiful park with sandy beaches and soaring dunes. We shared a tent and showered together in the park's facilities. One morning, we skinny-dipped in the Gulf at daybreak. Both of us splashed about in the waves like a pair of frisky seals while sunrise painted the horizon with shades of gold, pink, and green.

Whenever I saw Fergal naked—and this happened several times during the camping trip—my pulse quickened. How would it feel to have sex with him? But I kept those thoughts to myself. I had earned Fergal's trust when I hadn't made a pass at him the night we spent together, and now I wouldn't squander his friendship on the slim chance he might say yes to a request for intimacy.

He's your friend, Hunsinger. Isn't that enough?

On a Saturday afternoon in March, I returned home from Capital City, tired from caddying three rounds of golf on a particularly warm day. While I locked up my bike in the four-plex's stairwell, I heard Fergal play a familiar tune on his piano, and then a grin crossed my face.

I stuck my head through his open doorway. "That's music from *Pirates of Penzance*, isn't it?"

After Fergal turned on his piano bench, he arched his eyebrows. "*You* know Gilbert and Sullivan, mate?"

"Are you kidding? During high school, my drama club performed *Penzance*, and I played Frederic. We did *H.M.S. Pinafore*, too, and I played Ralph Rackstraw. I know every song in both shows."

Fergal rocked back and forth, laughing.

"My mum and dad perform in amateur theater, back in Melbourne. As a kid, I'd rehearse Gilbert and Sullivan numbers with them in our living room."

I took a seat next to Fergal on the bench. He wore a pair of boxer shorts—nothing else—and I smelled his piney scent.

"Do you know the 'Major-General's Song'?" I asked.

Fergal looked at me like I was daft. "Is the Pope Catholic?"

He struck the first chord, and then I commenced singing the silly tune, a monologue chirped by a pompous British army officer with a wealth of knowledge about science and military history, but who's utterly incapable of leading men into battle.

After I sang the tune, Fergal patted my shoulder. "You have quite the voice, mate. Keep going, please."

We continued until darkness fell. We performed "When Frederic Was a Little Lad" from *Pirates*, and then "We Sail the Ocean Blue" from *H.M.S. Pinafore*. We sang "When the Foeman Bares His Steel" from *Pirates,* too. I did the solos, and both of us joined in for the choruses. Fergal's scratchy baritone mixed well with my tenor; his piano accompaniments were precise and sure.

Neighbors gathered in the stairwell to listen, and soon a half-dozen people sat on the treads. One guy brought us two cold bottles of beer. People applauded in between numbers, and I beamed at their attention. I hadn't had as much fun in years. How I missed musical performing, and why had I quit?

When we'd finished our last number, Fergal gave me a wet smooch on my cheek while our audience cheered.

"You're the *best*, Andy. What a beautiful voice you have."

I felt so excited I wanted to grab Fergal by the shoulders and kiss him on the mouth, but I didn't, of course.

I mussed his hair instead.

Ten

IN 1977, EASTER fell on April 10, a day I won't ever forget.

I had driven to Pensacola from Tallahassee the night before. Sunday afternoon, after we'd attended services at First Methodist, I helped my mother prepare our family's Easter dinner: baked ham, scalloped potatoes in a cheese sauce, fresh green beans steamed with Vidalia onion, and a fruit salad. On the drain board, a chocolate layer cake with strawberry icing crowned a cut-glass serving pedestal.

In our living room, my dad and brother watched the Atlanta Braves play the Houston Astros on a console TV as big as my mom's cook stove.

Our home was a three-bedroom ranch-style cinder-block structure on a quarter-acre lot. My folks had bought the house with a VA loan, right after the army had discharged Dad from active duty. Most all the houses in the neighborhood had been built by the same developer.

Architecturally, they looked pretty much the same: carports, awning-style windows, brick accents, and screened lanais. But the developer had had the foresight *not* to bulldoze the native trees in the tract wherever possible. Instead, he built around them, so most houses enjoyed shade offered by live oaks, magnolias, and slash pines.

The year my parents bought our house, my mother planted dozens of azaleas along the flanks of the house and in beds surrounding the trees in our yard. By now, the shrubs were almost as tall as me. Mom kept them fertilized and pruned, and each Easter, they rewarded her with multitudes of pink and purple blossoms. Right now, our yard looked like a pageant float.

My folks had recently modernized the kitchen with new harvest gold appliances, Formica countertops, and fake-wood cabinets that tried to look like walnut but failed.

I found the changes less than appealing. What had been wrong with our maple wood cupboards, our old Frigidaire, and our tiled countertops? But I kept my mouth shut while I peeled and sliced potatoes at Mom's kitchen table. Rain had fallen the night before, and a scent of damp pine needles drifted in through an open window above the sink. Outside, a blue jay tootled on a slash pine's bough.

"You'd think the First Family were hillbillies, the way the media go an about them," my mother told me while she basted the ham with Coca-Cola. "Jimmy Carter's a Naval Academy graduate, and Rosalynn was valedictorian at Plains High School; they're sophisticated people."

I found it hard to concentrate on Mom's remarks. On the drive from Tallahassee the day before, I had decided I would tell my parents and brother I was gay.

It's time, I told myself.

I had rehearsed a speech. I would explain how I'd never felt attraction to girls, only boys. I would speak of my participation in the Bryant demonstration, my involvement with the Rap Group and AGA, and the gay and lesbian friendships I'd formed in Tallahassee. I would tell them about my brief relationship with Aaron, and how natural I had felt when we made love.

I had no idea what my family members' reactions would be. Homosexuality was a topic never discussed in our household—not in my presence, anyway. If my folks had any gay relatives or friends, they never mentioned them.

When I was in eighth grade, the Reverend Beauregard Davis, our minister of music at First Methodist, was arrested for indecency, after soliciting sex from an undercover police officer in a men's room at a Pensacola Beach county park. I recalled the expression on my mother's face when she read about it in the *News Journal* on a Saturday morning. She looked like she'd swallowed half a bottle of cod liver oil.

"I can't believe it," she told my dad while he studied the sports page. "Beau always seemed like such a *nice* young man."

Dad looked at Mom over the tops of his reading glasses. "Remember what Dr. King said, darling: 'There is some good in the worst of us and some evil in the best of us.'"

My parents had always professed unconditional love for me and my brother, so I didn't fear the kind of rejection certain Rap Group members had encountered when coming out to their families. My parents might be disappointed at my revelation, but they'd still love and accept me, I felt certain.

I wasn't so sure about my brother.

As tall as me, Jake had dark wavy hair, cobalt eyes, gleaming teeth, and a body like a gymnast's. He'd lettered in three sports at our high school, made honor roll every school term, and served in student government. His peers had chosen Jake to be their Homecoming King the previous fall, and his present girlfriend lived in a five-bedroom house overlooking a fairway at Pensacola Country Club. In September, Jake would attend Emory University on a full athletic scholarship. He'd goal-tend for the school's water polo team.

I'd heard Jake and his pals utter the word "faggot" many times during pickup basketball games in our driveway. "Suck my cock" was a frequent put-down. In Jake's world, queers were guys to be scorned and *never* respected no matter their accomplishments.

At school, Jake's friends had consigned non-athletes like me to a lower rung on the social ladder, and they always treated me with mild derision. Tough guys played ball or ran track, while pussies performed in school plays. Nonetheless, Jake and I had always shared a brotherly bond. Even as children, we formed a united front against our parents: no tattling, no taking sides with the folks. Most times, we tried to resolve our disputes on our own.

Our parents' conservative Methodist beliefs had never held sway with either of us.

"God's in heaven, protecting us?" I told Jake one night while we sat in lawn chairs in our backyard, studying stars. "Explain earthquakes and tsunamis that kill tens of thousands of innocent people. Explain the Nazi Holocaust or Joseph Stalin's mass killings in the USSR."

I quit attending church at age twelve—as soon as the decision was left up to me by my folks—and Jake followed suit on his own twelfth birthday. I called myself a humanist, while Jake declared himself agnostic. I'm sure my parents felt disappointed, but they didn't try to change our minds.

"We're all entitled our own personal beliefs," my mother told me.

At age fourteen, in a stupid act of rebellion, I took up smoking cigarettes, something my parents would not have tolerated if they'd known. I kept my Marlboros and breath mints stashed beneath a stack of sweaters in my bedroom closet, and though Jake knew about the cigarettes, he never squealed.

We had always shared our deepest secrets, Jake and I, ones we'd never reveal to friends or our parents. When Jake experienced his first wet dream, he told me about it the very next morning. When I skipped school three days in a row in high school to spend time at the beach with friends, Jake helped me write a note to the Dean of Men, using his deft forging skills to duplicate my mother's signature.

Whenever I performed in a community theater play, or my high school choir appeared in concert, Jake would always attend, along with my parents, even though they didn't require him to go. Likewise, I attended Jake's Pony League ball games and junior varsity football contests, even though I didn't much care for watching sports. I never thought twice about it. *Jake's my brother*, I told myself. *I need to be there.*

I don't want to imply all was blissful between Jake and me when I lived at home. We had our fair share of arguments and even a few fistfights. One of us might get sore at the other, and then we wouldn't speak for days; we'd sulk about the house like a pair of monks who'd taken an oath of silence. But we always made up in the end, as it seemed we couldn't do without confiding in each other for long.

A month before I left for college, Jake and I quarreled over something truly stupid: possession of our family's set of *World Book Encyclopedias*. I held the view I should take the books to FSU, to assist with my studies. Jake thought the set should remain at home.

"I'll need them for homework and essay assignments," he said.

My parents ruled in my favor.

"There's a set at the city's branch library," Mom told Jake at the dinner table. "You can ride your bike there in five minutes. Besides, college is difficult; Andy needs all the help he can get."

My brother's face turned brick red. After leaping to his feet, he shouted at me so loudly I'm sure the neighbors a block away heard him.

"They always take your side, *always*. No matter what I do to please them, it's not good enough. I can't *wait* 'til you leave. I mean it; I hope I'll never *see* you again."

After the blowup, we didn't speak to each other until the day I left for Tallahassee. I stood next to our pathetic Ford Fairlane, with my possessions in the trunk and my dad behind the steering wheel. An early morning breeze stirred the fronds on a sabal palm; they made a sound like cards being shuffled. I hugged my mother and kissed her tear-stained cheek. Then I extended my hand to my brother.

He wouldn't look me in the eye. Instead, he studied his sneakers while taking my hand and giving it the weakest of squeezes.

"Goodbye, Jake," I said. "I'll miss you."

Jake's face crumpled. After throwing his arms around my shoulders, he laid his cheek against my sternum. Then he bawled like a five-year-old.

"What is it?" I asked him. "What's wrong?"

"I don't want you to go. Who will I talk to?"

That was Jake for you: a bundle of vulnerability, guarded by a shield of bravado and talent.

Afterward, whenever I came home from school each summer, we spent much time together, doing simple things. We took walks through our neighborhood, and Jake would ask about college life. I described life in Tallahassee, and he listened raptly. He seemed fascinated, as though I were Marco Polo returned from a journey on the Silk Road, recounting my experiences. Sometimes, he dragged me into our backyard, along with a pair of worn ball gloves and a scuffed baseball. We played pitch and catch and talked about his future. Where would he attend college? What would he study? Would law or medicine be a good choice?

It occurred to me during these visits that Jake had no other confidants beside me. Our parents, as loving as they tried to be, weren't the most approachable people when it came to personal matters. And Jake's friends weren't the types to talk about their feelings, not ever.

Certain weekday nights, after our parents had gone to bed, we clambered atop our fuel oil tank, and then we crawled onto the roof of our house. We lay on our backs upon the still-warm asphalt shingles, with our fingers locked behind our necks and our elbows jutting. We stared into the night sky, saying little, just breathing the cool evening air and thinking private thoughts.

One such evening, during the summer following my sophomore year, we studied constellations on the roof while a Gulf breeze whispered in our long leaf pines. Earlier, we had played one-on-one in our driveway, and now we both sweated. Jake's body odor had a unique sweet-and-sour scent I could've recognized blindfolded. After rearranging his limbs, he spoke in shaky voice.

"There's something I want to talk about, something secret. If I do, you can't mention the situation to anyone—not even Mom or Dad, understand?"

"Of course."

Jake looked at me and squinted. "Do you promise? I'll get in trouble if—"

"Jake, I promise. Just tell me."

He drew a breath, let it out. "You know Tracey Bramlett? She's a girl I'm seeing."

"Which one is she? I can't keep track."

Jake turned toward me. After bending an elbow, he rested his cheek on the heel of his hand. "She talks with a Birmingham accent, has curly hair, and big boobs. Her dad has an insurance agency on Palafox Street."

I made a face. "Is she the one who's older than you, the one Mom's not fond of?"

Jake nodded.

"What about her?"

Jake rolled onto his back. "I got her pregnant, Andy."

I winced. My little brother screwed girls? He was only *fifteen*. How could it be?

"Do her parents know?"

"Not yet. She just told *me* three days ago."

I sat up. After I bent my knees, I rested my forearms on them. "Are you sure it's yours?"

"Pretty sure."

I didn't know what to say.

"Tracey says there's a doctor in Mobile, a woman who does...abortions."

I shuddered when he said the word. Sure, I knew about the procedure. The US Supreme Court had ruled a woman had the right to terminate a pregnancy early on, if she chose to—no questions asked—but I'd never actually known anyone who'd been a part of ending a baby's life. And then I thought of my parents. What would they say if they knew?

"It costs three hundred dollars," Jake said. "Tracey says she'll do it—her parents won't even know—but I have to come up with the money."

"You have your savings bonds from Mee-Maw, right?"

Jake grimaced. "They're in Mom and Dad's safe deposit box at Second National. I'd have to explain why I wanted them."

I nodded.

Jake rose to a sitting position. Like me, he bent his knees, rested his arms upon them. Moonlight reflected in a tear rolling down his cheek, and then his voice quivered when he spoke.

"I can't support a baby, Andy. And I don't want to marry Tracey, either; I want to go to college, like you. Why did this have to happen?"

My thoughts churned. I tried to imagine myself in Jake's position: a kid entering his junior year of high school, a boy full of promise, dragged into a life he didn't want or ever expect to face. I had a job for the summer, unloading tires and batteries off transfer trucks at Sears & Roebuck's automotive department. Already, I had saved one hundred fifty dollars. By summer's end, I'd have five hundred at least, a nice little cash reserve for my third year of college. The Sears job was hot sweaty work—I detested time spent there—but my wages were better than average for summer work. Did I really need to spend *my* hard-earned money to make up for my brother's reckless behavior?

This is Jake's problem, I told myself, *not mine.*

But then I thought of an Earth Day poster I'd seen taped to Biff Schultz's kitchen wall. The poster depicted a little girl planting a pine seedling; it included a quote from Dr. Seuss's book, *The Lorax.*

"Unless someone like you cares a whole awful lot, nothing is going to get better. It's not."

Who else would help with Jake's predicament? Who else but me could make things better? Sure, my parents would be suitably concerned at Jake's predicament—they'd feel badly for Jake—but they would never in a million years finance an abortion, nor would they allow Jake to pay for one from his savings. "You've made your bed," they'd tell Jake. "Now lie in it."

I didn't know Tracey Bramlett's parents, but it seemed they were typical middle-class Pensacola folks. At best, they'd send Tracey to live with out-of-town relatives until the baby arrived and was given up for adoption. At worst, they'd insist Jake marry Tracey. In either case, Jake's life would be hellish, his reputation tarnished beyond redemption. This was Escambia County, circa 1975, and both Jake and Tracey might be expelled from school, as well.

Lying next to Jake on the roof, I studied star clusters while my brain buzzed. At the time, I owned a surfboard I hadn't ridden since leaving for FSU. I had a gold chain my grandparents had given me for my sixteenth birthday. Together, the two would fetch two hundred dollars at a pawn shop, and my parents wouldn't even notice these items were missing if I sold them.

"I think I can help," I told Jake.

"I don't understand," he said. "What could *you* possibly do?"

To this day, I believe no one knows about Tracey's abortion, other than Tracey, Jake, me, and Tracey's doctor.

Jake's relationship with Tracey ended, along with the pregnancy, and thereafter Jake never mentioned Tracey's name again. The last I heard, Tracey had married a wealthy tobacco farmer. She'd been elected to the Escambia County Commission, running as a Republican and an Evangelical Christian.

Now, as we gathered in my parents' dining room for Easter dinner, I wondered if Jake would care "a whole awful lot" about *my* need for acceptance from him.

Would my revelation damage our relationship, maybe permanently? Would he shun me like a leper?

Halfway through our meal, my mother turned to me with her forehead furrowed. "Andy, you're only picking at your food. What's wrong? Are you not feeling well?"

I looked down at the barely touched meal on my plate, and then the room seemed to shrink. My vision blurred and I felt tightness in my chest. I drew a breath. Then I looked up at my mother and spoke.

"Mom, I'm gay."

My mother's face slacked while her eyes blinked.

My father dropped his fork; it tap-danced on his plate while his face turned as white as an eggshell. He looked as though he'd just witnessed a fatal car accident.

I continued. "I know Easter dinner might not be the best time to tell you this, but I feel you should know about my private life. I don't want to hide it any longer."

"Are you sure you're gay?" my mom asked. "Are you positive?"

Before I answered her question, I looked at Jake. He stared into his plate, his face expressionless. He looked as though he'd been stomach-punched.

I said, "I've known I was gay since I was twelve or so. I never liked girls, not in a sexual way."

My dad spoke up. "Son, have you actually been with another man?"

I looked at him and nodded. "It's what's right for me."

Dad lowered his chin; he drew circles on his plate with the fork he'd dropped.

"I don't wish to be *indelicate*," my mother said, "especially at the table. But exactly what do you and your lovers *do* when you're in the bedroom?"

Jake leapt to his feet; his face grew beet red. "For Christ's sake, Mom, you don't ask a guy something like that." Jake threw his napkin on the table. Then he strode from the room, heading for the hallway that led to our bedrooms.

"Jacob," my mother called, "come back and sit."

Jake didn't, and moments later, I heard a door slam.

My mother rose—it seemed she would follow Jake to his bedroom—but then my father seized her forearm.

"Leave him be for now; he's upset."

My mother sat. After she'd cleared her throat, she looked at me. Tears glistened in her eyes and her voice sounded throaty when she spoke.

"Don't you want to have children, Andy?"

"Children would be nice," I said, "but two men can't make a baby."

Mom looked into her lap, and then back at me. "I've heard homosexuals can sometimes change their behavior, through psychotherapy. They can lead normal lives, even father children."

"Mom, that's not going to happen. I'm okay with being gay; really I am. But I need to know you and Dad—and Jake as well—are okay with it too. I need to know you'll still love me, in spite of the fact I'm different."

"Honey," my mother said, "you *know* we'll always love you. It's just...some people will say cruel things when they find out. We don't want you hurt; we want you to be happy."

"I'll never be happy if I can't be myself."

When my dad rearranged his limbs, his chair frame squeaked.

"Do you have a boyfriend?" Dad asked.

"Not now, but I did for a while."

I talked about Aaron and our breakup. I told them about Jeff, and then I spoke of the AGA and the guys I'd met through the Rap Group.

"They're the first true friends I've ever had. I can be myself with them."

My mother chewed her lower lip; I could tell she was fighting an urge to weep, and who could blame her? Her eldest son was a faggot; he'd never give her grandchildren.

"Do you think," my dad asked, "this happened because of something your mother and I did when raising you?"

"You've been great parents," I said. "I couldn't have asked for better. But honestly, I think I was born gay. Nothing you could have done would have changed that, believe me."

My mother stiffened her spine. Then she looked at my dad.

"Darling, will you help me clear the table and load the dishwasher? I think everyone's quite finished with their meal."

"I can help," I said.

Mom shook her head. "Go talk to your brother instead."

When I knocked on Jake's bedroom door, he didn't respond. I twisted the knob, but he had engaged the lock.

"Jake, please open the door. I want to talk."

No response.

"I'm your brother," I said. "Please don't shut me out."

Sheets rustled and bedsprings squeaked. Then Jake opened the door. His eyes were red-rimmed and puffy, and he wouldn't look at me. His dark hair was tangled. After I entered the room, I closed the door behind me. Jake sat on his bed and I sat on his desk chair, facing Jake. He fixed his gaze on his sneakers.

"Tell me what you're thinking right now," I said. "I need to know."

When he looked up, his breath whistled in his nose. "I'm pissed. Not because you're a cocksucker—I guess I can handle that—but you *hid* it from me, like being gay was a secret you didn't trust me with. I thought we'd always been honest with each other, but now..."

"What?"

He looked at his lap. "I don't know *what* to think. I don't even know who you are right now."

"You have to understand," I said, "I only started having sex with men last summer. I wanted to be sure it was right for me before I told you or Mom and Dad about it."

Jake raised his chin, and then his gaze met mine. "You've led a double life, all this time. How many more secrets are you hiding from me?"

"You can ask me anything, and I'll answer truthfully. I mean it: just ask."

Jake narrowed his eyes. "How many guys?"

"Huh?"

"How many guys have you fucked with?"

I held Jake's gaze. "Two."

"Did you take it up the butt?"

The tops of my ears burned, but I kept on looking into Jake's eyes. "Sometimes I did. It may sound strange, but it felt very good to me."

Jake made a face. "Doesn't it hurt?"

"Not if it's done right."

"Did you kiss these guys?"

"One of them, yeah. Look, gay sex is not all that different from straight sex; I'm just working with different body parts than you do when you're in bed with a woman."

Jake made another face, like he'd swallowed something bitter. "What's it like, sucking another guy's dick?"

"*I* like it—a lot. In some ways, I think a man can pleasure another guy in ways a woman can't."

Jake grimaced. "I wouldn't want some guy's dick in *my* mouth."

I snickered. "You don't have to like cocks, Little Brother. It's my thing, not yours."

Jake's face clouded. "Don't laugh; this isn't funny. We're having a serious talk here."

I raised a palm. "Okay, all right, I'm sorry. Any more questions?"

Jake moistened his lips. "Have you ever thought about…"

"What?"

"Fucking *me*?"

I stifled a giggle. Sure, Jake was a good-looking boy, but he was my *brother*, for god's sake. Making love with him seemed incomprehensible, like having sex with one of my parents.

After reaching across the space between us, I mussed his hair. "Sorry to disappoint you, Jake, but as cute as you are, I've never wanted to get inside your pants."

Jake looked away and sucked his cheeks. Then he swung his gaze back to me. "Can we make a deal?"

"What's that?"

"Promise you'll never hide something like this from me again. We should always be truthful about everything we do, no matter what it is. I don't think I could stand it any other way."

At that moment, I realized just how lonely a person Jake was. I'd always been his confidant—the only person he truly trusted—and I had violated that trust. No wonder he felt upset. After moving to my brother's bed, I wrapped an arm about his shoulders.

"I promise, Jake," I said. "No more secrets, ever."

Eleven

COMING OUT TO my family released whatever inhibitions I'd previously harbored about sex and promiscuity, and then I became—quite frankly—a slut. No matter how many sexual encounters I had, I wanted more.

Shortly after Easter, Tallahassee's first gay bar, the Gate, opened for business, and this expanded my opportunities to meet men, exponentially. No more furtive glances or subtlety, *ala* the Pastime. Guys danced with each other at the Gate, kissed in the bar's dark corners, and left the place holding hands.

Located on Lake Bradford Road, the Gate was a mile south of Doak Campbell Stadium. The bar's proprietor was Darby, a bearded man in his late thirties with linebacker shoulders and a South Carolina drawl. The son of a Parris Island Lieutenant Colonel, Darby shared his double-wide mobile home with a freckle-faced boy named Beau, age sixteen, a high school dropout. The relationship between Darby and Beau was never fully explained. Was Darby a mentor to Beau, were they related, or were they lovers?

Who knew? But I never saw one without the other.

Word had it Darby's dad sent him periodic stipends, enough money to pay Darby's living expenses, and then some. In exchange, Darby kept his distance from his hometown of Beaufort, where his homosexuality would have disgraced his military family.

The Gate shared a building with the Owl Tavern, the latter a dump catering to bikers. The Owl had a reputation for fistfights and drug deals. Broken glass and crushed beer cans littered the property's asphalt parking lot. On Tuesday nights, both bars offered specials to their patrons—twenty-five-cent cans of Busch beer—and crowds from both establishments would spill into the parking lot. The gay boys wore sweaters and flared dress slacks, or blue jeans and long-sleeved T-shirts. The bikers sported leather gear and head bandanas.

An unwritten understanding existed between patrons of the Owl and the Gate: *leave us alone and we'll leave you alone.* Sure, occasionally a biker might holler "faggot" at a swishy gay boy, or maybe a crowd of Owl patrons would wolf-whistle at a drag queen passing by them in the parking lot, but otherwise the two subcultures ignored each other.

In the days before I'd come out to my family, I was cautious about approaching other men for sex. I'd wait for a sign, a flicker of interest. And, of course, this rarely happened, at least when it came to men I found attractive. But now, I didn't hesitate to hit on guys I liked. Who cared about rejection? If I struck out with one guy, I might score with the next.

Fortified by beer, I'd approach a cute FSU student or a handsome state government employee. I'd say, "Hi, I'm Andy. I don't think we've met."

Then things would take their course.

More than once, I shared a bed with an angelic FSU undergraduate named Pierre. He was a meteorology student from Baton Rouge, with a Cajun accent and a cute bubble butt.

A law clerk for the Chief Justice of Florida's Supreme Court screwed me silly on his waterbed, several times.

I hit on a Publix bagboy named Chris when he wheeled my groceries to my car. Chris was a high school senior with a Panhandle drawl, rust-colored hair that grew to his shoulders, and ample endowment between his legs. He'd visit my apartment when he was supposed to be studying at the public library, and then we'd take turns humping each other.

In the Gate's shadowy parking lot, I shared oral sex in my Vega with guys whose names I didn't even care to know: a long-distance trucker, a drywall hanger, a physicist, and a postal worker. Not once did I seek anything more than a physical relationship with these guys, nor did they look for something emotionally meaningful from me. Our meetings were sex for its own sake, nothing more, and I often wondered if my private life would always be this way.

Maybe love between two men isn't possible.

RUNNING WITH BIFF Schultz and his roommates became a haven for me, a respite from my frustration at not having a boyfriend. We gathered most every weekday afternoon, usually at the university track. I'd quit smoking cigarettes, and now I could run three miles in twenty-four minutes, just as Biff and his friends did. I purchased Nike "waffle iron" shoes and a pair of nylon running shorts slit at the thighs for ease of movement. The shorts had a built-in liner that cupped my genitals so they wouldn't bounce around during the run. I thought they looked pretty sexy on me.

I loved everything about running: the sweating, the rhythmic breathing, the feel of my heartbeat, and the sound of my feet kissing the Tartan turf while I glided around the oval with my friends. Sometimes we worked on "interval training." We ran a fast lap at six-minute pace, and then a slow lap at a ten-minute pace. Then another fast lap: over and over.

"It helps when you race competitively," Biff told me. "You make these bursts every so often; you pass many guys in the process."

On weekends, if Biff wasn't camping, the four of us traveled to Silver Lake, a twenty-acre spring-fed beauty west of Tallahassee, right after I'd finished caddying for the day. Miles of running trails snaked through virgin forest surrounding the lake. We ran in the shade of live oaks and long leaf pines; we crushed pine needles and oak leaves beneath our sneakers while we strode along at an easy pace, often for an hour or more.

We didn't talk much while we ran, and that was fine with me. During the first half hour, I'd reflect on my life: what I'd done, the changes I'd gone through since moving into McPhail's place, and where I would go in the future. Would I continue with my education in law school, or would I return to Pensacola? Would I ever find a boyfriend who'd accept the fact I was openly gay?

Then, halfway through a Silver Lake run, my mind would empty itself of thought entirely. I became a running machine, concentrating only on my breathing. I entered a trancelike state when I didn't even notice my surroundings or think of my companions any longer. I suppose what I experienced was something akin to a transcendental meditative state. All I knew was, I'd never felt more free and relaxed. By the end of a forest run, someone could have thrown rocks at me and I wouldn't have noticed or cared.

Afterward, we always spread blankets on the lake shore, took a swim in the placid waters, and snacked on simple foods: celery and carrot stalks, trail mix, and soy nuts. We guzzled apple juice or soy milk.

As months passed, I got to know Travis and Austin pretty well, both during our running sessions, and when visiting their house.

Austin planned to become a pediatrician; he would practice in Kingston one day.

"So many Jamaican children lack medical care," he told me. "It's my calling." Austin's dry sense of humor and dazzling smile kept us all grinning and laughing. His nickname for me was "Andy Boy." He liked teasing me about my attraction to guys instead of girls, but never maliciously. The four of us would lie on our blankets at Silver Lake, and then Austin might point to a good-looking college student swimming nearby.

"There's one for you, Andy Boy. You find him attractive, don't you?"

And I might say, "No, Austin. Actually, I prefer hunky Jamaican men, the kind with bushy hair and banana-sized dicks. How big is yours?"

Austin would lift his gaze to the sky and cackle.

Travis was quiet, almost to the point of secretiveness. He studied long hours in his bedroom, poring over medical texts at a beat-up desk facing a window. In his room, a bookcase held dozens of books on anatomy, physiology, chemistry, biology, and so on. A crucifix hung above his desk, and a framed print depicting Jesus in the Garden of Gethsemane decorated another wall.

"My family's Primitive Baptist," he explained to me one day. "We're very devout."

Every Sunday morning, Travis washed Biff's bare feet, and then Austin's, before Travis left for church. Kneeling on the bathroom floor, wearing only jockey shorts, he used a shallow porcelain basin, a fluffy purple towel, and soap scented with lavender to perform his tasks.

"It's a peculiar rite practiced by Primitive Baptists," Austin explained. "I know it seems a bit odd, but we let Travis do it because we love him. Plus, it's nice starting your week with squeaky-clean toes."

Travis kept a six-string acoustic guitar in his room, and sometimes he would teach me a few chords if I asked him to. As far as I knew, he never dated. School, running, and religion seemed to consume his life. He slept on a thin mattress without frame or box springs, resting on his bedroom's linoleum floor, and each night he knelt on the floor to say his prayers, bathed in the glow from a candle burning on his desk. He filled his room with plants of varying types and sizes: philodendrons, ferns, a corn plant, an areca palm, and a variegated green-and-purple coleus. The room was like a jungle.

"I've known him since high school," Biff told me. "He comes from a family of doctors. His dad's a vascular surgeon, so are his uncle and older brother. He always tells people, 'I was born with a stethoscope around my neck.'"

I liked my apartment, of course. But sometimes I grew lonely, and I always felt welcome when I visited Biff, Austin, and Travis at their house, a three-bedroom cinder-block building with a carport and a screened rear porch. The home sat on a lot shaded by live oaks and long leaf pines, on a dead-end street west of campus.

Biff's Volkswagen shared the home's carport with Travis's Oldsmobile station wagon, and three ten-speed bikes.

Biff and Austin both had girlfriends. Austin dated a Cuban-American girl, Maritza, who worked as a state legislator's aide at the Capitol. Biff's girlfriend, Carol Ann, was also a pre-med major, a pretty, slender girl with sad eyes and hair straight as straw; it grew to her waist. She was the first girl I'd ever known who didn't shave her legs.

Weekends, we often gathered at the house during early evening, to drink beer or cheap jug wine. In the shady backyard, I cooked chicken quarters on Biff's charcoal grill, basting the chicken in my homemade barbecue sauce. The girls prepared tossed salad or coleslaw, while Biff and his roomies cooked baked beans, garlic bread, and corn on the cob. We dined together on the screened porch—all of us seated on benches at a redwood picnic table—and I sometimes felt like an adopted waif.

After dinner, we smoked marijuana, using a bong we passed around the living room, and even Travis partook. He sipped from the wine jug, too, and I found these behaviors strange, considering his conservative upbringing. Didn't drug and alcohol use clash with his religious beliefs?

When I asked Travis about this, a little smile crossed his lips.

"Jesus often drank wine, and he never said smoking marijuana was wrong. Ganja's a natural substance; God made it. Why not smoke weed if it gives you pleasure?"

At Biff's house parties, music wafted endlessly from the stereo speakers: Fleetwood Mac, Jefferson Starship, AC/DC, and Iggy Pop. I'd relax on a bean bag chair, and then reflect on how happy I felt spending time with Biff and his circle of friends. Why had I wasted three years of my life hanging out with fraternity boys?

"Stay overnight anytime you like," Biff told me, and sometimes I did. I'd snuggle in a blanket on the living room sofa, listening to bedsprings squeak in Biff's bedroom, and hearing Maritza's sighs while Austin made love to her on his waterbed. Travis often played his guitar late in the evening, and I'd fall asleep to the sound of strumming beyond his bedroom door. He'd sing a Dylan tune or a Neil Young number in his baritone, or sometimes he sang the Delta blues—sad little songs about broken dreams and love gone bad.

But most weekend nights, I didn't stay. I'd leave around midnight to visit the Gate, in hopes of finding my own brand of love. Sometimes I scored, but most times I didn't, and I often ended up alone at my apartment. I lay in my bed and stared at the ceiling. Cars passed on the street out front, and glare from their headlights passed through the slats of my Venetian blinds.

Will this loneliness ever end?

MIDDAY ON A Saturday in May, the six of us—Biff, Carol Ann, Austin, Maritza, Travis, and I—organized a picnic outing at a state park on the banks of the Ochlockonee River, west of town. Rain had fallen constantly the day before; the course at Capital City was underwater in places, so I wasn't caddying that day. At the river, the ground was sodden and tree limbs sagged from the weight of dew. But now the sun shone, and birds tweeted in the park's towering oaks, magnolias, and pines. The river's tannin-stained water flowed past us on its journey to the Gulf of Mexico. Biff and Austin tossed a football back and forth while Travis strummed his six-string and I played gin rummy with the girls.

I had spent the previous evening at Franklin Street, preparing potato salad from a recipe I'd found in my Betty Crocker cookbook and then listening to Fergal play jazz music on his piano. I'd slept fitfully, as disturbing dreams kept waking me every hour or so.

In one dream, my brother, Jake, appeared in water polo attire: a slinky Speedo and one of those silly headgears with ear protectors that make a guy look like a Koala bear. But Jake wasn't playing water polo; he was drowning in a whirlpool in a swiftly flowing river that coursed through a dark and creepy jungle. He called to me for help, flailing his arms like a crazy man. I was in the river, too, but fully clothed. My shirt and jeans stuck to my skin. I tried to swim toward Jake, but the river's flow kept sweeping me away from him.

In another dream, my former boyfriend, Aaron, appeared as a blackjack dealer in a Las Vegas casino. He wore a shiny silk vest, a long-sleeve white shirt with French cuffs, and a diamond pinky ring. In the dream, I sat at Aaron's baize-covered table. A dozen people played the game, all elegantly dressed. Only one I recognized: Jeff, the serviceman from Eglin Air Force Base, the guy who'd deflowered me. He wore a white dinner jacket and black bow tie, and he wouldn't make eye contact with me. I kept asking Aaron to deal me in, too, but he ignored me as if he couldn't hear me or even see me, as if I were invisible.

I had never been to Las Vegas; I'd never been in a casino or played blackjack. And why was Aaron appearing in my dream?

Feeling frustrated and out of sorts, I finally lit a lamp around 5:00 a.m. I opened a recently purchased copy of *Blueboy* magazine, and then I jerked off to a photo spread of two guys butt-fucking in a locker room. The guy on top had a kielbasa for a cock. The other guy was skinny and blond and looked barely eighteen. After I came, I lay naked on the sheets while my chest heaved and sweat trickled from my armpits.

Within minutes, I dozed off.

When I woke, sunlight streamed into my room and birds chirped in the live oaks. My bedside lamp still glowed, the KY tube rested on the nightstand, and the *Blueboy* lay beside me on the mattress. I shook my head at the pitiful situation.

How romantic, Hunsinger. You're such a stud...

Now, at the river, the six of us dined on sandwiches, pickles, hard-boiled eggs, and the potato salad I'd made, at a concrete picnic table shaded by forty-foot bald cypress trees. The guys sipped from cans of Budweiser; the girls shared a bottle of sangria.

While Austin helped himself to a second serving of my salad, he gave me one of his backhanded compliments.

"You're quite the chef, Andy Boy; it's the best I've ever tasted. You'll make some guy a fine wife one day."

Everyone laughed, including me.

Maritza pointed a pickle spear skyward. "It's not fair. Austin has me, and Biff has Carol Ann, but Andy and Travis have no one."

She glanced around the table. "We need to find Andy a boyfriend, and Travis a girlfriend, the sooner the better."

My face grew warm, and then I lowered my gaze to my plate.

"It's a nice thought," Austin said, "but I think they can manage their love lives themselves."

"That's the *problem*," Maritza said. "They don't have love lives to manage."

I glanced over at Travis. He stared at Maritza with narrowed eyes, and then he spoke to her in the sternest tone I'd ever heard him use.

"I don't *want* a love life," he said. "I'm fine with being single, and I *don't* need your help."

Maritza crinkled her forehead. "I don't understand. No one wants to be lonely, do they?"

Biff cleared his throat. "Why don't we talk about something else?"

"Why?" Maritza said. "I'm only trying—"

"Sweet pea," Austin said to Maritza, "there's a nature trail a short distance from here; it follows the river. Finish your sandwich, and then we'll take a walk, just you and me."

Maritza's gaze traveled from face to face. She drew a breath, and then let it out. "Fine. Forget everything I just said."

Travis sat motionless; he continued to stare at Maritza like she'd insulted him. The tension at the table was so strong I felt it in the hair follicles of my scalp. What was going on? Was a quarrel about to erupt?

Say something, anything.

"Look," I said to Maritza, "at the risk of sounding desperate, *I'd* sure like some help. I'm not having any luck finding a boyfriend, no matter how hard I try. The best I can manage are one-night stands, and trust me, they're *none* too satisfying."

Everyone laughed, including Travis.

Maritza smirked at me. "What sort of boys do you like, Andy? What's your type?"

I scratched my head. "Let me think... How about a guy under thirty, with two arms, two legs, and a full set of teeth? Do you know anyone like that?"

Everyone laughed again.

Hours later, Biff gave me a lift home, and when we reached my place, I asked Biff a question. "I don't understand something: what happened between Travis and Maritza today? I've never seen Travis so cross."

Biff didn't answer until he'd parked and switched off his engine. A vertical crease appeared between his eyebrows when he turned to me.

"I'll tell you something about Travis—it's information few people in Tallahassee know—and you'll need to keep it to yourself."

I looked at Biff and crinkled my forehead.

Biff said, "Back in Jacksonville, Travis dated a girl named Merilee, a babe all the guys at our high school wanted. Merilee's folks liked Travis; they treated him like a son. During spring break, our senior year, they took him to Myrtle Beach on their family vacation.

"Merilee had a brother named Chip, a year younger than her. At some point during the vacation, Merilee's mom walked into the room Chip shared with Travis—without knocking. She found Chip and Travis, you know..."

Biff lowered his gaze while his cheeks reddened.

"What?" I said.

Biff's gaze met mine. "They were sucking each other's cocks."

I tried to imagine the scene in my mind: a shocked mom, two boys caught *en flagrante*.

"Jesus," I said, shaking my head.

Biff scowled. "Merilee's folks sent Travis home on a Greyhound bus. They called his parents, said all kinds of mean things about Travis, even threatened to call the police. The story spread at school like crazy; everyone knew about it."

"How awful," I said.

"*Worse* than awful: Travis caught all kinds of shit. People kicked and punched him; they called him nasty names. No one but me stuck by him, and *I* caught shit for doing that too. Things got so bad Travis transferred to a private school."

I squirmed in my seat, not saying anything.

Biff continued. "Travis was supposed to room with me our freshman year at FSU, but over the summer, he had a mental breakdown. He spent time in a facility, someplace in St. Augustine, a hospital where they treat people with screwed-up heads."

"Does Austin know about this?"

Biff nodded.

"I take it the girls don't?"

"That's right. And let's keep it that way, shall we?"

"Of course." Then I asked Biff, "Do you think Travis is gay?"

Biff raised a shoulder. "Who knows? Maybe you should ask him."

I worked my jaw from side to side, trying to imagine the humiliation and taunting Travis must have experienced back in Jacksonville. No wonder he'd seemed so introspective and mysterious since I'd met him. I had always felt an attraction to Travis—I liked his androgynous looks, lanky limbs, and baritone voice—but I'd never once suspected he was gay.

And what did it matter if he was?

He wasn't on the market for love, was he?

Twelve

I MET DEXTER Hayward at the Gate on the Friday night of Memorial Day weekend. I sat on a barstool next to Dexter, not because I planned to meet him, but only because all the other stools were occupied. The place was packed to the gills with students and townies. Couples danced to "Rubber Band Man" and the Bee Gees' "You Should Be Dancing," beneath pulsing strobe lights and a mirrored disco ball.

When it came to clothing, I'd always leaned toward the conservative side of fashion: button-down shirts, chinos, polo shirts, and traditional blue jeans. I guess my Pensacola upbringing had a lot to do with my tastes. But in 1977, the disco craze and the fashions that came with it made their appearance at the Gate. Guys wore white polyester pants that flared from the knee downward. They wore platform shoes and shiny Nik Nik shirts with gaudy motifs. Many patrons wore their shirts unbuttoned halfway down their chests to display gold chains hanging around their necks. Aviator sunglasses and caterpillar mustaches completed the look.

The crowd at the Gate that night looked like a gaggle of peacocks, and I found it hard to believe I was in sleepy Tallahassee, instead of Miami or New York. The Gate's patrons differed so much from the grungy elements one saw at the Pastime Tavern.

After I ordered a beer from a bartender with rings on his thumbs and all eight of his fingers, I turned my head toward Dexter. My gaze met his, and when he smiled, his emerald eyes twinkled. He spoke to me with a drawl as thick as molasses.

"I've seen you here before. It's about time we met."

We exchanged names and shook hands, and then Dexter explained that he attended Tallahassee Community College. He said he was twenty years old, but to me, he looked more like sixteen. Copper-colored freckles peppered his turned-up nose. His shock of yellow hair, pouty lips, and long eyelashes gave him a boyish look I found appealing. He wore a Nik Nik shirt with a pattern of tumbling dice scattered across a kelly-green background, along with a pair of tight-fitting button-fly Levi 501 jeans.

"Tell me about yourself," he said.

I talked about school, my apartment, and my involvement with AGA at the university, all the while taking gulps from my beer. While I rambled on, Dexter sipped from a can of Coke. He listened to my chatter as if my life was utterly fascinating, but when I'd drained my beer and turned to order another, Dexter touched my forearm.

"I have an idea," he said.

I looked at him and raised my eyebrows.

Dexter said, "I share an apartment with a straight boy—I can't invite you home—but my folks are out of town for the weekend. Want to go to their place for a while?"

Do it, idiot.

His family's homestead was a single-wide trailer in the outskirts of Havana, a town fifteen miles north of Tallahassee, once famous for growing shade tobacco, a variety used to make fine cigars. We reached the trailer via a red clay road bisecting a pine forest. The nearest neighbor, Dexter told me, was half a mile away. When we exited my car, a hoot owl's call was the only sound I heard in the surrounding forest.

Inside, Dexter flicked on a light. A battered sofa and a plaid Barcalounger faced a console TV. Framed photographs of Dexter and his much younger brother, an elfin carrot-topped boy with a toothy grin, sat atop the TV. The place smelled of cigarettes, but the kitchen was clean and a vase of freshly cut daffodils decorated the dinette table.

"We can't use my parents' bed," Dexter told me. "I wouldn't feel right if we did."

We made love in his little brother's room instead, on a double bed with Donald Duck sheets and a Star Wars bedspread. A total bottom, Dexter perched on the mattress on his hands and knees, and then I took him doggie-style. My hips smacked his compact rump each time I thrust.

After we cleaned ourselves up, we slept together spoon-style, like sardines in a tin. I wrapped my arm around Dexter's chest; I pressed my hipbones to his supple buttocks. I buried the tip of my nose in his hair—it smelled like Herbal Essence shampoo, a sweetly fragrant brand popular at the time—and then I fell asleep listening to him breathe. I slept through the night like I'd been drugged, feeling more contented than I had been in months.

When I woke in the morning, Dexter's head lay upon my chest, and one of his legs crossed my shins. His breath swept my skin. I studied his eyebrows and the curve of his nose. His features seemed as delicate as a flower's. Sunlight spilled into the room through a pair of awning windows.

Beyond the screens, a mockingbird tootled and a bushy-tailed squirrel hopped about the limbs of a live oak, looking like a circus acrobat.

I could stay in this place forever. How I've missed another man's affection.

"I want to attend pharmacy school," Dexter told me later that morning over corn flakes. "It's clean work and pays well, and sometimes you can snitch quality drugs: Quaaludes, Seconal, and such."

That weekend, an LPGA tournament took place at Capital City, and my caddying services weren't needed. I was free to do as I pleased, so I spent the entire three-day weekend with Dexter. We hung out naked in the trailer, smoking cigarettes and drinking beer. We prepared simple meals: beans and weenies, chicken with yellow rice, and bologna sandwiches. We showered together, brushed our teeth together, and watched TV together on the sofa. Every few hours, we'd hit the Donald Duck sheets, and then we'd try new positions: spoon-style, pogo-stick, whatever.

A gaggle of free-range chickens and a single rooster roamed the trailer's perimeter. Each morning, we served them breakfast from a feed sack stored under the kitchen sink. The chickens made a pleasant clucking sound while they ambled about the hard-packed earth, nipping at the seeds we'd tossed them.

Sometimes we sat on Dexter's concrete door stoop, wearing just our briefs. We smoked cigarettes and savored the shade offered by a towering live oak. Spanish moss beards festooned the oak's spreading limbs and swayed when a breeze blew. In late afternoon, crickets chirped and the horizon above the western tree line turned as red as the clay road leading to the highway.

Sunday afternoon, we pulled on our jeans and shoes, and then we walked through the pine forest, both of us shirtless and holding hands. Pine needles crunched beneath our feet; the air smelled of sap and damp earth. Mockingbirds chirped in the trees and a pileated woodpecker knock-knocked away. We came to a meandering creek; it babbled as it rushed across the surfaces of rocks and fallen tree limbs.

I turned my gaze to Dexter. Dappled sunlight reflected in his yellow hair. His shoulders were freckled like his nose, and his chest rose and fell with his breathing. I pulled him to me, and then we kissed. Our tongues rubbed and our lips smacked while the creek gurgled and gushed.

I felt as giddy as a teenager, as weightless as a feather.

I had always been a city boy—I'd never spent much time in the countryside—and now I understood why some people chose to live in such remote spots. I felt as though Dexter and I dwelled in a separate world, in a land where society's rules didn't dictate our behaviors, a place of freedom where we could do as we pleased.

That weekend we did intimate things I'd never tried before.

I lay face-up on Dexter's lap, stark naked, on the living room sofa. Using scissors, he trimmed my pubic hair to a wispy crescent. Then he dry-shaved my sac 'til it was as smooth as a twelve-year-old's. Shivers ran through me while he dragged the razor over my tender skin.

On Sunday evening, I tub-bathed Dexter, treating him like a little boy. He soaked in warm water up to his hips, splashing and dripping, and looking oh so cute. I sat tubside, on a stool his mom had used to bathe his little brother years before. I scrubbed Dexter's back and freckled shoulders, his limbs and his smooth chest. He stood, and then I soaped his genitals and the cleft between his buttocks. I shampooed his straw-colored hair, cleaned his ears with a washcloth, and I dried him head to toe with a fluffy towel. It sounds dumb, I know, but our little role-playing game in the bathroom was *fun*.

On Monday morning, when I drove us back to Tallahassee, Dexter held my right hand while I steered with my left. I hadn't felt so close to anyone since I'd been with Aaron so many months before. My weekend with Dexter had been more than a sexual encounter—at least for me— and now I hated the fact it would come to an end.

Would we share future weekends? Maybe become more than friends? We had talked of many things: our families, school, career hopes, and our high school days. But we hadn't talked about meeting another time.

Go on: ask.

I squeezed Dexter's hand.

"Are you busy next weekend?" I asked.

"I don't know," he answered. "Why?"

"I'd like to see you again, if that's okay."

Dexter pulled his hand away from mine. He rested his forearm on the passenger door's sill and stared out the window.

"What is it?" I said. "You don't like me?"

He swung his gaze back to mine. After drawing a breath, he moistened his lips. "I wasn't honest with you about my roommate; he's actually my boyfriend. He's a Leon County Deputy Sheriff. He's out of town for training right now; that's how come I could spend this weekend with you."

I turned my gaze to the windshield. My stomach churned while I flexed my fingers on the steering wheel. I felt like I occupied a free-falling elevator. For a moment, my vision clouded, and I honestly thought I might weep.

Of course he has a boyfriend, stupid. You were dreaming. Guys like him aren't just available; this was a one-shot deal, a weekend trick and nothing more.

Dexter laid a hand on my shoulder. "I'm sorry, Andy. It wasn't nice of me to lie, but you're so cute, and—"

I shrugged his hand away. Then I pounded the Vega's dashboard with a fist before I pointed a finger at Dexter's nose. His emerald eyes didn't look sexy now, only cagey, and I seethed at the knowledge he had played me for a sucker.

"Don't say you're sorry," I said. "In fact, don't say anything at all."

Thirteen

MY EXPERIENCE WITH Dexter—his casual lying and his exposure of my deep-seated neediness—made something crumple inside my head. A pall of self-loathing settled over me, and I quickly embarked on a course of self-abuse. I drank alcohol every night 'til I felt numb. I took tranquilizers and smoked marijuana. I even quit going to the track to run with Biff Schultz and his roomies, making the dumbest of excuses, time after time, for my nonappearance. I'd already completed my graduation requirements, so I didn't really care about my school performance; I skipped most of my classes in fact. But my work at Capital City suffered.

"You look like hell," Bucky Buchholtz told me on a Sunday morning when I showed up for work an hour late with a head-pounding hangover. "Go home and take a nap."

While I pedaled my bike home, I shook my head. I knew I wasn't treating myself well, but why take care of myself? Why worry about my future? I was a pitiful excuse for a queer, a guy who couldn't find a boyfriend to save his life. Who wanted me?

Nobody, it seemed.

In the past, I had sometimes fantasized about sadomasochism. I owned a few porn magazines with photos of men wearing leather vests and chaps, some of them restrained and gagged. Stories appeared in the pages of these magazines, tales of bondage, of rough sex and verbal abuse. The material had stirred my curiosity, and now, as I dwelled in the depths of self-hatred, I considered experimenting with S&M.

How would I feel if I groveled before another man, if he treated me like an animal and I submitted to his will completely? Maybe a dose of abuse was just what I needed. Maybe I could find a guy who'd treat me like the undesirable faggot I was. Maybe I'd like rough treatment. Why not find out?

A guy named Ray frequented the Gate. Tall and sinewy, maybe thirty-five, he always wore blue jeans and a leather vest. His buzz-cut hair, dark eyes, and tattooed forearms gave him an ominous look, one I found intriguing. Word had it he roughed up his tricks, before and during sex. But details were sketchy on just *how* cruel Ray could be.

On a Friday night, after I'd guzzled two bottles of Budweiser, I introduced myself to Ray. He sat on a barstool with the soles of his work boots resting on the stringers.

He nursed a glass of beer. His Winston cigarettes and plastic lighter sat next to him on the bar. The glow from an illuminated beer sign reflected in the dark stubble peppering Ray's face. His white T-shirt had yellow stains in the armpits, and his blue jeans were ripped open at one knee. When we shook hands, his callused palm rasped against mine like sandpaper.

I tried making conversation by talking about school for a minute or two, while Ray listened with a bored expression on his face. Then, when I asked about his work, he answered in a gravelly drawl.

"I'm assistant foreman at a sawmill in Perry. All day long, the saw blades scream like goddamned banshees. The pinesap stinks and so do the niggers. A mill's hot sweaty work, something a college boy like you wouldn't understand."

My cheeks burned from his insult, but I managed to blurt a response. "Look, just because I go to school doesn't mean I'm a pussy."

Ray's lips folded back to reveal his tobacco-stained teeth. "*All* college boys are punks, every goddamned one." He waved a dismissive hand. "Why don't you go talk with one of your Nancy-boy friends? We have nothing more to say to each other."

I looked around the bar, licking my lips and shifting my weight from one foot to the other. The possibility of returning alone to my empty apartment made me feel depressed and anxious. I needed a man's attentions, his flesh, sweat, and semen, more than ever. If I wasn't good enough for a redneck who worked at a sawmill, who *was* I good enough for?

I swung my gaze back to Ray. "Take me home with you."

He gazed at me and crinkled his forehead. "*What* did you say?"

"I said I want you to take me home with you—to Perry."

"What for?"

"Sex," I said. "Any kind you want."

Ray made a face. "What's your name again?"

"Andy."

"You wouldn't like the treatment I'd dole out, Andy. Believe me: you'll do yourself a favor if you find someone else."

Undeterred by Ray's comment, I continued. "Come on. Let's have some fun, you and me."

Ray looked at his beer while he drummed his fingers on the bar.

"I know you think I'm a punk," I said, "but I'm really not. You'll see."

Ray returned his gaze to me. "*Will* I now?"

I nodded.

He lit a cigarette, drew on the filter. Then he blew a stream of smoke.

After leaning toward me, he whispered in my ear. "I'm warning you, College Boy: if you come to Perry, I'll make you cry. That's a promise."

A shiver ran through me, but I felt reckless and desperate. Now I *had* to close the deal with Ray, or I'd totally lose respect for myself. Who cared if I collected a few bruises? A night with Ray would certainly trump jerking off alone in my bed.

"Let's do it," I said. "Let's go."

Ray's rusty pickup truck sat before a boarded-up shotgun cottage on a residential side street, two blocks from the Gate. The Ford's windshield was cracked, its tires slightly flat. The dome light didn't illuminate when we crawled into the cab, but a pale glow from a nearby streetlamp allowed me to see things. The truck's cab stank of burnt tobacco, stale beer, and body odor. Detritus littered the floorboard: crushed beer and soda cans, empty cigarette boxes, potato chip bags, candy bar wrappers, empty condom packages, and dirty-ass wipes.

Ray turned the starter three times before the engine finally turned over. After tossing his cigarette butt into the street, he turned and grabbed the hem of my T-shirt.

"Take this off."

I looked at Ray and crinkled my forehead. "Why?"

Ray slapped my cheek, not hard, but enough to make it sting. Then he pointed at my nose. "'Cause I *told* you to. Tonight, you'll do whatever I say, that's how things work. Either do it or get out."

Nodding, I rubbed the side of my face with the flat of my hand. Then I pulled off my shirt and tossed it onto the dashboard. The night air felt cool on my bare chest. Ray reached for my nipple; he pinched it between his thumbnail and index finger.

I flinched from the pain.

"You *are* kind of cute," Ray said. "We'll have us some fun at my place."

I stared out the windshield and didn't say anything.

Already I felt a slight uneasiness. Exactly what did "fun" mean to Ray?

Ray shifted gears, and then we drove in silence through the streets of Tallahassee, past the warehouses on West Gaines Street, then past our monolithic state capitol building on South Monroe Street. When we reached a stoplight on the Apalachee Parkway, Ray turned to me; he hooked a finger in the waistband of my jeans.

"Pull these down to your knees," he said.

I looked at Ray and made a face. "Pull *what* down?"

"Your britches, dumbass. I thought all you college boys were smart."

"Why should I pull my pants down? Why here?"

"'Cause I want to play with your goodies, that's why."

I glanced here and there. At 2:00 a.m., traffic on the Parkway was nonexistent, so we had our privacy.

Just do it, chickenshit. Submit.

I popped the button at my waist, ran down my zipper. After lifting my ass, I shoved my jeans to my knees. My genitals bulged in my white briefs. Looking into my lap, Ray flicked my crotch with a fingertip.

"Lose them jockeys, too: down to your knees."

My cheeks burned and my hands shook while I eased the briefs south. My bare ass stuck to the chilly vinyl seat. The stoplight changed to green, and then Ray accelerated. Wind rushed through the cab, making me shiver anew.

Ray reached his callused hand between my legs while I squirmed in the car seat. My heart thumped and my pulse raced. Already, things with Ray seemed a bit nutty and downright lewd. Who knew what lay in store?

By now, we had left Tallahassee's city limits. We drove through the tiny village of Capps. Then, after we passed the exit to US 19, the road turned toward the southeast. Ray continued squeezing and fingering my equipment. A half moon had risen; its weak glow silvered pecan groves we passed. The land rolled and the Ford's headlights cast two cones of yellow light. Ray was a man of few words, and we didn't say much of anything during the trip to Perry.

My pants and briefs remained at my knees, and Ray's hand remained in my crotch, stroking and squeezing my tender flesh. Despite my unease about what lay ahead, I'd decided I would do whatever Ray told me I must, no matter how humiliating or painful it might be.

Tonight, I told myself, *is all about submission to Ray's will. He's in control and you're not.*

Perry wasn't a big town: a shopping center with a Winn-Dixie, a McDonald's, a couple of single-story motels, a liquor bar, and two churches, one Baptist, the other Methodist. The town's only traffic light blinked at the Highway 98 intersection. A sour stench from a local paper mill wafted through the truck's cab. About a mile south of town, Ray turned off the highway onto a rutted dirt road. The Ford rocked and pitched; the chassis squeaked and groaned.

Our destination was a one-story cottage with a covered front porch and a pitched tin roof, surrounded by slash pines and scrub oaks. No grass or shrubs grew in the yard, only weeds. Ray shifted into park, turned off the engine, and killed the headlights. I glanced here and there. Ray, it seemed, had no neighbors. Besides the house, I couldn't see anything but blackness wherever I looked. When I reached for my shirt, Ray slapped my hand.

"Leave it there, and leave your britches down, too. Walk to the house just like you are."

When I exited the truck, my cheeks burned in shame. I felt like some kid who'd been spanked and then put in a corner with his pants down. The cool night air made me shiver. I strained for a noise of any kind, but there was nothing. On the way to the front porch, I tripped over a tree root, and then I fell to the ground with a thud.

"Jesus," Ray cried, "you're not only dumb, but you're clumsy, too." He kicked me in the rear, hard. "Get your ass up."

After rising, I stumbled toward the porch steps. It wasn't easy, climbing the steps with my pants lowered like they were. Ray's boot heels clunked on the treads behind me.

After placing a hand on my shoulder, he kicked open the front door. Then he pushed me into a room as dark as tar. A single shaft of moonlight entered through a double-hung window, casting a silver rhombus onto the bare wood floor. The place smelled of mildew.

Ray spun me around, grabbed the back of my neck, and brought my mouth to his. He pried my lips open, and then our tongues dueled while

Ray's chin whiskers rasped against my own. The firm muscles of his chest pressed against my sternum, and his hips met mine. I'd never had sex with a guy much older than me, and especially not a guy as hyper-masculine as Ray. My pulse accelerated, and then my armpits grew damp with excitement.

Ray pulled his mouth from my lips. "Get on your knees."

After I did so, Ray's belt buckle tinkled. He opened his pants, shoved them to mid-thigh. No underwear. Already, my eyes had adjusted to the darkness. I saw Ray's genitals and his dark pubic bush. When I drew a breath, I crinkled my nose. Clearly, Ray had not bathed after work that day.

I glanced up at his face. "Aren't you going to turn on a light?"

He chuckled. "This was my aunt's house. She's been dead four years; there's no electric service. But you don't need a light to take care of me, now do you?"

He slapped the top of my head, pulled my face to his groin. "Get to it, College Boy."

After a few minutes of thrusting, Ray withdrew. "Get on your feet."

I rose, wiping slobber off my chin with the back of my wrist. Ray led me down a dark hallway, and then into a bedroom. He lit a kerosene lantern, the kind with a glass chimney and a braided wick. The lantern rested on a battered bureau; its glow filled the room with caramel light, casting our shadows onto a wall. A burlap sack served as a drape, covering the room's only window. Aside from the bureau, the only furniture was a metal-framed four-poster bed with a badly stained mattress; the bed occupied the center of the room. Leather restraint devices, fashioned from belts, were fastened to each of the bed's four corners.

"Strip," Ray told me.

I felt an urge to bolt for the door. Who knew what Ray had planned for me? But I had come this far. I couldn't back out now, could I? Besides, Ray wasn't some freak who'd picked me up hitchhiking. He had a job; he was a regular customer at the Gate. The guy just liked his kink. Who knew, maybe I would too? I rubbed my chin with a knuckle.

Go on: do it.

I kicked off my shoes, pulled off my socks. After shucking my pants and briefs to my ankles, I stepped out of both. Then I tossed them into a corner. Ray's gaze traveled over me like a clothes iron pressing a pant leg.

"You've got a long night in store for you, College Boy, you know that?"

I glanced at the bed. "Are you planning to tie me up?"

"That's the general idea."

I swung my gaze back to Ray. "You've got to promise me, if I tell you to stop what you're doing—if I ask you to let me go—then you will, right?"

Ray crinkled the corners of his eyes. "Sure, College Boy."

Five minutes later, I lay facedown on the mattress, with my wrists and ankles buckled to the bedposts. Aside from shifting my hips or turning my head from one side to the other, I'd completely lost my freedom of movement. After he secured me, Ray left the room. He returned moments later, carrying a bottle of Boone's Farm apple wine and his doubled-up belt. He had fastened his jeans and removed his T-shirt. Dark hair dusted his chest. His biceps bulged, and the veins in his forearms looked like blue knitting yarn. When he drank from the bottle, his Adam's apple pumped.

After approaching the bed, he draped the belt across my shoulder blades. The buckle felt cold on my skin. When Ray sat on the mattress, the bedsprings squeaked while I squirmed.

Ray said, "You're in for a good pokin', College Boy; I know it's what you want. But first I'll need to strap your behind."

My vision went blurry. "You're going to whip me?"

Ray squeezed my ass cheek. "Sure am."

Get out of here, now.

"I didn't agree to a beating," I cried. "Let me loose, take me home."

Ray giggled. "Too late for that, College Boy. You're mine for a spell."

My voice shook when I spoke. Already I trembled like a kid in a spook house. Things had gone from kinky to downright scary, just like that.

"You said you'd untie me if I asked; you promised."

"Here's your first lesson in S&M," Ray said, wagging a finger while a shit-eating grin crossed his face. "Don't ever believe what a leather daddy tells you, at least not what he says *before* he ties you up."

What transpired during the next ninety minutes I'd like to forget, but never will. I was beaten, degraded, and violated. As the scene unfolded, I screamed like a guy getting stabbed to death. I blubbered like a child and pled for mercy, but received none. And when it all ended, I was sore and spent. My buttocks, thighs, and asshole burned. When Ray released my restraints, I rolled onto my back. I stared at the water-stained ceiling, and then I asked myself why the *hell* I'd ever left the Gate with Ray in the first place. What an *idiot* I'd been, an utter fool.

I worked my jaw from side to side.

You must never, ever lose control over your body like this again.

A half hour later, Ray drove me toward Highway 27. The two of us rode in silence; we stank of sweat and sex. I writhed on the truck's vinyl seat. Ray smoked as we drove through the night; his ash glowed in the truck's shadowy cab. The time was close to 4:00 a.m. The moon had reached its apex in the sky; it cast a silvery glow over live oaks, pecan orchards, and pastureland. When we reached the city limits of Perry, Ray pulled onto the apron of a darkened gas station. After shifting into park, he turned to look at me.

"Get out, College Boy."

"Aren't you taking me back to Tallahassee?"

Ray spat out his driver's door window. "Shit no; I'm tired. I'm headed home, and that's in the opposite direction from Tallahassee. This is as far as I'm taking you."

"But how am I supposed to get back?"

Ray raised a shoulder. "Not my problem, kid."

Arguing with Ray, I knew, would be futile. He had used me as a sex toy, treated me like an animal, and now he would dump me like a sack of garbage. After I exited the truck, Ray shifted gears and drove away without speaking to me again. I shook my head while I watched his taillights fade into darkness.

Asshole.

I shivered in the chilly, damp air. What should I do?

Off in the distance, a motel's illuminated sign glowed. I walked along the highway's edge with my hands in my rear pockets and my elbows jutting. The Bahia grass on the road's shoulder hadn't been mown recently, and fiddleheads brushed against the legs of my jeans. The only sound I heard, other than my footfalls, was the chirping of crickets.

Behind me, an engine growled. I glanced over my shoulder. A semi tractor-trailer approached, headed northward, and after I turned and stuck out my thumb, the truck's driver switched on his brights, making me squint. But he blew past me without slowing down.

Shit.

The motel was single-story with an exterior corridor and a dozen rooms. Several cars occupied the asphalt parking lot, rusty models with dented bumpers and cracked windshields. The lobby was dark, but a pay phone hung on a cinder-block wall in the corridor.

Who could I call?

I tried Fergal first, but he didn't answer, and I figured he was probably sleeping at Gina's. I tried Biff Schultz next. His phone rang ten times before someone answered in a sleepy mumble.

"Biff?" I said.

"No, this is Travis. Biff's camping this weekend with Austin."

Over the phone line, I heard a yawn.

"This is Andy, Travis. I need your help."

In less than an hour, Travis picked me up in his station wagon. Stars still gleamed in the night sky, and dew glistened in the motel's ragged lawn. As soon as I climbed into the car, Travis made a face.

"You look terrible, and you smell like a toilet. What happened?"

While Travis drove northward on US 19, I told him everything about my evening, and I didn't mince words. I spoke of leaving the Gate with Ray, the weird ride to Perry in his truck, the bondage, the fiery whipping I'd taken, and the rough sex that had followed.

Travis grimaced and shook his head. "I don't understand. Why would you go home with this guy in the first place?"

I stared out the windshield at two cones of light the station wagon's headlamps cast onto the asphalt road. "I've thought about that ever since I called you. I guess I *wanted* Ray's abuse."

Travis narrowed his eyes at me. "Are you a masochist? Do you get pleasure from pain?"

I shook my head. "I think right now I hate myself—I guess I felt I deserved a beating and I sure got one—but what a fucked-up situation. What is *wrong* with me?"

Travis turned his gaze back to the road, and he did not speak to me again until we reached Tallahassee. When we did, he told me, "I'm taking you to my house, but first we'll visit someplace special: a spot you should know about."

The Lake Talquin water tower stood a few miles west of Tallahassee's city limits, among a stand of slash pines, maybe two hundred yards south of Highway 90. Standing next to the tower's rusty ladder, Travis pointed upward, toward a wooden promenade with a metal railing. The promenade banded the water tank like a belt.

"Climb up there with me."

I made a face, looking upward. "Look, I'm sort of...scared of heights. Can't we just stay on the ground?"

Travis shook his head. "Come on, chickenshit; it's not that tall, really."

The tower's rusty ladder creaked as we ascended, Travis in the lead. My hands trembled, and I wouldn't allow myself to look down for fear I'd faint from fright. By the time we'd climbed to the tower's promenade, the sun had crested the eastern tree line, and now we both squinted in the dawn's brightness. Below us, birds chirped in the pines. A transfer truck roared past on the highway; its headlights were still illuminated. Off in the distance, Lake Talquin gleamed like a mirror. We sat on the promenade's wooden deck with our legs dangling over the edge. Gazing southward, we watched the sun burnish treetops.

I squirmed on my sore buttocks. Would I ever sit comfortably again?

Travis crossed his arms on the promenade's railing. Then he rested his chin on his arms. Sunlight reflected in his eyes, in the dark stubble shadowing his chin. I studied his delicate features, his craggy cheekbones, and thick eyebrows.

"I come here when I'm troubled," he told me. "Nobody knows I do; it's my private place. I feel a sense of peace when I'm up here, like I've escaped all the sadness in my life."

I didn't say anything.

Travis turned his gaze to me. "You should come here once in a while. Spend some time thinking about yourself and what you want from life; it might help you feel better."

I studied the roof of Travis's car. At that moment, I felt lower than pond scum, like the most worthless guy on the planet. I stank like hell. I was sore all over. I had been used and abused in the most horrid fashion. What kind of a loser was I? Would I ever feel good about myself?

An hour later, when we entered Travis's house, he pointed to the bathroom. "Go ahead: clean yourself up. Then I'll treat your skin."

In the shower, warm water streamed over my aching limbs, my raw buttocks, and steaming thighs. I scrubbed myself with a washcloth in frenzied fashion, as if by doing so I could wash away not only the stinks from my session with Ray, but the memories as well. Afterward, Travis had me lie naked on his mattress, on my stomach. Sunlight crept into the room, and birds chirped in nearby live oaks.

Down the street, a dog barked. Travis squeezed juice from an aloe plant onto my buttocks and thighs. Then he massaged the soothing juice into my skin.

For the first time since I'd left the Gate with Ray, I felt safe. Travis's touch seemed so gentle and caring, especially compared to the savagery I'd endured at Ray's hands.

"Feeling better?" Travis asked.

I nodded.

After he'd tossed a sheet and blanket over me, Travis closed the blinds.

"Look," I said, "will you do me another favor?"

"What's that?"

"Call the pro shop at Capital City around eight. Tell them I'm sick with a fever, okay?"

I still have nightmares about that night with Ray: the lantern's ghostly light; the shadows; the scents of kerosene, leather, and sweat; the crack of the belt against my flesh; the relentless, mind-numbing pain; and Ray's brutal penetration. A prison cell would have seemed like a hotel suite compared to the room where Ray assaulted me. To this day, when traveling through north central Florida, I won't pass through Perry. I'll take an alternate route, even if it adds extra miles to my trip. And aside from Travis, I've never told another soul about those miserable hours spent with Ray. They were, without a doubt, the darkest moments of my life.

Fourteen

I WOKE TO the sound of Biff and Austin's voices, to the clatter of tent poles and the rustle of camping gear.

Glancing at Travis's alarm clock, I saw the time was close to four in afternoon. I had slept over nine hours.

My ass and thighs still burned. After rising, I checked my appearance in Travis's bureau mirror. Purple welts crisscrossed my skin, from my waist to the backs of my knees. I rubbed my damaged flesh and shook my head. How could I have been so reckless? And who could possibly derive pleasure from a beating like the one I'd taken?

After stepping into my jeans, I eased them over my stinging flesh, and then I buttoned up.

Austin greeted me in the hallway. He was shirtless, wearing only cutoff jeans and hiking boots. The sun had lightened his hair a shade or two.

"Hi, Andy Boy. Taking a snooze, I hear?"

Nodding, I ran my fingers through my scalp. Then I scooted into the bathroom and closed the door. After I pissed and flushed, I stepped to the sink to wash my face. While waiting for warm water to flow, I studied my visage in the medicine cabinet's mirror. My hair was in tangles and my eyes were swollen from sleep. Two days' worth of stubble grew on my cheeks. A faint bruise appeared above my jaw, where Ray had slapped me in his truck outside the Gate. Another much darker bruise appeared above my collarbone, where he'd bitten me during sex. I shook my head. How I wished I could erase these markings, these reminders of my foolishness. How could—

A knock sounded on the bathroom door. "Andy, it's Travis. Can I come in?"

Once inside, he closed the door behind him. The fluorescent ceiling fixture reflected in his blue-green eyes when he spoke to me in a whisper.

"How are you? How's your skin?"

I puckered one side of my face. "I'm sore as hell, but I guess I'll be okay."

Travis stuck his hands in the back pockets of his jeans. "I didn't tell the guys what happened last night; I just said you were napping."

"Thanks," I said. "I feel pretty stupid right now; I'd rather they didn't know."

Beyond the door, Biff's laughter boomed.

Travis glanced at the door. Then he swung his gaze back to mine. "This will stay between you and me as far as I'm concerned. I know how to keep a secret when necessary."

I nodded, thinking about the story Biff had told me about Travis and the mess in Myrtle Beach. Of *course* he could keep a secret.

"Look," I said, "I'm sorry all this happened; I can't thank you enough."

A funny feeling swept through me, then. It started in my feet and crept up my legs. My knees began to shake. I felt an ache in my chest, as though I'd just had the wind knocked out of me. Tears clouded my eyes, and then I whimpered like a five-year-old.

Travis wrapped an arm around my shoulders. "Shhh. It's okay, Andy, don't cry."

"I feel like such an *idiot*."

"We all do stupid things in life," he said, "things we're sorry for. But you can't undo them once they've happened. You just have to learn from them."

I sniffled and swallowed. Then I babbled on. "Sometimes I think I should give up the whole gay scene; maybe it's not for me. Maybe I'm better off living like you do: alone. At least *you* have peace in your life. At least you didn't let some asshole tie you up and beat you like a dog."

Travis didn't speak for a moment. Then he said, "What works for me might not work for you. You're a guy who needs love, and that's okay. Don't use me as a role model. I'm unhappy and always will be."

Out in the hallway, Biff teased Austin about a raccoon that had spooked Austin when he'd left their tent to piss the night before.

"That thing was no bigger than a housecat. I can't believe how loudly you screamed."

Austin replied in a whiny voice. "We don't *have* such creatures in Jamaica. I understand they bite."

Biff snorted. "No self-respecting raccoon would bite a pussy like *you*."

I sniffled again. I felt safe with Travis's arm resting on my shoulders; I could have stood there for hours, feeling the warmth of his body, feeling his breath sweep my skin. But then he withdrew, and the moment passed.

"Blow your nose and dry your eyes," he said. "You have to be brave in moments like this. You can't let them know you've been crying."

"I know," I said. "I know..."

THREE DAYS AFTER my evening with Ray, when I came home from classes, I checked my mailbox in the four-plex's stairwell. A letter had arrived from the admissions office at FSU's College of Law.

Holy shit.

My hands shook as I tore open the envelope.

Dear Mr. Hunsinger:

We are pleased to inform you that your application for admission to Florida State University College of Law has been accepted for fall term, 1977. You will receive a registration package under separate cover. These materials should be completed and returned to the College at your earliest convenience.

The rest of the letter turned into a blur.

I closed my eyes, and then a shudder ran through my limbs. For a moment, I thought I might piss in my pants. I let loose a hoarse cry of joy just as Fergal entered the stairwell through the building's front door, wheeling his bicycle. He carried a backpack on his shoulders, and his marmalade hair looked like he'd just left a wind tunnel.

He looked at me like I was daft. "Something the matter, Andy?"

After I grabbed him in a bear hug, I lifted him from the floor, and then I shouted like a lunatic.

"I made law school, Fergal. I'm in."

ON THE SECOND Saturday in June, on a sunny and humid afternoon, I heard my name barked through a PA system, and then I strode across a temporary stage erected in Doak Campbell Stadium, wearing a ridiculous garnet-colored cap and gown. I shook the university president's hand, and then as I looked into the crowd, I raised a fist.

After post-ceremony photographs were taken, my parents treated me, my brother, all four of my grandparents, Bucky Buchholtz, and Biff Schultz to dinner at a barbecue place on Tennessee Street. I ate ribs until they came out of my ears and chased them down with cold draft beer.

My undergraduate days had ended, and I wasn't quite sure how I felt about it. I wasn't a beer-swilling fraternity boy any longer, and I certainly wasn't the same guy who'd moved into McPhail's ratty apartment only nine months before. So many changes had occurred since then.

Exactly who was I now?

WITH SPRING QUARTER'S ending, 80 percent of the student population at FSU left town for the summer. Not me. Why spend three months in Pensacola, working some crappy job and living with my parents? If I stayed in Tallahassee, I could caddy at Capital City most every day. I could keep my apartment *and* my privacy.

Not that I really needed privacy.

After the incident with Ray, I'd avoided the Gate, afraid I might see him again. How humiliating would *that* be? He'd made me cry and beg. He might've told people about our session in Perry so they'd know what a pussy I was.

I would do what Travis had done: avoid sex and romance all together. I had Fergal's friendship. I had Biff, Austin, and Travis to spend time with, as well. My right hand was always available, and it would never deceive me like Dexter Hayward had. KY Jelly was cheap, too.

School had ended for my brother as well. He would work as a counselor at a boys' summer camp in western North Carolina, but before he left, during the second week of June, he came to visit me for a few days. I showed him around campus, and then I drove him to Silver Lake for a swim. Jake had a fake ID. I took him to the Pastime, where we drank three pitchers of beer, munched on roasted peanuts, and smoked a pack of Marlboros.

Afterward, Jake vomited in the parking lot.

Biff, Austin, and Travis invited us to a farewell-for-the-summer dinner party one night. The next day, Biff would leave for Jacksonville to work as an intern at his dad's medical clinic.

"I'll keep the tongue depressor jars filled, take patients' blood pressure, and maybe bandage a wound or two. It'll be a learning experience."

Likewise, Austin would volunteer at a children's charity hospital in Port-au-Prince, Haiti.

"You wouldn't believe the poverty down there. Kids run around with no shoes; they all have tapeworms. Families live in plywood shacks. Maybe I can help them a bit, and it'll look good on my resume."

Travis, who was a year behind Austin and Biff in school, would remain in Tallahassee. He'd attend summer quarter classes, remaining in the house by himself until Biff and Austin returned in the fall.

Carol Ann had already left Tallahassee for the summer—she didn't attend the dinner party—but Maritza was there, dressed in a halter top, short-shorts, and high heels. We stood under the long leaf pines in the backyard, sipping from cans of beer and yakking away, while Travis sat on a bench playing bottle-neck guitar. He played a style of Delta blues, using open tuning. He wore a thin stainless-steel tube on his left middle finger, and he slid the tube up and down his guitar's neck, forming chords and plucking individual notes as well. The sound he produced was both raw and edgy.

The night was warm. Biff, of course, wore nothing but a pair of sandals. His cock wagged to and fro as he walked about. All the other guys soon shed their shirts, and when Maritza's gaze fell upon Jake's athletic physique, she flickered her eyebrows.

"Andy," she said, "you never told us your little brother was so *cute*. I'll bet all the girls are after him."

Jake lowered his gaze while his cheeks reddened.

"Don't mind her," Austin told Jake. "Cuban women are all man-crazy."

Our hosts made sure Jake wasn't left out of conversation. They asked about his college plans, what sort of music he listened to, and which sports he enjoyed. In response, Jake chattered away like he'd known my friends all his life.

"And tell us," Austin said to Jake, "how was it, having Andy Boy as your older brother? Was he a good role model, or just a pain in the ass?"

"Andy's the best," Jake said. "I could always share my deepest secrets with him."

"Awww," Maritza said.

Jake told Austin, "Andy's talented, too. Do you know he has a great singing voice?"

Travis stopped playing his guitar. Then everyone swung their gazes to me.

"You sing?" Biff said.

"I *used* to, I—"

"He sang in his high school choir," Jake said, "and in several musical plays." Then Jake turned to me. "Remember when you played Lieutenant Cable in *South Pacific*?"

"Ah-*ha*," Biff cried. "You've been holding out on us, haven't you, Hunsinger?"

"Look," I said, "except for singing a few tunes with my neighbor, it's been years. The only place I perform now is in the shower."

Travis looked at me. "Do you know the words to the Beatles' song, 'Blackbird'? It's on *The White Album*."

"Sure," I said. "I've listened to it a hundred times."

He patted the bench he occupied. "Come sit while I re-tune my guitar. Then you'll sing the melody, and I'll sing harmony, okay?"

I sat next to Travis. While he adjusted his tuning keys, I guzzled the rest of the beer I'd nursed. Excepting that one evening when I'd performed with Fergal, it had been years since I'd sung before others. I felt a bit embarrassed, but still…a tinge of exhilaration crept through my bones while my pulse quickened. I'd always loved performing back in Pensacola. Why be shy about singing in front of this group of friends?

The others gathered in a semicircle around Travis and me. Travis plucked the opening note of the song, and then we hummed until we both sang in key.

Travis looked at me and raised his eyebrows. "Ready?"

I nodded.

Travis fingerpicked the song while we both sang. I was a tenor, Travis a baritone, so he sang a chord level below me. Combined with reverberations from the guitar's metal strings, we created a pleasing resonance, one as pretty as any song I'd ever been a part of.

Our voices echoed off oak tree trunks, off the cinder-block walls of Biff's house. During the song, when I looked at Biff, he grinned like a kid with a birthday cake. I didn't want the song to end—my spirits soared like the music itself—but when Travis and I finished the number, our listeners burst into applause.

Biff whistled through his teeth.

"I *told* you guys he could sing," Jake hollered.

A shiver ran through me. I looked at Travis. Then he gave me his lazy smile.

"We need to do this more often, Andy."

Biff grilled pork chops over charcoal. We teamed the chops with baked sweet potatoes, steamed yellow squash, and a pan of cornbread I'd baked from scratch at my apartment. Afterward, in the living room, the stereo blared. When Biff brought out the water pipe, I wondered just how Jake would react. I'd never really discussed drug use with him, but when Austin passed him the pipe, Jake took a deep pull. He held his smoke without coughing.

I took a few hits myself, and once the marijuana hit my brain, the room developed a two-dimensional look. THC affected different people in different ways, I knew. In my case, I always grew introspective when stoned, and that night was no exception. I thought about law school and what lay in store for me. Would Biff's description of my first year prove true?

Already, I'd received a schedule of classes and a list of books I'd need to buy. My professors, a letter informed me, would post reading assignments. I should complete these before the first day of class. I shook my head when I read the letter. Would I spend my days and nights in the law school library, immersed in my studies? Would I never see my friends or family? Would I surrender my Capital City job?

Still...

Maybe a total immersion in law studies would be for the best. I could forget about finding a boyfriend and focus on my career instead.

My gaze fell upon Travis. He sat alongside Biff on the sofa. Biff handed Travis the water pipe, and then Travis took a pull. He held his smoke several seconds before exhaling a blue cloud. The glow from a battered floor lamp reflected in his dark eyes. His hair hung loosely, brushing his shoulders, and because he was shirtless, I could watch his chest and arm muscles move under his smooth skin. To me, Travis had never looked as beautiful as he did right then.

Beneath that stoic demeanor, what sort of emotions bubble? What are his demons, his dreams and hopes?

I tried to imagine conversing on a personal level with Travis. How would he react if I asked if he were gay or if I asked about the Myrtle Beach incident? I could probably expect a response like the one Travis had thrown in Maritza's face, during our picnic by the river. My questions might sour the friendship we'd developed since I'd first visited the FSU track, and I didn't want that to happen.

Austin passed me the water pipe. After drawing a deep toke, I closed my eyes. Then I held the smoke in my burning lungs.

Stop thinking so much, Hunsinger. It's not good for you.

Hours later, around midnight, I handed Jake my car keys. "Drive us home, will you? I'm tired and a little too stoned to get behind the wheel."

"You'll have to direct me," Jake said. "I don't know the way."

We cruised Tallahassee's deserted streets. The Vega's headlights shone upon Spanish moss beards hanging among limbs of live oaks lining both sides of the road. Jake was still shirtless, and I studied his carved chest, his rippled belly, and the thin line of hair spilling from his navel. Dark stubble smudged his cleft chin.

My handsome little brother. How I loved him.

"I like your friends," Jake said, "especially Biff. I've never met anyone like him."

"Biff's his own man, that's for certain. He doesn't give a shit what anyone thinks of him; he just does as he pleases."

Jake snickered.

"What?" I asked.

"Biff said the same thing about you: 'Andy's the ballsiest guy I know.'"

"Did he really?"

Jake nodded. "He's right, you know. Not many guys have the courage to be openly gay. If you tell everyone you suck cock, certain people lose respect for you."

I shrugged.

"So, how do you deal with that?" Jake asked.

I rearranged my limbs. "Being yourself actually makes things easier; you know who your true friends are. Take Biff, for instance. He's totally straight, but he doesn't care if I like boys. Being queer doesn't define me in his eyes. It's the same with my neighbor, Fergal, and with good old Bucky Buchholtz. They might not understand the whole gay thing, but they know I'm still a decent guy. I'm still Andy Hunsinger."

Jake bobbed his chin. "Mom and Dad are okay with it, too, I think."

"Are they?"

Jake rocked his head from side to side. "Okay, they seemed a bit shocked at first, right after you told them. We discussed you often at the dinner table. I think they worried about your happiness, but now it's like you've become a Buddhist or Hari Krishna—a little weird, but nothing to get upset about. I think they've seen past it."

Go on: ask...

"What about you?"

Jake crinkled his forehead. "What?"

"Are you okay with me liking boys?"

Jake turned his gaze to the windshield. "I'm fine with it, really. It's just..."

"What?"

"You don't seem too happy, Andy."

I stiffened my spine. Then I rested my arm on the sill of the passenger door. Cool night air rushed through the Vega's open windows, ruffling my hair.

"I'm *not* happy, Little Brother, not at all."

Jake looked at me and shook his head. "I don't understand. You have such cool friends. You'll attend law school; you have your own apartment and the caddying job. What more do you want?"

"A *boyfriend*, Jake: a guy who cares about me, someone I can hold at night. But I can't seem to make it happen."

"How come, what's wrong?"

I grimaced and shook my head. "I sure don't know. I don't have your looks, of course, but I'm not ugly, either. I should be able to find someone. But every time I meet a guy—someone I like—it doesn't work. Either he doesn't feel attracted to me, or he's straight, or he's fucked up emotionally. Or, of course, he's already taken."

I blew air out of my nostrils. "I can't win."

When we halted at a stoplight, Jake drummed his fingers on the steering wheel. "Maybe you're trying too hard. Maybe you seem a little too desperate, know what I mean?"

I shrugged.

"How long have you dated guys now," Jake asked, "a year?"

I nodded.

"That's not very long. I have friends in Pensacola who've never been in bed with a woman. A few have never even been on a *date*."

"But that's different, they're high school boys. I've graduated from *college*; I'm twenty-two years old, for Christ's sake."

The light changed to green, and Jake accelerated. At my direction, he turned onto Apalachee Parkway. Then we headed south toward Franklin Street.

"Look," Jake said, "I don't know anything about gay life, but I *do* know this: you have a lot to offer someone. You'll find a guy eventually; I know you will."

Back at my apartment, after we brushed our teeth and used the toilet, Jake yawned while he pointed to the sofa in the living room. "Do I have to sleep on that thing again tonight? There's a loose spring in the seat; it jabs your ribs like crazy."

I shrugged. "You can sleep with me if you'd like; there's room enough for two."

Jake looked at me and raised his eyebrows. "If I do that—crash in your bed—you won't grab my cock when I'm asleep, will you?"

I waggled *my* eyebrows. "I just might."

Jake kneaded the back of his neck, feigning indecision while he swung his gaze to my bedroom. "I think I'll take my chances with you, Big Brother."

I rubbed my hands together while I stared at Jake with my lips curled back. "I haven't lured a straight boy into my bed in months. This'll be fun."

Jake cackled while he followed me to the bedroom.

We both undressed, down to our briefs. Then, after we'd crawled under the covers, I killed the lamp on the nightstand. Beyond the window, our resident whippoorwill sang his sad and spooky tune. Jake bent an elbow, and then he propped his cheek against his hand. His breath swept my skin and I smelled the toothpaste he'd just used.

"Remember when we were kids," he said, "and we camped out in Dad's pup tent in our backyard?"

"Yeah, sure I do. I hope you don't still snore like you used to."

Jake giggled. "I always loved it, lying next to you and listening to crickets chirp. I always felt safe."

There in the darkness, I mussed Jake's hair. "I'll always be here for you, Little Brother."

Jake repositioned himself. He draped an arm across my chest and rested his cheek on my shoulder. His skin felt warm against mine.

"Good night, Andy," he whispered. "I love you."

Fifteen

"ITCHY *WHAT*?" I said.

I spoke on the phone with Travis early on a Tuesday morning in July.

"Ichetucknee Springs State Park," Travis said. "It's only a ninety-minute drive from here."

"What's there to do?"

"Tubing, there's a six-mile stretch of river. The water's seventy-two degrees and clear as gin. We'll float downstream until the Ichetucknee meets the Santa Fe; it's a great way to spend a hot day."

I twisted the phone cord around my finger while sweat beaded on my upper lip. *Should I go?*

I wasn't working that day. At the time, business was dead at Capital City, at least on weekdays. Even on weekends, only the most dedicated golfers ventured onto the course. On a typical summer day, Tallahassee's temperature and humidity levels would both reach ninety by 10:00 a.m. On Saturday and Sunday mornings, I broke into a sweat whenever I pedaled my bike to the club; I wouldn't even bother to put on my polo shirt until I cooled off in the club's air-conditioned locker room. Morning rounds were somewhat bearable, but afternoon sessions became endurance tests for both caddies and golfers. Heat shimmered over the fairways, and the greens became anvils. One afternoon, Dustin Ausley collapsed on a fairway. An ambulance took him to Tallahassee Memorial, where an ER doctor diagnosed him with heat stroke.

Bucky Buchholtz had fled for the mountains of western North Carolina, where he, Eddie, and Flo were renting a cottage for two weeks.

Fergal was spending the summer in Melbourne.

"It's wintertime there," he'd told me. "No sweating like here in Florida."

The whole city felt like a steam room, and the few folks I saw on the sidewalks moved like their feet were mired in molasses.

I hadn't seen Travis since the farewell dinner party, weeks before, and the thought of spending an entire day with him appealed to me. Closing my eyes, I imagined us floating in a cool stream.

"Well?" Travis said.

"Sure, I'll go."

I dressed in swim trunks, a faded T-shirt with the FSU crest silk-screened on the chest, and rubber flip-flops.

In the kitchen, I made two ham-and-cheese sandwiches.

I shrouded both in plastic wrap while listening to a mockingbird tootle in a slash pine just outside the kitchen window.

By the time Travis picked me up in his station wagon, the sun had crested the tree line east of the four-plex.

Already, the morning felt steamy. Travis wore a Fabulous Furry Freak Brothers T-shirt, a pair of jeans with the legs cut off at mid-thigh, and leather sandals. As usual, his dark hair was disheveled; it brushed his shoulders and tumbled over his ears. He greeted me with a smile and a handshake.

"I've missed you, Andy; it's been too long."

My face grew warm at Travis's remark.

He's "missed" me? Really?

I tossed a bath towel and a small ice cooler into the backseat. The cooler held the sandwiches I'd prepared, along with sodas and a jar of pickles. Sunlight glanced off the station wagon's hood. While we drove down Franklin Street, Travis fished a pair of aviator-style sunglasses from his glove box.

"It'll be *stinking* hot today," he said, perching the sunglasses on his upturned nose. "I hope the river's not too crowded."

We traveled in a southeasterly direction on Highway 27, and my scalp prickled when we passed through Perry. I thought of the night I'd gone there with Ray and the abuse I'd endured at his hands. I saw the motel where Travis had picked me up after that awful night.

Neither of us mentioned the incident, which was fine with me. We drove in silence mostly, past endless pine forests. Stink from paper mills drifted into the car. Heat shimmered on the asphalt pavement before us. Air rushing through the station wagon's open windows was too warm to even cool our skins. The sill of the passenger door was hot as a griddle; I couldn't rest my arm on it. Sweat gathered in my armpits, on my forehead, and between my legs. I longed for the air-conditioned coolness of Capital City's locker room, for my bedroom and box fan.

After turning east, we crossed the coffee-colored Suwannee River. Then we entered the small town of Branford with its brick and glass storefronts. Morning sunlight bore through the car's windshield, and I squinted in the brightness.

"I need shades," I told Travis. "Let's make a stop."

We found a convenience store with a revolving rack of knockoff sunglasses and a little mirror. A fat girl in a red smock, with acne and hairy forearms, sat behind the counter, smoking a cigarette and watching a small portable TV. I tried on pair after pair of sunglasses, each time asking Travis if he thought the sunglasses looked good on me.

"Face it," he said. "They all look terrible 'cause they cost next to nothing. Just choose a pair and let's get going."

I bought a pair with metal frames and round purple-tinted lenses; I thought they made me look like John Lennon or Ozzy Osbourne. In the car, Travis looked at me and shook his head.

"What?" I said.

He turned down one corner of his mouth. "With any luck, you'll lose those sunglasses in the drink."

Once we'd reached the Ichetucknee River, we rented tubes from a vendor just outside the state park. The tubes were black and fat, each about five feet in diameter with multiple orange patches. Four students from nearby University of Florida joined Travis and me in the bed of the vendor's pickup truck for a ride to the head of the river. We trundled down a red clay road, all of us clutching our tubes as we passed beneath live oaks that completely shaded the road. Already, it seemed the temperature had dropped by ten degrees. The woods on either side of the road were so thick I could only see a few feet into the forest.

Inside the park, the river's beauty stole my breath. The Ichetucknee was fed by a fresh-water spring called Blue Hole, and the spring's name was certainly apt. As a kid on a school trip to Washington, DC, I'd viewed the Star of Bombay sapphire on display at the Smithsonian Institution, an amazing gem with an azure hue one rarely sees in nature. Blue Hole had that same unearthly color. Groups of bathers splashed about the spring while others sunned themselves on limestone outcroppings rimming the spring. Children's laughter and shrieks echoed through a stand of towering cypress trees.

"I'm hot and sweaty," Travis said. "Let's take a dip before we tube."

After we'd both shed our shirts and footgear, my mouth grew sticky while I watched Travis's muscles move under his fair skin. His broad shoulders tapered to a trim waist, and his belly muscles rippled like a washboard. His nipples were dark and as tiny as raisins. A thin line of hair trickled from his fuzzy navel and into the waistband of his shorts. When he waded into the spring, goose bumps popped up on his skin. He clasped his arms in his hands. Then he looked at me with a grin on his face.

"It's cold as ice," he cried.

I stepped to a rock ledge that hung over the spring. Then I dove in headfirst. The chilly water pricked my skin like a thousand needles, and the sound of rising bubbles filled my ears. The spring's temperature was nearly twenty degrees less than the air above it. I thought of the hot drive we'd just made in Travis's station wagon, and I marveled at the spring's natural coolness.

Who needed air conditioning?

I swam through crystalline water to the shallow area where Travis stood waist-deep with his feet planted in the spring's sandy bottom. I stood alongside Travis, and then we both shivered like little boys in an ice storm. Droplets of water glistened on Travis's shoulders, in his dark hair. Sunlight reflected off the spring's placid surface.

Travis said, "I think my balls crawled up inside my body."

We both chuckled while we continued to shiver. "How long will the tube trip take?" I asked.

"If we stop for lunch along the way—and we should—it's about three and a half hours. You'll like the ride; the river's beautiful."

"You've been here before?"

He nodded. "My folks are big on outdoor activities. When my brother and I were kids, my family camped all over the state of Florida, from the Keys to the Panhandle. I think I was nine or ten when we stayed here."

The river proved as pretty as Travis had said. The water was just as clear as Blue Hole's. The river's width varied from thirty to sixty feet, and in most places the depth was less than three feet. Beneath the surface, exotic water plants undulated with the river's flow. We glided at a speed of two miles per hour, passing beneath ancient cypress trees with buttressed trunks and lacy branches. Using a length of bailing twine he'd found in a trash can, Travis had tethered our cooler to his tube, and now he trailed it behind him in the cool water.

As much as I'd cursed the sun's intensity earlier that morning, I felt glad for its presence during our trip. The water remained seventy-two degrees throughout the river's six-mile length, and I'd have been cold that day without the sun warming my shoulders and belly.

"Weekends, this place gets really crowded," Travis said.

But we encountered few other tubers as we slid past the stream's forested banks, listening to the water gurgle and the cries of birds echoing in the trees. We passed a hammock where a flock of wild turkeys, perhaps ten or so, pecked at the marshy ground. As we floated, Travis pointed out various species of trees I wasn't familiar with: sweet gum, Florida maple, turkey oak, swamp chestnut oak, wax myrtle, and red mulberry. He knew his flowering shrubs, too: arrow-wood, possumhaw, elderberry, and dahoon.

"Plants and trees have always fascinated me," Travis said. "My dad keeps a greenhouse at our home in Jacksonville. He grows orchids and bromeliads."

"Your folks sound pretty cool," I said.

He raised a shoulder, let it drop. "They can be...demanding. They set high standards for themselves *and* for their kids."

I nodded. "Biff told me many of your family members are doctors."

Travis bobbed his chin.

"I guess you will be, too?"

He pursed his lips, and then he spoke with a tone of resignation in his voice. "That's the plan."

"You don't sound too excited about it."

Travis trailed a few fingertips in the chilly water, creating ripples on the surface.

"Practicing medicine's okay, I guess. But I don't have the passion for it like Biff and Austin, or like my dad and brother do. I'd sooner do landscape design, maybe own a plant nursery or tree farm. Does that sound weird?"

"Not at all," I said.

"What about your folks?" Travis asked me. "Have they always expected you to practice law?"

I shook my head. "That was my idea, not theirs."

We dined on a sandy riverbank, seated in our beached tubes. We chewed our sandwiches and munched on pickle spears. The fresh air and sunshine made these simple foods taste special. Even the sodas we drank seemed to carry more flavor than they usually did. Travis's damp shorts clung to his body. Between his thighs, his genitals bulged beneath the denim. I studied the dark hairs dusting his calves and the smoothness of his thighs. Because he hadn't shaved that morning, stubble blued his face.

I asked myself, *How would it feel to kiss his lips, to feel my whiskers rasp against his while I ran my fingers through his hair?*

Between my legs, I stiffened. Then I tore my gaze from Travis.

Cut it out, Hunsinger. Remember, he's not interested in love.

Once back on the river, we floated in silence. My full stomach and the sun's warmth made me drowsy. My chin kept dropping to my sternum as we drifted along, and I was nearly asleep when Travis roused me with a question.

"Have you seen that man from Perry again—the one who roughed you up?"

Heat rose in my cheeks. I looked at Travis and shook my head. "Do you think I like bondage and torture?"

Travis narrowed his eyes. "I don't know *what* you like, Andy. You seem to have a hard time deciding."

I lowered my gaze. Then I looked at Travis again. "You're right, I guess. I seem a bit lost right now, but at least I haven't quit trying like..."

Shut up, Hunsinger.

"Like me?" Travis said.

I didn't answer him; I gazed at treetops instead.

"Has Biff told you about my Myrtle Beach debacle?"

I nodded, but I kept my gaze fixed on the cypress trees we passed.

Travis said, "Do you know how it feels to think your life is over?"

I thought about the day of the Anita Bryant demonstration.

"I think I do," I said.

"After Myrtle Beach and all the miserable shit that followed, I entered a very dark place inside my head, one I thought I might never escape. They locked me up in a psych ward, you know."

I nodded. "How long were you in?"

"About three months, but it seemed like more. Most of the time they kept me sedated with Seconal. I wandered the halls in a bathrobe like a sleepwalker."

"Are you gay?" I asked.

Travis raised his eyebrows. "I guess, but I'll never let myself love another man. Gay sex is forbidden by my faith, plus my family won't tolerate it. My folks have told me, more than once, 'We love you, but not your homosexual urges. Be a good man and make us proud: *control* yourself.'"

I made a face. "You'll go through life alone?"

He nodded.

"That's crazy, Travis."

"Is it?"

"Look, I know your faith's important to you, but I don't understand. How can loving another man be a sin? Did Jesus ever say homosexuality was wrong?"

Travis shook his head.

"And your family's not being fair," I said. "It's like they've put you in jail."

Travis snorted. "You sound like Biff. He's told me a dozen times, 'Grow some balls. Tell your family to fuck off.'"

Behind us, a group of bathers, a mix of high school boys and girls, approached on inflatable rafts. Their laughter rang through the surrounding forest. Travis and I fell silent. We hugged the riverbank, allowing the kids to float past us. One boy on a raft held hands with a girl on another raft. They floated side-by-side, gazing at each other and whispering back and forth. They looked awfully happy.

Once the kids rounded a bend in the river and their voices faded, Travis and I recommenced floating, and then I told him about my friends at AGA.

"This fall," I said, "you should come to a meeting with me."

Travis made a face. "Why? What would that accomplish?"

"You could be yourself among people who'll accept you. It's liberating, believe me."

Travis gazed into the river's crystal-clear water. "Let's talk about something else."

I LAY ON my bed in my Franklin Street apartment. My bedroom was dark, but faint moonlight entered through the windows and I stared at the water-stained ceiling. Hours before, Travis had dropped me off, following our tubing excursion, and ever since then, I couldn't get him off my mind. I remembered every detail of our conversation. I visualized the delicate contours of his face. I pictured his lanky limbs, creamy skin, and long fingers. I heard his baritone voice inside my head.

After seizing a tube of KY Jelly I kept in my nightstand drawer, I stroked myself while visions of Travis loomed in my head. When I came, I groaned so loudly Fergal would have heard me downstairs, had he been there. My chest heaved and my breath whistled in my nose. While my pulse slowed, I stared at the ceiling, feeling utterly satisfied.

If imaginary sex with Travis was that good, what would the real thing feel like?

For a fleeting moment, I thought of getting dressed, jumping into my Vega, and driving to Travis's home. I would seize him in my arms, plant a kiss on his cheek, and tell him how much I cared for him. But then I recalled what he'd told me while we floated downstream, earlier that day:

"I'll never let myself love another man."

Now, in my bedroom, I stared at the ceiling and shook my head.

Shit...

Sixteen

MY MOTHER CALLED on a weekday afternoon in late July. "Your father's had a heart attack, Andy."

"What?"

"He's in surgery right now."

My knees turned to jelly. I had to sit in my rocking chair, or I'd have fallen to the floor. My voice trembled when I spoke.

"How serious is it, Mom?"

A second or two passed. Then Mom answered. "They're not sure he'll make it. You'll need to come, now."

I rode to Pensacola with Bucky Buchholtz, in his Chrysler convertible. We hardly spoke during the three-hour drive on Highway 90. Bucky kept working his jaw from side to side; he flexed his fingers on the steering wheel while we flew past pine forests and pastureland.

"I can't believe this," I'd told him earlier. "Dad's always been so healthy; he's never even smoked. I thought he'd live to be a hundred."

"He damned sure better," Bucky said. "I can't imagine life without Drake Hunsinger. Who will I hunt and fish with? Who...?" Bucky's voice broke like a teenager's.

He kept his gaze straight ahead while a tear rolled out of the corner of his eye. Sniffling, he shook his head. Then he cleared his throat.

"Look at me, I'm crying like an old lady."

"It's okay," I said.

Bucky looked at me with a stricken expression on his face. Then he returned his gaze to the windshield.

"Your dad's the finest man I've ever known, a true friend, a good husband and father, and a damned fine bomber pilot. When he's in a cockpit, he doesn't know the meaning of the word fear."

I tried to imagine my father piloting a B-17 in the skies over Germany, while flak exploded all around him and Messerschmitts peppered his plane's flanks with bullets. Dad had always seemed mild-mannered and averse to conflict. The times he'd quarreled with my mom I could have counted on my fingers, and he had never struck me or my brother. He said his prayers each night and never missed church on Sunday. Yet this same man had rained destruction on his enemy, time and again. He had bombed bridges, factories, train stations, oil refineries, and chemical plants. No doubt he'd caused dozens or maybe hundreds of deaths.

Did he feel guilty about these deeds?

I had never asked him the question. In fact, early in life, I'd learned not to ask him anything about the war.

Whenever I did, he quickly changed the subject, and when I asked my mom why, she answered carefully.

"Men who fought in that war don't like to discuss their experiences. They saw things too awful to describe, I'm afraid; things they prefer to forget."

By the time Bucky and I reached Pensacola, the sun had dipped its lower edge behind the taller buildings to the west. Traffic was light and few pedestrians appeared on the city's sidewalks. Bucky maneuvered the Chrysler through downtown's narrow streets, past structures dating back to the Civil War. Baptist Hospital sat on West Avery Street, a red brick five-story structure with Florida maples spaced evenly in the hospital's freshly mown Bahia lawn. I had passed the building a thousand times while growing up, but never went inside.

We found Mom in a hallway, just outside the Intensive Care Unit on the hospital's fourth floor. Dressed in a light blue pantsuit, she sat on a straight-back chair with her hands resting in her lap and her gaze fixed on her leather pumps. When she heard our approach, she rose. Dark crescents smudged the lower halves of her eye sockets, and her shoulders sagged as though she carried cinder blocks in both her hands. When her gaze met mine, her upper lip quivered.

"Oh, Andy..."

I took her in my arms, and then I squeezed as hard as I could without hurting her.

"It's going to be okay, Mom; I know it will."

Mom let me go. Then she hugged Bucky. "It's good of you to come," she told him.

"Martha," Bucky said. "I wouldn't be anywhere else right now."

Mom sat in her chair. Then she spoke to us with a tremble in her voice. "He came home from work around noon. His face was as pale as an eggshell. He said he wasn't feeling well—he said he needed to lie down—but never made it to the bed. He clutched his chest, and then he collapsed on the kitchen floor."

Bucky jingled the change in his pants pocket. "Jesus," he muttered.

I chewed my lower lip while my stomach roiled and my knees shook. For a moment, I feared I might pass out. How could this be happening?

"I thought the ambulance would *never* arrive," Mom said. "I didn't know what to do, so I knelt on the floor and held his hand. I kept telling him, 'Hold on, Drake. Help's on the way. You have to hold on.'"

"Where is he?" I asked.

She pointed to a pair of swinging doors just a few feet from us.

"What caused this, Mom? I don't understand."

She pulled a hank of hair from her brow. After tucking it behind an ear, she explained.

"The doctor said something called 'plaque' had clogged the arteries feeding blood to your father's heart. They don't yet know how much damage was caused; it's too early to tell."

"Can I see him?"

She nodded. "But he's under sedation; he's not conscious."

"I just want to see him," I said.

The ICU hummed with activity. Several nurses in scrubs tended a dozen or so patients in beds, with scrims separating the patients. My dad lay with his upper body elevated. A blanket covered his lower body. He wore a green hospital gown. A heart monitor stood beside his bed; it bleeped and blipped. Clear liquid dripped into Dad's arm from a tube hooked to a bag hanging from a metal stand.

Dad's eyes were closed. His chest rose and fell. His hands lay limp on his blanket; his face was the color of cake flour. He seemed to have aged ten years since I'd last seen him. And how long had *that* been? It took me a moment before I realized I hadn't come home since Easter, three months before, when I'd broken the news about my personal life.

A wave of guilt washed over me. Why hadn't I visited home more often? What was so important in my life that I couldn't make time for my folks?

You're a selfish ingrate, Hunsinger. Look at all he's done for you, and think of how little you've done for him.

When I took one of Dad's hands in both of mine, his palm felt cold and moist. I shivered beneath the glow of a fluorescent ceiling fixture. The grayness in the hair at Dad's temples seemed to have spread upward toward the crown of his head since I'd last seen him. The furrows in his forehead and the crow's feet at the corners of his eyes seemed deeper than before. Had all this happened recently, or had I been so consumed with my own personal issues that I'd failed to notice my father's aging?

I thought back to Jake's Tallahassee visit, weeks before. What was it he'd said about my folks' attitude toward me being gay?

"I think they've seen past it."

Maybe so, but then again…maybe not. Maybe the stress I'd dumped into their lives was somehow linked to my dad's present condition. Didn't stress cause heart attacks? My eyes clouded, and then my tears dripped onto Dad's hairy forearm. He drew a deep breath. Then he let it out, but his eyes remained closed.

"Oh, Daddy," I whispered. "I'm so sorry if I hurt you."

MY BROTHER ARRIVED in Pensacola, the morning after Dad's heart attack, just after the sun rose. Jake had driven all night from North Carolina. His hair was tousled, and stubble shaded his face. His hand shook when he brought a glass of orange juice to his lips.

We sat in our kitchen's breakfast nook at the Formica-topped table: Jake, Mom, and I. Odors of fried bacon and freshly brewed coffee scented the air. Beyond the nook's casement windows, a blue jay flitted about the branches of an azalea shrub, glancing here and there, perhaps looking for bugs to eat. His tail feathers twitched.

My mother looked as shell-shocked as Bucky's brother, Eddie. She wore no makeup. Normally, she kept her hair perfectly coiffed, but that morning, her chestnut tresses looked as wind-tossed as Jake's. Dark crescents remained beneath her eyes, and her shoulders slumped. She wore a terrycloth robe with her monogram stitched on one pocket, a Christmas gift Jake and I had bought her many years before. Eschewing breakfast, she stared into her coffee cup.

I felt like hell and probably looked worse. Mom and I had remained at the hospital well past midnight. Bucky had driven back to Tallahassee, but I spent the night at my parents' home, in my old bedroom among mementoes from my childhood and adolescence: Little League trophies, yearbooks, my framed high school diploma, and so forth.

I slept fitfully, tossing about my bed like I wrestled with a demon. Visions of my dad—little vignettes from the past—kept filling my head: Dad carving our Thanksgiving turkey, using an electric knife for the first time and marveling at its precision; Dad taking Jake and me horseback riding at an Okaloosa County ranch when I was nine and Jake five; Dad and Bucky grilling venison in our backyard after they'd hunted in Montana; Dad and Mom renewing their wedding vows before a crowd of a hundred friends and family, on their twenty-fifth wedding anniversary.

And so on.

It surprised me how many events I recalled so vividly.

Some I hadn't thought about in years, but now they bubbled up like lava from the recesses of my brain. I supposed we often take these sorts of family experiences for granted. We fail to pay them the homage they deserve until we learn there might not be any more of them, until it's too late to create more memories.

Now, in the breakfast nook, Jake jabbered about his camp counselor job while Mom and I listened stoically.

"I supervise a cabin with a dozen campers between eight and thirteen years old. They're all rich kids from the South: Georgia, the Carolinas, Florida, and Alabama. One kid's a bed wetter, another cries in his sleep, and one boy has Tourette's Syndrome; he can't sit still. You wouldn't believe how screwed up so many kids are."

Mom rolled her eyes and shook her head. "Try teaching junior high school English for a year. I fear for the future of our country at times."

I talked about the guys I caddied with at Capital City. "Money spoils kids, I believe. Rich boys develop an attitude, think they're better than those who don't come from wealth."

I spoke of the incident involving Dustin Ausley and Jerry Justus, after my appearance on TV at the Bryant demonstration. I described how Dustin had called me a fag, and then how Jerry assaulted Dustin in the caddy tent.

Jake ceased chewing on a piece of toast; he pointed a finger at my nose. "If *I'd* been there, I would've punched that kid's face in."

My mom looked at my brother and scowled. "Jacob, your father wouldn't approve of what you just said. Violence never solves a problem. It just makes things worse."

Jake started to reply to Mom's remark, but then the wall phone rang before he could. All three of us leapt to our feet, but my mother raised a palm to Jake and me.

"Both of you stay where you are," she said. "*I'll* take this call myself."

Mom clenched her jaw. Then she lifted the receiver, said hello in an even voice. A ten-minute conversation ensued. The party on the other end did most of the talking. Mom said things like, "Yes, I see," or "All right, okay," and not much else.

Jake and I sat on the edge of the breakfast nook bench with our gazes fixed on our mother. What was going on? My heart slammed against my rib cage. Was my dad alive or dead? If Dad was gone, how would our family bear it?

At long last, Mom said, "Thank you, Doctor, for all you've done. God bless you." Then she hung up and turned her face to us. "Your father's okay. He's actually sitting up and talking."

Mom thrust her face into her hands. Her shoulders shook while she wept.

Jake and I hugged each other so tightly our joints crackled.

"Thank God, Little Brother," I whispered. "Dad's alive."

DAD'S SURGEON BELONGED on a daytime soap opera; he was silver-haired with a baritone voice, a deep suntan, a lab coat, and a stethoscope hung about his shoulders. He met with Mom, me, and Jake in a conference room overlooking Baptist Hospital's parking lot. Morning sunshine poured into the room through Venetian blinds, casting bars of light onto the room's mint green walls.

"We performed a double bypass procedure," the doctor told us. "We relieved the blockage in his arteries—his heart's pumping well, considering—but he'll be weak for at least a month. He'll need help getting out of bed, with bathing, and using the toilet."

Mom chewed her lower lip. "Drake's a big man. I'm not sure I could lift him."

"*I* can," Jake said. "I'll quit my job and come home, right away."

Do something, Andy. For once, be a help instead of a burden.

"No, you won't," I told Jake. "You need to save money for school."

Jake lowered his gaze and didn't say anything.

I looked at Mom. "I'll come home. Business is slow at the country club this time of year. Bucky won't mind if I'm gone for a month."

Mom raised her eyebrows. "You're sure, Andy?"

I nodded.

Seventeen

JAKE DROVE ME to Tallahassee on his way back to North Carolina. After I'd packed all my summer clothing in the Vega's trunk, I called Travis; I asked him to water my houseplants once a week.

"I'll leave a key in my mailbox," I told him.

Then I drove to Pensacola on Highway 90, passing through Panhandle towns like Quincy, Chipley, and DeFuniak Springs, little burgs with one or two traffic lights and Winn-Dixie shopping centers.

Mom wouldn't report for work until the third week of August. Dad, of course, would spend most of his time in bed. We'd be together—the three of us—all day and night, seven days a week, for a spell. And how would that be? I had my own place now; I was used to coming and going without explaining my plans. I ate what I wanted to, slept as late as I chose to. Would that all change? I was twenty-two years old now, no longer a kid. Would my parents expect me to revert to the role I'd played back in high school, the dutiful son?

I thought about Jeff Dellinger, the serviceman I'd dated the previous summer. We hadn't spoken in nearly a year. For all I knew, he'd transferred to another base, but...maybe not. Okay, Jeff hadn't really been a "boyfriend," per se. Our meetings had been sexual encounters, nothing more.

But sex for its own sake was better than no sex, right?

I seized my wallet and rummaged through it with one hand. A minute or so passed before I located a scrap of notebook paper with Jeff's phone number scribbled on it. Studying the number, I thought of Jeff's lanky limbs, his dark hair and eyes.

Call him, dumbass, as soon as you get to Pensacola.

I stopped for gasoline in Marianna, another small town with a single traffic light. Heat shimmered over the asphalt road. Brick buildings in the old downtown were mostly vacant, their storefronts papered. But the Jackson County courthouse, a three-story beauty built of dimpled block with stately columns and a cupola, still hummed with activity. Uniformed deputies conversed with briefcase-toting lawyers on the sidewalk. Beneath a live oak with spreading limbs, a Confederate soldier statue stood guard. The Stars and Stripes and the Florida state flag hung as limply as dishrags in the still afternoon.

At a Sinclair station, a gangly high school kid with auburn hair, a turned-up nose, and freckles pumped my gas and cleaned my windshield. After giving me change for a twenty, he pointed to a sticker on my Vega's rear window.

"You're an FSU student?" he asked in a scratchy tenor.

I nodded.

"I hope to go there after I graduate next year. I can't wait to leave Marianna."

I glanced left and right. "Is it so bad here?"

When he looked at me and bobbed his chin, I saw desperation in his emerald eyes, the same I'd often seen in my bathroom mirror when I was his age.

"People here can't see past the ends of their noses. Everyone thinks the same, acts the same. Know what I mean?"

I nodded. "But it's different in Tallahassee."

He raised his eyebrows. "Is it?"

"You can be yourself, whatever that is."

He studied a transfer truck that blew past on Highway 90. Then he swung his gaze back to me. "Do you think a kid from a town like this could cut it at Florida State?"

"Of course," I said. "Why not?"

He shrugged. "I've never been more than fifty miles from Marianna. I'm a hick, you might say, not too...worldly."

I shook my head. "Don't let life scare you. Get out there and try your best. You'll get what you want if you do."

He tilted his head toward a shoulder. "I don't know..."

"Look," I said, "I know leaving home can be frightening. FSU's a big school—25,000 kids—but you'd find your place there. Most everyone does; it only takes a little time."

He extended a hand. "I'm Carter."

We shook. "I'm Andy," I said. "Tallahassee's only an hour's drive from here. You should pay a visit, take a tour of campus."

"But I don't know anyone there."

I chuckled. "You do now."

After I pulled a writing pen and a napkin from the Vega's glove box, I scribbled my name and phone number on the napkin. Then I gave the napkin to Carter.

"I'm spending the next month in Pensacola," I said. "But in September, I'll start law school in Tallahassee. Call me then, you can drive over and I'll show you around. How's that?"

A grin spread across Carter's freckled face. "You're serious?"

"Sure," I said. "I only live a mile from campus; it's no problem."

Carter stuffed the napkin into the hip pocket of his Dickies work pants.

ONCE HOME, I had much to do. Mom and I moved my parents' bed into the garage. Then a rental service delivered medical devices to my folks' home: a hospital bed with an electric motor that raised and lowered the mattress at either end; an aluminum walker, the kind with wheels on the front legs; a stainless-steel bed pan, and a set of walkie-talkies Dad could use to call Mom or me if he needed help. Mom borrowed a portable TV with rabbit ears from a friend, and I set it up in my folks' bedroom, atop the bureau.

"I'll sleep in Jake's room," Mom told me, "so I don't disturb your father when I get up at night."

They brought Dad home in an ambulance. Two guys in white scrubs wheeled him into the house on a stretcher. Then they helped him into the hospital bed. Dad was still as pale as cake flour, and his cheeks looked sunken, like he'd lost twenty pounds. Silver stubble dusted his chin and cheeks. His breath wheezed while he maneuvered from the stretcher to the bed, with both guys holding him up by his elbows. His voice sounded raspy and weak when he spoke.

After the ambulance fellows left, the first thing Dad said to me was, "Get me out of this damned hospital gown, would you? I'm tired of my ass hanging out for the world to see; I want real pajamas, something a little more dignified."

I helped him into a pair of briefs, and then his PJs while he huffed and puffed.

"I'm as weak as a kitten," he told me. "Doc says it'll be a while before I can walk on my own."

"That's why I'm here," I said. "I won't leave until you're better."

He looked at me and raised an eyebrow. "When does school start?"

"The day after Labor Day."

"I don't care what happens," Dad said, pointing a finger at my nose. "You're going back to Tallahassee at the end of August. We've never had a lawyer in the Hunsinger family—you'll be our first—and nothing, I mean nothing, will get in the way of that."

"Dad—"

"I mean it, Andy. Nothing."

My mother brought Dad's lunch on a bed tray: a bowl of tomato soup and a dish of saltines.

Dad studied the food. "This is *it*? How about a McDonald's cheeseburger instead?"

My mother put her hands on her hips; she spoke to Dad like he was one her students. "Doctor Lipton says no heavy foods, period."

Dad grimaced and shook his head. Then he picked up his spoon and dipped it into the soup.

My mother looked at me and rolled her eyes. "I need to talk with your father privately. Why don't you take an hour's drive somewhere?"

I looked at Dad, then her. "You're sure it's okay if I leave?"

Dad set down his spoon and glared at me. "Jesus Christ, don't treat me like a child."

"Go on," Mom said. "We'll be fine."

I drove the Vega across Pensacola Causeway to the beach highway. Then I turned west and drove to Gulf Islands National Seashore, a federal park with soaring dunes and sand as white as table sugar. The Gulf was emerald green, as clear as tap water, and groves of sand pines swayed in a gentle breeze. As a teenager, I had tent-camped several times on this stretch of coast with my friends. We built sandcastles, roasted weenies, drank beer, and even skinny-dipped in the Gulf while the sun glowed above the western horizon. People said the park looked the same as it had when Andrew Jackson was Florida's first governor: undeveloped and pristine, a part of Florida most tourists never saw when they visited.

I parked the Vega and kicked off my sandals. Then I walked along the shore with my hands in the pockets of my shorts. Waves struck the sand, making slushy sounds. The breeze tossed my hair about and plastered my T-shirt to my chest. Above me, the sun kept disappearing behind cumulus clouds that looked like tattered cotton balls, skating across a brilliantly blue sky. The air smelled briny and fresh, so different from torporific Tallahassee's.

My thoughts churned.

What if Dad *didn't* get back on his feet by the end of August? If I left for Tallahassee, he'd likely have to stay in a nursing home, something I couldn't bear to think of.

Still...

Competition for slots at the law school had been fierce. If I no-showed next month, they'd give my place to someone else, and then I wouldn't have another shot at admission, would I? But if I returned to Tallahassee in September and Dad was still bedridden, my brother would insist on staying home; he'd give up his scholarship and spend his days toting Dad to the bathroom. He'd enroll at community college, like many of my friends from high school had done, and then he might never leave Pensacola. I couldn't bear to think of *that* either. My handsome, bright little brother had places to go, things to do.

And I could not imagine my mother living at our home alone while Dad occupied a bed in a nursing facility, halfway across town. My parents weren't just spouses, they were best friends; they did everything together. They weren't sociable people; they didn't join civic organizations or attend neighborhood parties, though they'd been invited many times. After work and on weekends, they always stayed home, working in the yard or reading on the lanai.

The few times they went out, they attended Jake's sporting events or my stage productions.

Without Dad around, Mom would wither like a houseplant someone forgot to water.

Up ahead of me, a park ranger in an olive drab Jeep approached, kicking up sand with his rear tires. The Jeep's engine growled; sunlight glanced off its windshield. The ranger waved when he passed me, and then I waved back. He wasn't much older than me, and I wondered what working such a job might be like, spending five days a week by the seashore, keeping an eye on the park, with no pressures to deal with and no one to speak to but seagulls and turtles.

Then I shook my head.

That's not you, Hunsinger. Like Jake, you have places to go, things to do.

The sun pounded my shoulders and the top of my head. My armpits moistened and sweat trickled down my ribs.

I shed my T-shirt. Then I sat cross-legged at the foot of a sand dune. I gazed at the churning Gulf while I tried to imagine myself living in Pensacola, without all the things most important to me: my apartment, Fergal and Biff, my job at Capital City, my independence, and, of course, Travis.

Travis.

When I'd called to ask him to water my houseplants, he expressed concern about my dad. He asked many questions about Dad's condition, and then wished Dad the best.

"I'll pray for him, Andy, and for you, too. I'll ask God to watch over your family."

I appreciated Travis's gesture, but to me belief in an Almighty who controlled our lives was a concept for people frightened by life, folks who feared what lay in store for them when they died. I didn't for one moment believe God would heal my father.

Now, as I sat there in the sand, I knew I'd never need religion in my life. The world didn't scare me like it did Travis. Yes, life could be tough at times; I was still finding my way. But one way or another, I would shape my surroundings to suit me. And when I died, be that in five years or fifty, I wouldn't leave Earth in fear. Whatever was out there was...*out* there.

Okay, Hunsinger, you're thinking too much. You're here for a month, and you might as well make the most of it.

My knees crackled when I rose. I dusted sand from the seat of my shorts, and then I made my way back to my car.

Hours later, after I'd helped my dad bathe and my Mom clean the kitchen, I drove to a strip mall on the Mobile Highway. Standing in a phone booth, my hand shook when I dialed Jeff's number at the Eglin BOQ. The booth's interior felt stuffy; sweat beaded on my upper lip and forehead.

I recognized Jeff's baritone the moment he answered. "Jeff, it's Andy Hunsinger. Remember me?"

Jeff didn't answer for a few seconds. When he did, he spoke in a whisper.

"How've you been, Andy?"

"Pretty good, and you?"

"*Not* so good, I'm afraid."

"Why, what's wrong?"

"It would take a while to explain."

I twisted the phone receiver's cord. Beyond the booth's glass door, traffic whizzed past on the highway.

Go on: ask him.

"I was hoping we could get together."

Another long pause ensued. Then Jeff spoke *sotto voce*. "If you'd like, we can meet. I'm free Saturday."

My pulse accelerated. "Can we—"

"The usual place," Jeff said. "I'll see you in the lobby, at 3:00 p.m."

Jeff hung up before I could say anything else.

THE DAYS DRAGGED by. Mornings, I got my dad out of bed, and then I helped him to the bathroom so he could use the toilet and shave. Many days, Mom went to her school to prepare for her first classes, and I was left alone to fix breakfast for Dad. I'd bring him his meal on a tray, along with the newspaper, and then I watched TV in the living room, or I rode Jake's ten-speed bike around our neighborhood.

By 11:00 a.m., the temperature reached the lower nineties. Pensacola became a steam bath, and I found little to do but hide in the air conditioning with a book. I read Herman Wouk's *The Winds of War*, and then James Michener's *Hawaii*, both lengthy novels I chose because they kept me occupied. I spent four or five hours a day reading, just to kill time. Every day, I fixed Dad's lunch, and then I brought my own to the master bedroom as well, so we could chat while we ate. We talked about sports, about my upcoming law school experience, and Jake's move to Emory University.

Dad said, "It's going to feel a bit lonely around here, with just your mom and me rattling around the house. I hope I don't make her crazy."

I drove Dad to appointments with his cardiologist, surgeon, and physical therapist. The therapist, a short man with piercing brown eyes and a lisp, gave Dad homework.

"I'm having a treadmill delivered to your home. I want you to walk at least fifteen minutes per day at a two-mile-per-hour pace. We need to rebuild strength in your heart."

Most evenings, after I took a steamy three-mile run in a nearby park, I showered, and then I prepared dinner for my folks and me. I didn't mind; it helped pass the time and gave my parents time to spend together while I banged pots and pans in the kitchen. I made lasagna, tuna casserole, and baked chicken with wild rice. Heeding the doctors' advice, I didn't fry food, and I tried to limit the amount of red meat we consumed.

One night, I prepared a chef's salad, replete with boiled eggs, chipped ham, and a medley of garden produce: tomatoes, cucumbers, purple onion, and bell peppers. I even prepared my own ranch dressing from a recipe I found in Mom's copy of *Joy of Cooking*. Another night, we dined on fresh flounder filets I'd baked in a lemon and mushroom sauce.

"You're spoiling us, honey," my mom told me. "We might not *let* you leave for Tallahassee if you keep this up."

One afternoon, after I'd helped Dad to the bathroom and then back to bed, he pointed to the chair beside his bed.

"Sit a spell," he told me. "I want to talk."

A thunderstorm had rolled into town from the Gulf, and rain drummed the roof above our heads. Each time a thunderclap sounded, the windows rattled. Puddles formed in our backyard and branches on Mom's azaleas thrashed about when the wind gusted. I sat with my hands in my lap, looking at Dad. The lines in his face seemed deeper than ever before. He wheezed like an asthmatic and his skin was eggshell pale. Behind his horn-rimmed glasses, his pale blue eyes focused on me. Glow from the nightstand lamp reflected in his gold wedding band.

Dad cleared his throat before he spoke.

"Not long before this heart attack happened, I spoke with Bucky by phone, for a good long while. He told me about the Anita Bryant situation. He talked about the mess at the country club, too."

I lowered my gaze while heat crept into my cheeks.

"Andy, look at me."

My gaze met my dad's.

"I want you to know I'm proud of you for sticking up for yourself. You and your friends gave that Bryant woman a dose of her own medicine."

My eyes watered, but I kept looking at my dad while he continued.

"Bucky told me about the board meeting at the club and how impressively you spoke. A lot of guys wouldn't have had the courage. I don't know *I* would have."

"Does Mom know?"

Dad nodded. "She feels just as I do. We're both so proud."

I couldn't help it: a wave of guilt washed over me. My lips quivered and my eyes watered. I buried my face in my hands and wept.

"Shhhh," Dad said. "There's nothing to cry about."

I spoke, in between sniffles. "I fear I've let you and Mom down."

"How so?"

"I'll never live a normal life. I won't get married or have kids."

Dad shrugged. "Bucky never has, and he seems happy. Marriage isn't a panacea, you know. It's not for everyone."

I nodded.

"A man has to be true to himself, son. I don't have to tell you that. However you choose to live and whomever you choose to live with, it's fine with your mother and me. We only want your happiness, understand?"

I nodded, blinking out a few more tears. Then I said, "Dad?"

"What?"

"Please don't die anytime soon. Promise me you'll do whatever the doctors say."

Dad grunted. "You sound like your mother."

"I don't care what I sound like. I love you, and I don't want to lose you."

Dad reached out and squeezed my shoulder.

"Don't you worry," he said. "I'll stick around a good long while."

Eighteen

THE HOTEL'S LOBBY hadn't changed since I'd last been there: Formica reception desk, Naugahyde sofa and chairs, mildewed carpet, and a rack holding brochures for local tourist attractions. In one corner of the lobby, *Wide World of Sports* appeared on a console television. The guy behind the desk had a face the color of boiled ham; he puffed on a cigarette while perusing the *Pensacola News-Journal*.

I checked my wristwatch. The time was 2:50 p.m.; I was ten minutes early. I glanced here and there. What to do?

I seized a brochure distributed by the National Park Service. The brochure described Fort Barrancas, a red brick structure with a "water battery" overlooking Pensacola Bay from a bluff. According to the brochure, the fort had been the site of the Battle of Pensacola, fought between British and American forces, during the War of 1812. Andrew Jackson had led the Americans to victory there.

I shook my head in disbelief, feeling a bit disgusted with myself. I had lived in Pensacola all my life. A historical gem existed, practically beneath my nose, yet I had never visited the fort. Why?

"Andy?"

When I looked up from the brochure, I barely recognized Jeff. He had always been slender, but now he looked haggard. His thick, dark hair was disheveled, his skin was pale, and a few acne pimples dotted his cheeks. His civilian clothes hung on his frame like a scarecrow's attire: T-shirt, blue jeans, and rubber sandals.

I rose, and then we shook hands while the guy behind the counter rustled his newspaper.

Jeff let his gaze travel from my forehead to my feet. "You look great."

"Thanks," I said. "You do, too."

Jeff grimaced. "No, I don't."

I followed Jeff down an outdoor corridor, and then up a flight of stairs to his second-floor room. Already, my pulse pounded. Jeff's butt cheeks moved beneath the seat of his jeans, and the thought I'd soon see him naked made my mouth go pasty. How many months had it been since I had touched another guy?

Jeff's room looked like others we'd occupied in the past: queen-size bed with a quilted comforter, dime-store artwork bolted to the walls, a laminate desk and chair, a bureau with a mirror. A wall unit blew cool air into the room, fluttering the drapes above it. In the tiled bath, a paper strip banded the toilet seat, and gauze-thin towels hung from a chrome bar. The shag carpet was worn to its weft in places. The shade on the nightstand lamp was yellowed with age.

Despite the changes in his appearance, Jeff still looked sexy to me. I liked his dark hair and eyes, thick brows, lanky limbs, and baritone voice. After he sat on the edge of the bed, I sat beside him and rested my arm about his shoulders. Jeff responded by shoving his hands between his knees. He stared at his feet while his jaw worked from side to side; he looked like a kid waiting outside the principal's office.

Go on: do something.

I nuzzled his ear, very gently.

Jeff flinched. Then he shrugged my arm off his shoulders.

I drew back and made a face. "What is it?" I asked. "What's wrong?"

Jeff swung his gaze to me; he glared at me like I'd done something inappropriate.

"Don't touch me—not right now."

"Why?"

Out in the corridor a group of boys—they sounded like college students—passed by our door, laughing and chattering away. Though the plastic drapes were closed, we heard their conversation clearly. All of them sounded a bit drunk.

One boy called another a cocksucker.

Jeff lowered his gaze. He kept silent until the group wasn't within earshot. The wall unit's hum was the only noise in the room, and Jeff's voice cracked like a teenager's when he spoke.

"Something bad happened, Andy, something awful."

"What? Tell me, are you sick?"

When Jeff's gaze met mine, tears glistened in his eyes. "There's a gay bar in Fort Walton Beach, the Red Door. Ever heard of it?"

I shook my head.

"It's a small place, very discreet. I've gone there lots of times, to meet men, usually other guys from Eglin."

"So?"

"The MPs sent a—"

"The *who*?"

"The military police; they sent a pair of undercover detectives to the Door. The detectives wrote down license plate numbers in the parking lot. Then they made notes on servicemen they saw in the club. I made the list."

I winced. "Are you in trouble?"

Jeff nodded. "My CO informed me three weeks ago: I'll receive an undesirable discharge."

I squirmed on the mattress. "I don't understand. Why?"

Jeff looked at me like I was nuts. "You can't have sex with men when you serve in the US military; don't you know that?"

I lowered my gaze and shrugged. What did I know of military matters? I'd never considered whether or not an openly gay man could serve.

"It doesn't seem fair," I said. "Why do they care?"

Jeff ran his fingers through his hair. "They *do*," he said, "believe me."

"Can you fight it?"

Jeff shook his head. "I'm a goner; I'll even lose my veteran's benefits: health care, my VA loan, the works."

"That's terrible," I said. "I wish I could help somehow."

Jeff looked at me with his watery eyes. Then he touched my cheek with a fingertip. "Let's have sex," he said.

We hooked the chain on the door. Then I took my clothes off while Jeff did the same. Once we were naked, Jeff pointed to his reflection in the mirror.

"Look at how skinny I am. I've lost ten pounds since all this happened. Food doesn't interest me anymore."

I took Jeff in my arms and hugged him. I rested my chin on his shoulder, patted his rump. His familiar scent, a mixture of wet pine needles and damp earth, made my pulse quicken.

"You still look handsome to me," I said. "You were my first, you know."

Jeff wrapped his arms around my waist. Then we swayed like two dancers at a high school prom. The soles of our feet scuffed the room's worn carpet while Jeff's hips rubbed against mine. His voice shook when he spoke.

"It's like the end of my whole world. Everything I've worked for, ever since I joined ROTC in high school, will go down the drain."

What was there to say?

"You had a life before the military," I told him. "You'll find one afterward, too."

"You don't understand. My dad's career navy and my older brother's a marine. A military life is all I ever wanted. Now..."

"Come on," I said, "let's hit the bed."

Before he crawled between the covers, Jeff produced a tube of jelly. He fetched hand towels from the bathroom, too. It had been nearly a year since we'd had sex; I was more experienced now, and I wondered just how things would unfold in the coming hour.

Looking at Jeff made my heart race. My mouth grew sticky and a shiver ran through me. Yes, he was super thin right now, and his skin was as pale as milk. But still, he was handsome. His chest was defined, his nipples dark, and his belly was rippled. As soon as he lay beside me, I seized the back of his neck—I brought his face to mine—but when I tried kissing him, he resisted. He looked at me and knitted his eyebrows.

"What are you doing?"

"I want a smooch."

Jeff made a face. "When did you start kissing men?"

"Since I met my first boyfriend in Tallahassee. Do you have a problem with it?"

Jeff turned away from me. He lay on his back, placed his hands behind his neck, and then stared at the popcorn ceiling.

"It's one thing to fuck around with another guy," Jeff said. "It's another to turn completely queer. There's a big difference, you know."

"Is there?"

Jeff looked at me. Then he returned his gaze to the ceiling without answering.

I lay beside him on the flimsy coverlet. "Since I last saw you, I've kissed many men, even guys whose names I didn't know. Straight people kiss. Why shouldn't two gay men?"

Jeff kept his gaze fixed on the ceiling. "I'm not gay, not entirely. I only need a man's touch now and then. It's a release for me, that's all."

I bent an elbow. Then I rested my jaw on the heel of my hand. "You're telling me you're straight, that you're attracted to women?"

"I don't know, I—"

"Jeff, look at me."

He did.

"A guy who takes another man's cock up his butt is gay. A man who fucks another man in the butt is gay. Why are you so afraid to admit who you are? Why does kissing me scare you?"

Jeff blinked a time or two. "If I do that—if I kiss you—I'll cross a line."

I couldn't help it, I chuckled.

"What's so funny?" Jeff asked.

"You're not going to sprout fairy wings if we suck face, you know."

Jeff lowered his gaze, but a thin smile crept across his face. Then he snickered and shook his head. "I guess you're right, and what does it matter, anyway? I'm already screwed."

I reached for Jeff's ear, tugged at his lobe.

Jeff looked at me again. His voice sounded tired when he spoke. "Okay, Andy. Let's do it."

He turned toward me. Our hips and chests met, and then our mouths touched. Our lips parted and our tongues dueled. I explored his teeth and the walls of his mouth, probing with my tongue. Our sloppy smacking and the air conditioner's chugs were the only noises in the room.

Jeff's hand traveled south, to caress me between my legs.

His attentions made me slightly dizzy, like I'd swallowed a shot of vodka, and right then I realized how badly I'd missed sex. Since my episode in Perry with Ray, I'd been celibate, but how much sense did *that* make? Sex was a necessary part of life for me. I needed it just like food, drink, and sleep. Depriving myself of intimacy made no sense. The sights, sounds, and smells of sex thrilled me in a way nothing else could.

So I made a promise to myself, there in the hotel room. When I returned to Tallahassee in September, I would pursue another man's love, relentlessly, even if I had to humble myself, and even if I had to settle for less than perfection. At least for now I had Jeff, and I knew what I wanted from him.

Jeff did not demur when I made my request. He lay on his back with his head resting in a stack of pillows and his arms wrapped around the back of his knees, holding his legs aloft.

"Andy?"

"Hmmm?"

"Take it slow; it's been a while since...you know."

I looked into Jeff's dark eyes. He looked like a little boy instead of a grown man, and it seemed to me we had actually *switched* roles since the last time I'd seen him. I was no longer the novice or the fumbling kid who'd allowed Jeff to call the shots and set the limits. Unlike Jeff, I'd become a man who wasn't afraid to be himself.

Jeff's viewing himself as *partially* gay puzzled me.

Why had kissing scared him so? Kissing men didn't make me a sissy or a pervert. On the contrary, I felt it *enhanced* my masculinity *and* my self-assurance. *I* set the rules and boundaries in my private life, not the military police, or Raymond Connor, or the pastor at First Baptist in Tallahassee. Who were these people, anyway? What gave them the right to limit *who* I might love and *how* I might love them?

As Biff Schultz might say, they could "go fuck themselves."

I mussed Jeff's hair, and then I smooched his forehead. "I'll be gentle."

The veins in Jeff's neck popped out when I entered him. He closed his eyes and clenched his jaw.

"You okay?" I asked.

He nodded. "Go ahead, Andy."

I commenced thrusting my hips while Jeff grunted and sighed. I felt electric all over, like I'd plugged myself into a wall socket. Minutes later, when I came, my whole body jerked three or four times.

"Jesus *Christ*," I hollered.

The sound of my voice bounced off the walls. My lungs heaved like I'd just finished a three-mile run. I wrapped my arms around Jeff's sweaty neck, and then I pulled his face to mine. Our lips met first, our tongues next, and then we slobbered like two teenagers. Jeff's earlier reluctance to kiss me seemed to have disappeared like a puff of smoke from a campfire.

"Can we do this again?" I asked Jeff, already hungry for more.

"Sure," he said. "I'll meet you here next Saturday, same time."

I rested my sweaty cheek on the curve of Jeff's neck, and then I listened to him breathe.

Next Saturday's so far off. I could do this every day.

Nineteen

A FEW DAYS after my encounter with Jeff, I rose before daybreak. I drove to Tallahassee in darkness, squinting at the glare from headlights of transfer trucks on Highway 90. I would collect my mail at the apartment. Then I'd visit the law school to buy books and write down my reading assignments for the first day of class. Law students, it seemed, hit the ground running.

My mother stayed home that day to look after Dad. "I'll write lesson plans," she told me. "Just do what you need to do; we'll be fine."

The drive to Tallahassee from Pensacola on Highway 90 was boring as hell, especially in the darkness. I couldn't even see the usual progression of cow pastures, pecan groves, and slash pine forests, not until I reached Gadsden County. At that point, I was thinking about Jeff and his Air Force difficulties when I came upon a disgusting scene, one that made my breakfast roil in my stomach. Someone, probably a transfer truck driver, had struck a good-size deer during the night, and now, as the sun crested the eastern horizon, several turkey buzzards gathered about the animal's bulky carcass on the shoulder of the road. The buzzards looked like diners at an all-you-can-eat buffet. A shudder ran through me, and then I returned my gaze to the road.

Had the deer died instantly when it was struck, or had it suffered a while before it succumbed?

By the time I reached my apartment, the sun had crested the trees to the east and dew glistened in the crabgrass. Already, the day was heating up. Folks drove down Franklin Street with their car mufflers growling, headed for jobs in the monolithic state office buildings surrounding the Capitol.

A mockingbird eyed me from a live oak's limb, as though I were an intruder on the property.

In my building's foyer, I found my mailbox empty. My front door was unlocked, and I crinkled my forehead in puzzlement while I pushed the door into my living room. What was going on?

Travis sat at my dining table, wearing nothing but white briefs. His hair was disheveled and he hadn't shaved. He studied a chemistry text while dining on a bowlful of breakfast cereal.

"The landlord's having our house tented for termites," he explained. "I didn't think you'd mind if I stayed here a few nights."

"Of course not," I said. "You know you're always welcome."

He pointed to a stack of envelopes and circulars on the coffee table. "I emptied your mailbox."

I sat on the sofa. Then I leafed through the mail. There wasn't much of interest: a utility bill, an invitation to join the Law Student Association, and my car registration renewal papers. The rest was junk I tossed into a wastebasket.

"Your bed's comfortable," Travis said. "I'm jealous."

I thought of Travis's bedroom and his thin mattress resting on the floor. Then I thought of Travis lying in *my* bed, and despite the morning's sultry temperature, I shivered.

Go on: say it.

"You can sleep in my bed anytime you'd like, you know; whether I'm gone or not."

Travis gazed at me, and then he narrowed his eyes.

Shit.

For a moment, I thought he might lash out at me like he had at Maritza that day at the river, but he didn't say anything.

"Look," I said, "what I just said was meant to be a joke."

He raised his eyebrows. "Was it?"

I lowered my gaze and shrugged. "Partly, anyway."

Travis rose from the dining table. His buttocks jiggled in his tight-fitting briefs when he walked to the kitchen to rinse out his cereal bowl. Moments later, he joined me on the sofa. He placed his bare feet on the coffee table, joined his hands behind his head. A sour scent, not unpleasant, wafted from his dark armpits. He rubbed his lips together while he stared at the ceiling. I hadn't been this close to Travis since our Ichetucknee trip; his presence made my heart pump and my mouth go dry.

What should I say?

"How's summer school going? Are you—"

Travis cut me off with a flinty stare. When he spoke, his voice sounded reedy. "Please, don't toss small talk in my face like I'm some kind of idiot. I know you think I don't own a pair of balls."

Travis's aggressive attitude took me by surprise; it was totally out of character. What was going on?

When I didn't say anything, Travis kept on.

"You see me as a chickenshit who won't stand up for himself. But I'm not, Andy; I'm just...struggling right now. Why can't you understand that?"

I shrugged. "I don't see why being gay frightens you so."

Travis kept his gaze locked onto mine. "I already explained when we tubed the Ichetucknee: the Myrtle Beach thing—"

I hissed in frustration. "How long ago was that? Four years?"

He nodded.

"You're letting one event dictate how you'll live the rest of your life? How much sense does that make?"

After Travis lowered his hands into his lap, he twiddled his thumbs. "Ever heard of Troy Perry? He founded a Christian church for gay men in Los Angeles."

I shook my head.

"He's written a book, *The Lord Is My Shepherd and He Knows I'm Gay*. I've read it five times since I bought it."

I raised my eyebrows. "It must be a good book."

Travis nodded. "Perry talks about a variety of Old Testament passages, including the few that seem to condemn homosexuality. He says many ancient Biblical laws don't make sense in today's world."

"How so?"

Travis babbled like a vacuum cleaner salesman. "Deuteronomy, in chapter twenty-two verses thirteen through twenty-one, says if it is discovered a bride is not a virgin, she must be immediately executed by stoning. Then, in chapter twenty-two, verse twenty-two, Deuteronomy says if a married person has sex with someone else's husband or wife, both adulterers must be stoned to death. In today's world, if we took these passages literally, we'd sling rocks day and night."

I nodded.

"In Mark chapter twelve, verses eighteen through twenty-seven, the Bible says if a man dies childless, his widow is required to have intercourse with each of his brothers in turn until she bears her deceased husband a male heir. We'd have some very unhappy widows in today's society if we followed Saint Mark's words to the letter."

"Maybe," I said, "you should lend that book to your folks."

"I plan to," Travis said. "Labor Day weekend, I'll visit Jacksonville for a family reunion. I'll give Perry's book to my father."

"Do you think he'll read it?" I asked.

Travis raised a shoulder. "We'll see."

FSU'S COLLEGE OF Law wasn't a place I'd ever visited as an undergraduate. The three-storied red brick structure stood a few blocks east of the university's main campus on its own parcel of land. The Law Student Association operated a used bookstore on the school's second floor, and that's where I bought my texts for fall quarter. These were not the sort of texts I'd studied at FSU. Most were "case books," thick collections of court decisions from all over the United States, involving contracts, torts, civil court procedures, real property, and criminal law. All were bound in faux leather, dyed various colors: dark blue, brown, forest green, and crimson. Gold lettering on the spines had all but worn away.

A pair of students staffed the bookstore: a guy wearing wire-rimmed eyeglasses and a long-sleeved T-shirt, and a flaxen-haired girl in bib overalls. While I made my selections, they joked about the work lying in wait for me.

"The library's just down the hall," the guy said, pointing. "You should pay a visit, maybe choose a study carrel. It'll be your second home for the next nine months."

I winced.

"Who's your torts professor?" the girl asked.

I consulted the schedule of classes I'd brought with me. "Someone named Vanderbleek."

The two looked at each other, and then at me.

The girl shook her head. "He eats first-year students for lunch."

In a seating area outside the bookstore, adjacent to a plate-glass window, I plopped into a vinyl-upholstered chair. Then I leafed through each book I'd bought. Previous owners had used yellow felt-tipped pens to highlight passages on most every page. I kept looking for photos or illustrations, but found none. The material seemed as dry as old cornhusks, and the language used in court decisions seemed stilted and lifeless.

The smallest volume, titled *Powell on Real Property*, wasn't much larger than a paperback novel. The first few pages discussed various forms of property ownership: fee simple, life estate, tenancy in common, joint tenancy with rights of survivorship, and so forth.

After five minutes of reading *Powell*, my gaze lost focus.

Would I really have to learn this material, just to become a trial lawyer or a judge? I had no interest in real estate or contracts. Why bother studying them? I shook my head.

Maybe I wasn't cut out for the legal profession. Had I made a mistake by enrolling here?

Although classes would not commence for three weeks, the law school bustled with activity. A balding man in a tweed sports jacket talked with a guy whose beard grew to his sternum; they discussed a recent Supreme Court decision involving "search and seizure." A dozen students from every sort of ethnic background—Hispanic, Asian, African, and Native American—sat in a circle on the carpet nearby. Sunshine reflected in the lenses of one girl's eyeglasses while she discussed the outcome of that summer's "moot court" competition. People kept entering or leaving the library's swinging double doors. Each person carried a stack of books; the books seemed a part of their bodies, like their livers or kidneys. Would the same be true for me in the months ahead?

My torts text was a brown monster, four inches thick. The book's former owner had penned the following inside of the cover: "Are you a first-year law student? If so, take my advice: bend over, stick your head between your legs, and kiss your ass goodbye."

Aye-yi-yi...

WHEN I RETURNED to my apartment, Travis was gone.

I entered the bedroom, where my bed was neatly made. I lay upon it, on my belly. Then I buried my nose in a pillow, wondering if I might detect the scent of Travis's dark hair, but I could not. Had he slept naked in my bed? Had he touched himself while lying between my sheets?

If I wasn't needed back in Pensacola, I would likely have stayed the night in Tallahassee. Perhaps I'd even share my bed with Travis. If so, how might he respond if I made a pass? Had the book by Troy Perry caused a change in Travis's view toward gay sex? Would he let me kiss him? Would he let me do more than that?

I turned onto my back, and then I stared at the ceiling.

A cobweb waved at me from one corner. Beyond the windows, songbirds tootled. I thought of Travis's lanky limbs, his rippled belly and blue-green eyes. How would it feel to...?

Be responsible, Hunsinger. Forget Travis and forget sex for now. Get your ass in the Vega and go.

I got up and left.

Twenty

I THOUGHT SATURDAY might never come.

The days following my visit to Tallahassee dragged over me like soggy blankets, as though someone had poured molasses into the works of my wristwatch. I ceased reading novels. Instead, I devoted many hours to my legal texts.

I read court decisions, studied rights and responsibilities of tenants in common, or I focused on provisions of the Uniform Commercial Code: "Section 2-315. Implied Warranty: Fitness for Particular Purpose. Where the seller at the time of contracting has reason to know any particular purpose for which the goods are required and that the buyer is relying on the seller's skill or judgment to select or furnish suitable goods, there is unless excluded or modified under the next section an implied warranty that the goods shall be fit for such purpose."

Aye-yi-yi...

When I wasn't studying or caring for my dad, I'd think of Jeff and our afternoon spent at the Pensacola Beach hotel. While with Jeff, I'd felt like a starving man invited to a banquet. I couldn't get enough of his scents, the sound of his voice, and the feeling of his fingers touching my skin.

We'd had sex twice that day, actually. The second time, Jeff rode *me*—hard—sending jolts of pleasure through my body. Even the soles of my feet grew warm. When I came, I shouted so loudly I'm surprised the hotel manager didn't pay us a visit.

Now, at my folks' home, sexual tension crackled within me. For relief, I took three-mile runs or I bicycled fifteen miles. I performed push-ups and sit-ups in my bedroom, and I pleasured myself frequently. Visions of Jeff made my sexual imagination sizzle whenever I'd stroke.

To kill time, I spent hours in the kitchen, experimenting with new recipes: linguini with homemade clam sauce, Greek moussaka, trout almandine with potatoes au gratin, and corned beef and cabbage. I even baked an angel food cake using a special pan I found in the recesses of my mom's pantry.

When my mom saw the cake, she made a face. "I haven't used that pan in ten years. What's gotten into *you*, son?"

I wanted to say, "I got *laid*, Mom, by a really cute guy. I'm walking on air."

But, of course, I didn't. Instead, I simply grinned and shrugged.

Each day, my dad seemed a bit stronger. Color had returned to his cheeks, and his breathing wasn't as labored. Midmornings, he dutifully walked on his treadmill. While in bed, he read the newspaper or *National Geographic*, or he watched shows on PBS: the news, or travel and history programs. Once a week, Mom visited the public library on West Gregory Street; she checked out a half-dozen books for Dad to read, everything from fiction anthologies to novels and Civil War history books.

One afternoon, I brought Dad a snack on a tray: a slice of my angel food cake and a glass of milk. He lay with his upper body elevated, in his pajamas, and when I entered, he set aside a biography of Stonewall Jackson. After I placed the tray before him, he studied the cake, and then he shook his head.

"You're spoiling me, son. You know that, don't you?"

I grinned and bobbed my chin. "I *like* spoiling you."

Dad puckered one side of his face. "It needs to stop. Understand: I appreciate all you do. But soon, I'll get out of this goddamned bed, once and for all. You'll start school, and then everything will return to normal."

"Will it?"

He looked at me and narrowed his eyes. Then he took a bite of cake. After he chewed and swallowed, he arched his eyebrows.

"Damn, that's good." Dad looked left and right. Then he lowered his voice to a whisper. "Don't tell your mother I said so, but this cake is *far* better than hers: so fluffy and moist."

I waggled my eyebrows. "That one's between you and me, Dad."

I WOKE AT 8:00 a.m. on Saturday. Bars of morning sunlight spilled into the room through the slats of my Venetian blinds. I lay on my back with hands clasped behind my neck, staring at the ceiling and listening to cool air rush from the air conditioning register. A pleasant aroma of percolating coffee wafted from the kitchen, where my mom rattled dishes and silverware. How many thousands of mornings had I woken from sleep in this room? How many breakfasts had I shared with my family, watching Jake study the newspaper's sports section while my parents chatted about the day ahead? Before my dad's heart attack, I had taken such things for granted.

Not anymore.

Of course, I felt no desire to live at my parents' home for any length of time—I needed my independence and privacy—but knowing my room was still here and waiting for me offered reassurance. The thought my parents were still here, going through their routines of daily living, made me feel safe and secure.

But change was part of life, wasn't it? Change never stopped unless you were dead, right? How must my parents feel about Jake's absence from their lives? Sure, he'd return from his summer job soon, but only for a brief stay before he'd drive north to Emory University and all that awaited him there. My folks would become "empty nesters," and how would they handle the change? Of course, they'd still have their jobs, their gardening, and their hobbies. But the house would certainly be a quieter place with both Jake and me gone.

My thoughts turned to Jeff. I had seven hours to kill before I'd hold him in my arms, seven hours before I'd feel his warm breath on my skin. What would I do between now and then?

I could study my law books, of course. But the thought of spending my day indoors didn't appeal. After rising, I opened my desk drawer. Then I studied the Fort Barrancas brochure I'd found in the hotel lobby at my last meeting with Jeff. According to the brochure, the Park Service offered guided tours of the fort at 11:00 a.m. each Saturday, free of charge.

I chewed my lower lip, thinking. Mom wasn't working; she could look after Dad. Why not take the tour? Afterward, I could run three miles on the beach, perhaps take a swim in the Gulf. I could always shower in Jeff's room afterward. Why not?

In the kitchen, sunlight poured in through the windows.

My mom bustled about in her bathrobe and slippers. I whistled while buttering the pancakes my mom served me along with a rasher of fried bacon.

"*You're* certainly chipper this morning," Mom said.

I spoke of my plans to visit Barrancas and then the beach, omitting any mention of my plans with Jeff. I wasn't quite sure how Mom would react if I told her I'd meet another man at a hotel for casual sex. She'd likely consider it tawdry, so I kept my plans with Jeff to myself.

After I finished breakfast and read the newspaper, I packed a zippered canvas bag with things I'd need: sunscreen, beach towel, a change of clothes, my running shoes, running shorts, and so forth. I dressed in khaki shorts, a T-shirt, and leather sandals. Outside, the temperature and humidity had already risen. My Vega's interior was an oven. When I opened the driver's door, a blast of hot air hit me. Dampness gathered in my armpits, and sunlight glanced off the Vega's hood when I backed out of my folks' driveway.

I put on the cheap sunglasses I'd bought in Branford to ward off the morning's glare.

A neighbor I knew pushed his mower around the green expanse of his lawn. I waved as I passed him, and then he waved back. Two kids played catch in the street. I slowed so they could get out of my way. In the park near my folks' home, a group of guys my age played basketball on the outdoor court. Most were shirtless, and I studied their lean physiques while I idled at a stoplight. One guy reminded me of Travis: long dark hair, lanky, with fluid movements.

How sexy...

Behind me, a motorist honked his horn. When I glanced in my rearview mirror, I saw a guy shake his fist. Then I realized the traffic light had turned green while I'd stared at the guys playing basketball. Accelerating, I shook my head.

Pay attention to your driving, Hunsinger.

Fort Barrancas sat on a bluff overlooking the entrance to Pensacola Bay, a perfect spot to defend against naval invasion. I learned much history as I toured the facility, following a female park ranger in her Smokey the Bear hat. The British had first built a "redoubt" on Barrancas bluff in 1763, just a crude fortification fashioned from earth and logs. Then the Spanish built two structures there around 1797: one a masonry water battery at the foot of the bluff, the second an earth-and-log fort. A half century later, American engineers remodeled the water battery. They built a massive fort on the bluff, with brick walls three feet thick. And then they built a second brick fort on the opposite side of the harbor's mouth. The two American-built structures still remained in place, much as they were a hundred years before.

A uniformed Cub Scout troop from Panama City—a jumble of navy blue and yellow, accompanied by a harried den mother—took the tour as well. Little boys fidgeted and smacked their chewing gum; their voices echoed off the walls of tunnels we passed through while they elbowed one another's ribs or raced up stairways.

A breeze blew my bangs into my eyes when we clambered to the top of the fort to view Pensacola Harbor. Sunlight reflected off emerald water. Gleaming pleasure yachts bobbed alongside shrimp boats with gauzy nets hanging like bat wings from their booms. I tried to imagine cannons of the water battery firing on enemy vessels assaulting the harbor. Between the guns at Barrancas and those at Fort Pickens on the opposite side of harbor, how could an enemy ship stand a chance? A "turkey shoot" was what my dad might call the situation. Off in the distance, Pensacola's lighthouse hulked, black and ominous against a cloudless azure sky. How many ships had it guided safely to anchorage in the harbor's placid waters?

The tour took about an hour, leaving me with little to do during the next three hours. While the Cub Scout troop piled into a station wagon, I leaned against my Vega's fender and weighed my options. If I ate lunch, I couldn't very well take a three-mile run on a full stomach, now could I? So, I drove to Fort Pickens State Park on the opposite side of the harbor, where remnants of another nineteenth-century fort stood. Built of brick with sloping walls and arched supports, Pickens loomed high above the sand dunes, another reminder of the harbor's strategic importance during nineteenth-century wars.

In the men's room, I changed into my running shorts and shoes, the latter a pair of Nike waffle irons I'd come to love. Then I ran at a nine-minute-per-mile pace on hard-packed sand. Waves slapped the shore while I glided along, feeling the sun on my bare shoulders. My feet felt like they barely touched the ground. Sea oats on the dunes fluttered in the breeze. I passed families picnicking on blankets and then a group of servicemen in swimsuits, all with tattoos and crew cuts, each man with a girlfriend to smooch with. Farther down the beach, I passed two guys my age, both with hair growing past their shoulders; they tossed a Frisbee back and forth.

When I'd run for half an hour, I wasn't even tired, so I kept on going. Running seemed effortless that day. My arms chugged and my breath huffed. My heart beat a steady rhythm. Eventually, all thought drained from my head, and then I became a running machine, skipping along the shore, feeling almost weightless. By the time I stopped, I'd logged ten miles. My skin shone with sweat, my hair was a damp mop, and my running shorts stuck to my skin. I felt exhausted, but in a good way.

I found a drinking fountain at a picnic pavilion, where I must have swallowed two quarts of water in less than a minute. How *good* the water tasted. Then I kicked off my running shoes and waded into the Gulf of Mexico. The salty water's temperature wasn't much cooler than the air's, but still the water felt refreshing. I floated on my back, gazing up at the sky, and at that very moment, I think I felt more comfortable in my own skin than I ever had before.

AT JEFF'S HOTEL, the same florid-faced guy sat behind the reception desk, smoking his cigarette and reading *Sports Illustrated*.

I had rinsed off under an outdoor shower at the park, following my swim, but I still wore my running shorts, along with a T-shirt and sandals. I carried my canvas bag in one hand, a six-pack of Budweiser in the other.

"Has Jeff Dellinger checked in?" I asked.

The desk clerk nodded without looking at me. "Room twenty-four."

I bounded up the outdoor staircase, taking the steps two at a time. Already, my pulse raced. It seemed like a *month* since I'd seen Jeff, instead of a week.

I rapped on Jeff's door. "Jeff, it's me, Andy."

No answer.

I knocked again. "Jeff?"

No answer.

Jeff's drapes were closed. Inside, a radio played a popular country-western song, "Daytime Friends" by Kenny Rogers. The lyrics described an affair between two married persons, a relationship they hid from everyone they knew. I glanced here and there. Maybe Jeff was buying cigarettes at the convenience store down the street? Maybe he'd taken a stroll along the shore? Maybe—

A noise sounded inside Jeff's unit, something akin to a firecracker going off, and I flinched when I heard it.

What the hell?

Right away, I sensed something wasn't right. I felt a prickle in my scalp and dryness in my mouth. Why wasn't Jeff answering? What was going on?

I pounded on the door. "Jeff, are you in there? Are you okay?"

No answer.

Moments later, when the office manager used a pass key to open Jeff's door, a sulfurous scent wafted from the shadowy room, and then I crinkled my forehead in puzzlement. Had Jeff ignited an entire matchbook? The manager flipped a wall switch, and then his hands flew to his face.

"Good God Almighty."

Jeff lay on the queen-size bed with his back propped against the headboard. He wore his Air Force uniform: a light blue short-sleeved shirt with epaulets, navy-blue pants, patent leather shoes, navy-blue garrison cap. His head lay against one shoulder. His face was pale; it lacked expression, as if he were daydreaming. A starburst of fresh blood, as broad as the headboard and reaching as high as the popcorn ceiling, gleamed on the wall behind him, dotted here and there with bits of Jeff's skull, brain tissue, and shreds from the blown-out backside of his cap. Jeff's pistol lay on the threadbare carpet.

Blood drained from my head. My knees liquefied while my vision blurred. For a moment, I thought I'd pass out. I turned and stumbled into the outdoor corridor. After bending over the metal balustrade, I puked up the lunch I'd eaten only ten minutes before. The contents of my stomach painted the hood of a Buick parked beneath me.

Inside the room, the hotel manager phoned the police while the radio played on, describing the lives of Kenny Rogers's secret lovers and their nefarious courtship.

ACCORDING TO THE *News Journal*, the police found a copy of Jeff's "undesirable discharge" order on the desk in his room. Using a felt tipped pen, Jeff had scrawled the following on the order's face:

"Fuck the Air Force. And fuck you all."

IN THE HOURS following Jeff's suicide, I wondered, over and over, how Jeff must have felt during the final moments of his life. Was he lonely or just angry? Had he purposefully awaited my arrival before pulling the trigger? Had he wanted me to witness the carnage? If so, why? Was he punishing me for sharing in the furtive sex life that had cost him his chosen career?

We had made love, passionately and tenderly, just a week before his death, and now I found it hard to believe he was gone. I recalled the sound of his voice, the scent of his skin, and the warmth of his body when I thrust inside him. I remembered the soothing sound of his heartbeat when I laid my head on his sternum after our sex.

That last meeting with Jeff, he likely shared more intimacy with me than he had shared with anyone else during his short life. He allowed me to kiss him—a first for Jeff, it seemed. And yet I'd never met a member of his family, nor had I ever met any of his fellow airmen. I was little more than a secret he hid from other people in his life.

Had he ever mentioned my name to a single soul before he died?

I doubted it.

The fact Jeff felt ashamed of our lovemaking made me angry, not just at Jeff, but at any person who didn't have the balls to lead a truthful life. I could not respect people who wouldn't stick up for themselves, who wouldn't tell the self-appointed arbiters of social propriety to get lost.

Saying "fuck you" in a suicide note didn't count for much, not in my book. Jeff's statement was a chickenshit move, like hurling an insult at a bully after he's already left the room. What was the point?

Did I mourn Jeff's passing? Sure, I did. How could I not have? He had opened a gate to a new world for me; he had led me into a magical garden, and I felt grateful to Jeff for these gifts.

Still, I could not respect his decision to end his life. There was no honor in that sort of surrender, was there?

Twenty-One

ON LABOR DAY weekend on an overcast Saturday, Jake and I stuffed our clothes, shoes, and books, including twenty-two volumes of the *World Book Encyclopedia,* into the trunk and rear seat of my Vega. I would drive Jake to Emory University in Atlanta. Then I'd return to Tallahassee to begin my legal education. I'd enter a new chapter in my life.

My dad sat on a folding metal chair in our driveway, watching us work and giving Jake advice on everything from study habits to Atlanta-area landmarks Jake needed to see.

"Visit Stone Mountain, ride the gondola. And Lake Lanier's a nice place to spend a warm day at this time of year."

Dad could walk without assistance now, albeit slowly. Color had returned to his cheeks and his breathing wasn't labored, but he still slept twelve hours per day. His activities remained limited to reading, watching TV, or listening to sports on the radio.

The night before, while Mom had washed dishes and I dried them, I asked Mom a question. "Are you sure you and Dad will be okay without me?"

Mom looked at me and pursed her lips. Then she returned her gaze to the dishwater. "I'm not sure about anything anymore. But your dad and I will somehow manage on our own."

"Mom, I could always—"

She silenced me with an icy stare. "Your father would have a fit if you didn't go back to school. Don't even *think* about staying here with us."

Now, on the driveway, Jake sported his best bravado. He cracked jokes and wondered out loud how long it might take him to find a new girlfriend up at Emory. But I knew just how hard the moment was for him. Sure, he'd spent his summer in North Carolina—he'd had a taste of living away from home—but this was different. Jake had spent his entire life in Pensacola, always in the same house, surrounded by friends and family he'd known forever.

Emory was three hundred miles from Pensacola, in a city where he knew no one. And he'd face rigorous academic and athletic challenges at the university, all without my parents' daily support and encouragement.

I had no doubt Jake would succeed, but life wasn't going to be easy for him in the coming months. He'd face tests, over and over, by his peers, his water polo coach, and his classroom instructors. He of course knew this, and I'm sure he felt scared out of his wits. But he wasn't going to let my folks know just how frightened he was at the moment.

My mother put on her game face as well. "At last peace and quiet will reign around here," she told my dad while she stuffed a blanket and two pillows into the Vega's overflowing trunk. "For the first time in twenty-two years, we'll have the house to ourselves."

But I knew Mom's heart bled. Jake was her baby, her Little Prince, her golden boy, and now he would leave the nest where she'd sheltered him since the day of his birth. Sure, he would come home for holidays and perhaps summer breaks, but this day represented a huge shift in our family's dynamic. Jake was departing.

Before Jake and I left, the four of us gathered in our living room; we stood in a circle. Each of us held hands with the person on either side of us. We bowed our heads and then my father intoned a prayer.

"Lord, this morning our boys embark on important missions: for Jake, college, for Andy, law school. Keep them safe in their travels. Help them make the right decisions in the months ahead. Thank you for all your blessings, Lord, especially for the love we share as a family. In Jesus' name we pray."

We all four said, "Amen."

Jake and I exchanged hugs and kisses with both our parents, and then we left. We headed north on US Highway 29. The land rolled by. We passed through farmland where peanuts and soybeans grew on vast swaths of cleared property. After crossing the Florida-Alabama state line, we encountered slash pine forests so dense I couldn't see twenty feet past the edge of the roadway. The day was damp and overcast. Rain spotted my windshield.

Jake turned on the radio; he twisted knobs, trying to find a station worth listening to. But this was south Alabama, where rock 'n roll didn't sit well with folks. All the stations Jake found played either country-western or gospel music. At one point, I heard a few verses of "Daytime

Friends" before Jake turned the knob again, and then I thought of Jeff Dellinger.

Of course, I hadn't attended Jeff's funeral. I didn't even know where Jeff's family lived; that's how little he'd ever told me about himself. But I imagined Jeff's body resting in a freshly dug grave, and then a shiver ran through me.

He's dead. Let go, Andy.

Before long, we merged onto I-65, a four-lane highway divided by a grassy median. The land continued to roll.

At the time, federal law had reduced speed limits on all interstate highways to fifty-five-miles-per-hour, to promote fuel conservation. I drove sixty. We passed transfer trucks, Greyhound buses, and military convoys. The rain's intensity grew. The Vega's wipers worked back and forth, making slapping sounds, while my tires hissed on the slick roadbed.

Jake rearranged his limbs. He drummed the dashboard with his fingers, raised and lowered his passenger window several times. Then he chewed a hangnail. He kept fiddling with the radio's knobs, producing little but static and gibberish, until I finally switched the radio off.

"Try sitting still, Little Brother. You're driving me batty."

Jake twisted here and there in his bucket seat. The vinyl upholstery crackled under his weight, and I was reminded of my sex with Aaron at Alligator Point, so many months before.

"I can't help it," Jake said. "I'm nervous as shit."

I nodded. "I don't blame you; today's a big day."

Jake cracked his knuckles. "Can you remember your first day at college?"

"Sure, I do; just like it was yesterday. And I'll tell you a secret if you promise never to repeat it."

Jake looked at me and gathered his eyebrows. "Go ahead."

"Dad drove me to Tallahassee. A tropical storm brewed in the Gulf. Rain fell so hard you could barely see the car ahead of you, a dreary day. We arrived at campus and all these kids were moving into my dorm, Smith Hall, an ugly place that looked like a prison.

"For some reason—I can't remember why—Biff Schultz hadn't arrived yet. So, I had the place to myself."

I stared out the windshield, flexing my fingers against the Vega's steering wheel.

"After we'd carried all my things up to my room, Dad took me to McDonald's for lunch, and then he drove me back to the dorm. He left me there on the sidewalk. Rain still fell, and I can remember standing there at the curb, watching him drive away. I felt so damned *sad*."

Jake made a face. "Sad about what?"

"I was *lonely*, Little Brother. I didn't know a soul in Tallahassee. And I guess I'd never realized how much I loved my life in Pensacola. I swear, if Dad would have let me, I'd have returned home with him that very day. But I didn't, of course. He and Mom would have been so disappointed."

"What happened next?" Jake asked.

"I went to my ugly-ass room. Then I lay on my bed and bawled like a baby."

Jake looked at me and blinked his eyes. "Did you really?"

I nodded.

Jake turned his gaze to the windshield; he worked his jaw from side to side and rubbed his lips together. "Do you think Dad and Mom pampered us? Is that why leaving home was hard for you? Is that why *I* feel like crying right now?"

I kept quiet a minute or so. Then I spoke.

"I think we got lucky—I'm talking you and me—to have the parents we do. I didn't know *how* lucky until Dad's heart attack happened. That's when I realized nothing lasts forever, especially not who or what we love the most. It's all slipping away, in little increments.

"Just the same," I said, "you can't go back, and neither can I. We have to move forward, even though it hurts like hell."

Jake chewed another hangnail. "I should have enrolled at FSU. Then we could have lived together. We'd have each other instead of no one."

I shook my head. "You have to get out there on your own; you'll never become the person you're meant to be until you do. Trust me on that, will you?"

Jake drew a breath. Then he let it out.

"Can I call you," Jake said, "whenever I need to, even if it's at 3:00 a.m.?"

I thought of all the lonely nights I'd spent in Smith Hall, especially when the rain fell and I'd press my cheek to the screen on the window near the head of my bed. I recalled the wind sweeping across nighttime Tallahassee, how it stirred the branches of live oaks, and how it tossed Spanish moss beards about.

My lips parted into a tiny smile, and then I patted Jake's shoulder. "Of course, Little Brother, of course you can."

THE MORNING FOLLOWING Labor Day, one hundred and twenty first-year law students, including me, crowded into our school's main lecture hall, a semicircular room with tiered seating and desks descending from the rear of the room toward a podium with a lectern and microphone. The lectern stood before an enormous chalkboard. A crush of conversation filled the room, sometimes punctuated by a guy's throaty laugh or a woman's cackle. Fluorescent overhead lights cast their milky glow upon heads and shoulders. Most students were my age, an equal mix of males and females. People dressed casually: T-shirts, blue jeans, sneakers.

I didn't see a single person I knew.

Yawning, I stretched my limbs. I'd slept fitfully the night before: I tossed and turned while the whippoorwill sang his tune and a full moon bathed me in silvery light. I couldn't stop thinking about my parents, and about Jake. Were they okay?

Now, a man with a mane of silver hair entered the hall through double swinging doors behind me. He descended a flight of steps bisecting the hall, with a vinyl-clad notebook under an arm. He wore charcoal dress slacks, a navy-blue blazer, a bow tie, and wing-tipped lace-up shoes. A corncob pipe protruded from his face like an outrigger. When he reached the lectern, he fiddled with the microphone, causing pops and rumbles in the hall's loud speakers. Then he put down his pipe and cleared his throat.

The hall fell as silent as an empty church. Then the man at the lectern spoke in a stentorian drawl. He sounded like Colonel Sanders, the fried chicken mogul.

"Good morning, ladies and gentlemen. I am Robert Mabry, Dean of the Florida State University College of Law. If you are a geology student, you came to the wrong building this morning."

People chuckled.

As Mabry spoke, his head swiveled. His gaze traveled from face to face in the crowd.

"I'm here, first of all, to welcome you. Our faculty and staff are glad you're here, and we look forward to getting to know you; we truly do.

"I am also here to caution you. Law school is tough; we will work you like you've never before worked in your life. We will challenge you intellectually, physically, and spiritually. And some of you—a healthy percentage, in fact—will not survive the process.

"Have a look, right now, at the persons seated on either side of you. Go on, look..."

Nervous conversation erupted while folks looked here and there at their neighbors. Then we all looked back at Mabry.

"I'm here to tell you, ladies and gentlemen, it's quite likely at least *one* of your neighbors, and possibly *both*, will not be here when we return from Christmas break. Every year, we have a thirty-three percent attrition rate among our freshmen class. That's a sad but true fact."

Great, just great.

Mabry's basso boomed.

"The law is a jealous mistress, ladies and gentlemen. She will consume your every waking hour, and then she'll haunt your dreams. This quarter, you will read more material than you did in two *years* of undergraduate study. Your books shall be your constant companions, supplanting your friends and family. You will learn to speak a new language, and learn to analyze matters in a peculiar manner known only to those who study the law.

"I've often heard this said: Your first year we scare you to death. Your second, we work you to death. And the third...we *bore* you to death."

A ripple of laughter moved through the hall.

"Students, the law demands sacrifice. But she also rewards the diligent, not just with lucrative careers, but with intellectual stimulation and the ecstasy of courtroom triumph. Few persons will ever know the thrill of winning a jury verdict in a criminal or civil trial. It's better than liquor, better than drugs, and even better than *sex*, some say."

Mabry gripped the edges of the lectern, leaned toward the crowd.

"I urge you: *apply* yourselves like you never before have. Put yourselves to the test. Survive the crucible, if you can. Do your level best."

Mabry picked up his pipe and notebook. "Let's get to work."

And then he strode from the hall.

THREE DAYS LATER, on a Friday afternoon, I lay on my living room sofa with a pencil stuck sideways between my teeth. I studied a New

Jersey appellate decision rendered a dozen years earlier. The decision permitted a consumer who'd bought a defective automobile to sue the car's manufacturer, despite the fact no contract existed between the carmaker and the consumer.

I had read the case back in Pensacola and would likely read it again.

That morning, a girl in my torts class had stood before sixty of our fellow students in a lecture hall. She "recited" the New Jersey case, discussing the court rendering the decision, the principal issues in the case, and how the court had disposed of those issues.

Afterward, Professor Lars Vanderbleek, an enormously fat and rheumy-eyed guy, brought the girl to tears through use of the "Socratic method" of teaching. He questioned her at length about the finer points of the case, going into details I had not even considered.

"Exactly what does 'privity' *mean*, in the context of this decision?" Vanderbleek asked the girl.

"It's a contractual relationship between two parties," the girl said.

"Which parties?"

"In this case, no contractual relationship existed."

Vanderbleek scowled. "Of *course* one did. The plaintiff had a contract with a car dealer, correct?"

"Yes, but—"

"Why not let the plaintiff sue the car dealer?"

"The dealer was bankrupt, he—"

"Oh, so the dealer's financial irresponsibility results in the *manufacturer* paying the piper. Is that fair? Is that justice, Miss... What's your name again?"

"Jamieson, sir. Maxine Jamieson."

Vanderbleek rubbed his chin with a knuckle. "Do we simply pin the tail on the donkey with the moneybags? Isn't that what the court is doing here?"

"The car was defective, sir, and—"

"*Allegedly* defective. This case was still in the pleadings stage when the plaintiff appealed the trial court's dismissal of his claim against the manufacturer, correct?"

"That's true, but assuming—"

"Assuming?" Vanderbleek thundered. "Don't ever assume *anything* when you walk into court. Be *prepared* for any and all possibilities. And do the same when you enter my classroom. Understood, Miss Jamieson?"

And so on.

Now, as I lay on my living room sofa, light slipped from the room. Already the sun had descended behind buildings to the west. Just when I reached to switch on a floor lamp, my phone rang.

My caller was Biff Schultz.

"Hey, cocksucker, I heard about your dad. Is he okay?"

I told Biff about the weeks I'd spent in Pensacola. Then I asked about his summer.

"I worked my ass off, but I learned a lot. If you break an ulna, I'll know how to set the bone and cast it. Or I can take your temperature anally; I *know* you'd like *that*."

I shook my head. "You're *not* funny, Biff. But I still love you."

"Listen," he said, "I need your help, and right now."

I groaned. "I have to study tonight. Then I caddy in the morning. I—"

"This is *serious*, Andy. I'm worried about Travis."

My scalp prickled while I rose to a sitting position. "Why? What's going on?"

Biff cleared his throat. "He spent Labor Day weekend in Jacksonville with his folks. Things blew up while he was there—a major quarrel. I'm not sure what the problem was—he wouldn't say—but now he's talking crazy shit: quitting school and going home to live with his parents. I've never seen him so down."

I thought of the day Travis and I had floated on the Ichetucknee River. What was it he'd said about his parents?

"They can be...demanding. They set high standards for themselves *and* their kids," Biff continued. "The fucker promised he'd run with me at the track this afternoon—we agreed on five o'clock—but then he no-showed. When I came home, after my run, he wasn't here. His station wagon's gone. He's already packed up half his shit in cardboard boxes: shoes, clothes, books, you name it."

Pacing the floor, I chewed my lips while I twisted the phone receiver's cord around my index finger.

Travis, what's going on? What happened?

"Tell me what I can do," I said.

"Help me find him. I'm sure he's somewhere in Tallahassee, but I don't know where."

I rubbed my chin with a knuckle. "I think *I* do."

THE SKY HAD darkened by the time I reached the Lake Talquin water tower, via the clay road Travis had shown me so many months before. Glow from my headlights fell upon Travis's station wagon. After parking my Vega, I walked to the tower's rusty ladder, but I couldn't see much because of the pine forest's darkness. I cupped my mouth with my hands. Then I hollered as loudly as I could, trying to overcome rumble of traffic passing on Highway 90.

"Travis, are you up there? It's me, Andy."

No answer.

Shit. "Travis?"

No answer.

Go on, Hunsinger: get your ass up there.

The ladder creaked beneath my weight as I ascended. Whenever I gripped a rung above me, rust flakes stuck to my hands and others sprinkled my face. I grimaced and shook my head. I hated heights; they frightened me. How old was the tower? Was the ladder even safe to climb? My breath huffed, and I prayed a rung would not give way beneath my feet. A jetliner, preparing to land at Tallahassee's airport, flew directly overhead. It passed so low I wondered if it might scrape the tower's apex. The roar of the jet's engines made the tower tremble.

I found Travis seated on the promenade's wooden deck on the west side of the tower. His legs dangled from the deck's edge while his arms rested on the railing. He wore a T-shirt, blue jeans, and his Nike running shoes. His dark hair draped his shoulders.

My chest heaved from my climb, but a light breeze cooled my sweaty brow. I waited until a transfer truck had passed and its roar had faded before I spoke.

"Travis, what's going on?"

He didn't look at me—he didn't seem startled by my sudden appearance—but when he spoke, his voice sounded lifeless.

"Go away, Andy."

"Why? What are you doing here? And why are you packing up your things at the house?"

When Travis looked at me in the darkness, I barely saw the whites of his eyes.

"Does it matter?" he said.

"It matters to me."

"Why?"

Just go ahead and say it.

"Because I love you; I have for a long time."

"You once let a man beat you in the name of love. Is that what you want from me: abuse?"

I drew a breath and then let it out. "Of course not. I took that whipping because I hated myself. I told you that when it happened, I—"

"Do you still hate yourself, Andy?"

I lowered my butt to the promenade's deck. Then I swung my legs over the side as Travis had done. We weren't five feet from each other. I stared into the night sky. Orion's stars glowed in the west; I studied the constellation's sword and belt while wondering how to answer Travis's question.

Do I hate myself?

"Not anymore," I said. "What about you?"

"My family hates me, I can tell you that."

Uh-oh.

"You gave them that book to read, didn't you?"

Travis didn't say anything.

"I guess Reverend Perry's message wasn't a hit?"

Travis shook his head. "Why do they have to be so rigid? Why can't they love me for who I am, whatever *that* turns out to be?"

I didn't have an answer. My parents had accepted me for who *I* was— albeit with some difficulty—but I had never doubted for one single moment that I was their beloved son, and always would be. I thought of my last conversation with my dad, back in Pensacola, when we'd talked about Anita Bryant and the board meeting at Capital City. He told me he was *proud* of me for being true to myself. I could not imagine belonging to a family like Travis's. If you loved someone, you wanted them to be happy, right?

When another transfer truck blew past, the truck's headlights illuminated Travis's face. He looked pallid, and dark smudges appeared beneath his eyes.

"Travis?"

"What?"

"Don't leave Tallahassee. Come to my place instead."

He turned his face toward mine. "I have to go home to Jacksonville. My folks won't give me money for school, not right now."

"Are you serious?"

He bobbed his chin.

"Forget them," I said. "Stay with me, at least for a while. I'll buy the food and pay the light bill. You can pay me back later on, if you want."

Travis made a face while he shifted his buttocks on the boards beneath him. "Are you asking me to be your boyfriend? Is that what you're suggesting?"

I shrugged. "Maybe; I mean—"

"I'm not even positive I'm gay," Travis said. "I don't know *who* I am 'cause I've never allowed myself to find out."

"We can change that."

Travis looked away. "I'm a weird guy, Andy. I don't think you'd want to deal with my problems. You deserve someone who's not as messed up as me."

I wasn't giving up that easily. After all, I was Andy Hunsinger.

"Will you give it a chance? Will you try, at least?"

Travis raised his knees; he rested his forearms on them. Then he moistened his lips. "Ten minutes ago, I seriously considered jumping over this railing in front of us. Death would certainly have solved all my problems. And who knows, maybe the afterlife's a more pleasant place to live."

I swallowed while trying to imagine Travis leaping from the tower. I thought of how grief-stricken Biff and Austin would have felt. And I thought about Jeff Dellinger and his recent suicide. How could people feel so discouraged by their circumstances that they chose to end their lives? I'd gone through unhappy times myself lately, but never once considered killing myself.

"Why didn't you jump?" I asked.

Travis looked at me and raised his eyebrows. "*You* showed up, that's why."

I drew a breath, and then I let it out. A shudder ran through me when I thought of how close Travis had come to ending his life.

Keep pushing.

"Look, stay with me a few weeks; see how things go between us. If you decide it doesn't suit you, then I'll understand. You can go to Jacksonville and face whatever waits for you there."

Travis rubbed his lips together. "If I do that—if I live with you a while—you can't expect too much."

My heart pounded. "I don't expect anything. Just be yourself, that's all I ask."

Travis gazed into the darkness for a moment or two. Then he looked at me and nodded. "All right, Andy, okay."

I closed my eyes and let out my breath. Then I peered down at our cars; they seemed so far away. For a moment, I felt a bit dizzy, as if I might pass out. I swung my gaze to Travis, and then I cleared my throat.

"I know you like this place," I said, "but I've told you before: heights scare me. Can we go now?"

WHEN WE REACHED my apartment, Travis phoned Biff. "I'll stay with Andy a while; I'm not sure how long. We'll see. Thanks for worrying about me, but I'll be fine."

After Travis hung up, I asked him, "Are you hungry? I can make you a sandwich."

He stared at his feet and shook his head. His hands hung at his hips. He kept clenching and then relaxing his fingers.

"I couldn't eat a bite right now," he said.

"Why? What's wrong?"

Travis's gaze met mine. "I'm nervous. I don't know what we're supposed to do, now that I'm here."

I raised a shoulder and then let it drop. "We don't have to *do* anything."

A little smile crossed Travis's lips. "I don't think you asked me here to watch TV."

"Let's not force things," I said. Then I pointed to the sofa. "Have a seat; I'll get us two beers."

Moments later, we sat side by side, sipping from cans of Budweiser. Lamplight reflected in Travis's dark hair and his eyes. His silky drawl enchanted me while we talked, and I could not believe he was here, that I had convinced him to stay with me. The thought we would likely share my bed that evening had my pulse racing, my hands shaky.

"You should have heard my dad," Travis said. "We sat in our kitchen: I, my dad and mom, discussing Troy Perry's views. Then, all of a sudden, Dad stood up and *threw* the book across the room. He shouted like a lunatic; he called Perry a Philistine and a pervert.

"Dad said, 'No son of mine will lie with another man. Homosexuality is a sin in the eyes of God, and I won't let you shame our family.'"

Travis shook his head. "I kind of lost control, then; I shouted, too. I'll bet the whole neighborhood heard me."

"What did you say?"

"I told them, 'I might be gay, or maybe I'm not. We'll see. But God made me the way I am for a reason. It's not your place to judge me. I'm your son and you should love me, no matter what.'"

Travis sipped from his beer. Then he swallowed. "My mom started sobbing; I'll bet the neighbors heard her, too. She kept hollering, 'Stop it, both of you. We're supposed to be a family.'

"My dad kept on. He said he wanted me home, right away. He plans to enroll me in a 'treatment program,' someplace in Fort Lauderdale where they turn gay men straight. He even showed me the brochure."

"That's crazy," I said. "Your dad's a surgeon, an educated man. How can he—"

"You don't understand Primitive Baptists," Travis said. "They take the Bible literally, every jot and every tittle, no exceptions."

I shook my head. "You're twenty-two years old, entitled to make your own decisions. Don't let them treat you like a kid."

Travis drained his beer. Then he yawned. "I haven't slept in two days."

I glanced at my wall clock. The time was a little past nine. The day's events had sapped my energy, and I felt tired as well.

Go on: ask him.

"I have an idea," I said.

Travis looked at me and crinkled his brow. "What?"

"Let's take a shower...together. Then we'll go to bed."

Travis didn't respond right away. Instead, he lowered his gaze and chewed his lips. The room was so quiet I heard my pulse throb inside my head. When Travis finally spoke, he kept his gaze fixed on his lap.

"That's fine, Andy. Let's do it."

AFTER I'D LIT the candle on my bedroom bureau, I killed the overhead fixture. We undressed in the semi-darkness, tossing our discarded clothing into my laundry hamper. Travis seemed to hesitate before he slipped his thumbs inside the waistband of his briefs. But then he peeled them to his ankles and kicked them aside. Already he had stiffened. His pubic bush was dark like the hair on his head.

I grew stiff as well.

I extended a hand toward Travis. He came to me and I wrapped my arms around his waist. He gathered his arms about my neck, laid his chin on my shoulder. Our hips met. His skin felt warm, and I savored his sour scent. I kissed his cheek, nuzzled his ear.

"You're trembling," I said. "Why?"

"'Cause I'm a chickenshit."

I kissed his neck, beneath his ear. "I won't hurt you. And I won't ask you for anything you don't want to give, understand?"

We stood there in candlelight, holding each other and swaying a bit. Then Travis spoke. "I've wanted this for a long time, ever since that first day you came to the track to run with us. Remember?"

"Sure I do."

"Since then, I kept on asking myself, 'Why can't *you* have the courage Andy has? If he can do it, why can't you?'"

"I'm not so brave," I said. "Life's actually easier, once you're out of the closet. All the fear just sort of...evaporates."

Travis cleared his throat. "Like I said at the water tower, don't expect too much from me. I've never done much besides jerk off."

I nibbled Travis's earlobe. Then I said, "That kid in Myrtle Beach, was he your boyfriend?"

Travis blew air out his nose. "Not even close. We just fooled around, a one-time thing. After that he never spoke to me again."

"Jesus..."

"Do you know how many nights I've knelt beside my mattress and prayed to God, asking him to make me straight? I actually believed distance running might help me ignore my attraction to men. You know: the energy release and all. But then you started running with us, and my urges only grew each time I saw you."

I shook my head, thinking of all those nights I'd lain in bed, thinking of Travis. All that time, he'd thought of me the same way.

"Why didn't you tell me?" I said.

"Because I had so much to lose, and I still do. Once I make that leap—once I declare myself gay—I'll lose my family. I'll be an orphan, on my own completely."

"That's not true," I said. "You'll still have me."

Moments later, we stood in my shower. Warm water pounded Travis's shoulders while I worked up lather with soap and a washcloth. I knelt before him and commenced scrubbing his feet.

"That feels nice," he said. "For once, someone's washing *my* toes."

"Didn't Jesus clean his disciples' feet once?"

"He did, just before the Last Supper, to express his love for them."

I scrubbed the fronts of Travis's furry calves and his smooth thighs. Water gurgled in the drain as I worked. Our voices echoed off the shower's tiled walls.

"Turn around," I told him.

After he did, I scrubbed the backsides of his legs. His buttocks were compact and rounded, and a dark stripe of hair grew in the cleft between them. I re-soaped the washcloth and worked it between his cheeks, nudging his pucker in the process. He flinched, but did not pull my hand away. Instead he asked a question.

"What's it like, getting penetrated by a man?"

I had to think for a moment, before I answered. "There's pain involved at first—you have to learn to relax—but having a guy inside me is...transforming. I feel his presence, not just down below but in every part of my body."

I rose to scrub Travis's back, his shoulders, and then his nape.

"That feels great," he said. "No one's bathed me like this since I was little."

I chuckled, and then I patted his firm rump. "I'll do this anytime you like. Now, turn around."

I scrubbed his chest and belly. Then I had him lift his arms, so I could wash his dark armpits. His hair lay plastered to his skull and water beaded on his nose and cheeks. He looked so beautiful I couldn't help myself. I seized the back of his neck and brought his mouth to mine.

He didn't resist.

Our lips met, and then we tongue kissed while our chin stubble rasped. When I reached between his thighs to caress him, he groaned deep in his throat. I pulled my mouth from his, and then I looked him in the eye.

"Is oral sex enough for now?"

A little smile crept onto his lips. "It's fine, Andy. You lead the way."

I knelt before him on the tub's porcelain floor—not the softest surface but it would serve. Then I took him into my mouth.

Travis groaned again. "That feels so good."

By now, air in the bathroom had grown steamy, as though a fog bank had rolled into Tallahassee. The whole scene—Travis and me together and naked, me on my knees tonguing his rigid flesh—had an otherworldly feel to it.

Travis rested his hands on my shoulders; he rocked his hips, picking up my rhythm. He plunged until a shudder ran through his body. His chest heaved, and then a wail escaped from his throat. I swallowed every drop of his seed as though it were something sacred. To me, in fact, it was. I had taken his life force inside my own body, and now Travis was a part of me.

I ran my hands up and down the backs of his legs. The dark hair on his calves gave way to the smoothness of his thighs. Distance running had hardened every muscle beneath his waist. His legs felt as though they'd been carved from marble.

"Andy?"

I looked up and raised my eyebrows.

"That was amazing," he said, "but what about you?"

Moments later, Travis knelt before me like a supplicant.

I stroked myself, using soap as lube, while the shower drummed my back. I savored Travis's androgynous beauty: his upturned nose, full lips, and thick eyebrows, his blue-green eyes and sooty lashes. When I came, my body jerked like someone had nudged me with a cattle prod. My semen flew everywhere.

Travis's gaze met mine while I caught my breath. And then we both smiled at each other.

WE SLEPT TOGETHER spoon-style, with Travis's back pressed to my chest and my arm wrapped about his slender waist. I fell asleep moments after we hit the mattress, right after our shower. I felt exhausted by all that had happened that day.

When I woke, early morning sunshine poured into the bedroom through the eastern windows and a scent of pine needles wafted through the screens. In a nearby tree, a squirrel barked. I checked the clock on the nightstand. *Shit*. I was due at Capital City in an hour.

Travis had changed position during the night. His cheek rested on my sternum, his arm draped my waist, and one of his legs crossed over one of mine. I studied the contours of his face while his breath swept my skin. Sunlight reflected in his dark hair; it fanned out across my chest and his shoulder. We lay beneath a thin cotton bedsheet. On the windowsill, my box fan hummed, fluttering leaves on a corn plant in one corner of the room.

I found myself wondering whether the previous night's events had truly occurred. Had it all been a dream? But Travis was here, in my bed. I felt the warmth of his skin, listened to his soft snoring, watched the rise and fall of his chest. His pulse throbbed in his temple that lay upon my chest.

It's real. He's here.

Now, it's your job to make sure he stays for good.

I smooched the crown of Travis's head—his hair smelled like rainwater—and then I spoke in a whisper.

"Time to wake up."

Travis chugged his knees. His eyelids fluttered open, and then he yawned.

"Hey, Andy."

"Good morning," I said. "How'd you sleep?"

He kissed my chest. Then he returned his cheek to my sternum. "Better than I have in years. Why is that? Because your bed's more comfortable than mine?"

I chuckled deep in my throat. "I think you know."

Twenty-Two

A FEW DAYS after Travis moved in with me, Biff Schultz phoned.

"How's the love nest?" he asked. "Are you two cocksuckers getting along?"

"Everything's fine," I said. "I'm not a fatalist, but I think Travis and I are meant to be together; it just took us a while to get here."

Biff snorted. "You know, you have *me* to thank for all this."

I crinkled my forehead. "How so?"

"Remember when I first asked you to run with us? It wasn't long after your Anita Bryant thing."

"Sure, I remember."

"Well, once I learned you were queer, I knew you'd be perfect for Travis."

"What?"

Biff hissed. "Hunsinger, sometimes you're *so* dense. Why do you think I invited you to the track?"

IT SEEMED TRAVIS'S relationship with his family, following their Labor Day blowup, wasn't quite as dire as he'd thought. Days after he moved in with me, his mother sent him a check to cover Travis's fall quarter expenses.

"Your father doesn't know about this," she wrote, "and let's keep it that way until he cools down. He still loves you. Give him time, and he'll come around."

"Good old Mom," Travis said, shaking his head.

"I don't understand," I said. "Where did she get the money?"

Travis shrugged. "Her grandparents left her a small trust fund; it's hers to spend as she pleases."

So, Travis studied his pre-med courses while I faced the challenge of law school. Each weekday morning, Travis and I showered and shaved.

We packed brown bag lunches and shared a hasty breakfast. We kissed each other goodbye, and then we were off to school on our bikes.

Chilly weather came early that year. The morning air reddened our cheeks as we pedaled through neighborhoods where smoke rose from chimneys. We both wore flannel shirts and blue jeans, and yet we rarely broke a sweat on our journeys toward campus. I hated the moment when I turned west onto Call Street and Travis continued northward toward FSU's main campus. We always waved goodbye. Travis might blow me a kiss, and then a lonely feeling would wash over me, as though I'd lost something special.

Travis's clothing and shoes occupied my bureau and closet. His underwear and socks commingled with mine in a drawer. His collection of plants gave the apartment a jungle-like appearance. On shelving we'd created with concrete blocks and plywood, Travis's multitude of biology books stood next to my law texts.

Okay, the place was overcrowded, but I didn't care. I wasn't alone anymore.

Each afternoon, before we prepared dinner, we made love in my bed, and our passion for each other seemed unlike any I'd experienced before. I found Travis sensual in a way I hadn't found Jeff, Dexter, or even Aaron to be. Just kissing Travis seemed like a visit to a deeply erotic place.

Of course, we had our issues.

Travis was a nervous sleeper; he thrashed about between the sheets; he talked gibberish that often woke me, and then I'd lie awake for an hour or more, staring at the ceiling. He also had a habit of drinking from a glass of water and then leaving the half-empty glass wherever he'd set it down.

One afternoon, I collected *eight* glasses from various places in our apartment: the top of the toilet tank, the nightstand, Travis's desk, and so on. Afterward, when I confronted him about the situation, he only shrugged.

"It's important to stay hydrated," he told me.

But these were small quirks of his personality I could easily overlook. His pluses, as they say, far outweighed his minuses.

Every Sunday morning before he left for church, Travis washed my feet in our little bathroom, using the basin, the lavender-scented soap, and the fluffy towel he'd used when ministering to Biff and Austin. And every evening before joining me in bed, he knelt on the floor to pray, bathed in the glow from a candle he kept on our dresser. Travis kept a King James Bible in our bedroom, and most every day, he read from it for an hour or so.

I, of course, did not attend church with Travis, nor did I join him in prayer. I tried to respect his religious beliefs, and he tried to accept my lack of faith. We had an unspoken understanding between us: we would not let our divergent views on religious matters interfere with the love we felt for each other.

We dealt with sexual issues, too. At first Travis resisted anal intercourse. "It seems unnatural," he told me. But finally, he acceded. I let him take me on my back with my legs slung over his shoulders. He had never looked as beautiful as he did right then: his brow sweaty, his dark hair fluttering over his shoulders, his mouth agape while he thrust inside me. Every muscle in his upper body was visible under his skin.

When it was over, Travis whispered in my ear, "That was incredible, Andy."

And all I could think was, *Incredible's an understatement.*

Then, one afternoon in late September, while we made love in our bedroom, Travis stroked my cheek with his thumb. He whispered so quietly I barely heard him over the din of traffic passing on Franklin Street.

"I shouldn't always be on top, Andy. I think it's time I felt you inside *me.*"

What followed was the most memorable sexual experience of my life, eclipsing even my first time with Jeff Dellinger. I will never forget the details. Afternoon sunshine slanted into the bedroom, casting bars of light onto Travis's fair skin. Veins in Travis's neck swelled, and then his jaw clenched when I entered him. The scents of sex and our sweat filled the room. Travis's cries bounced off the bedroom walls while I thrust inside him. More than once, he called my name—and then Jesus', too— when he came. My orgasm shook my body like I'd been shot with a stun gun. My vision blurred and my chest heaved. I shouted like a lunatic, and then I collapsed on top of Travis: sweaty, spent, and thoroughly satiated.

As each day passed, I grew more comfortable with Travis's presence in my life. Beneath his stony exterior dwelled a gentle soul who'd suffered greatly, who needed my love and attention—as much as I could give—and I didn't hold back. We spent most of our evenings on our living room sofa, studying in our underwear. Travis lay with his head in my lap, and every so often, I ran a hand through his hair; I stroked the hairs on the back of his forearm, or sometimes I raised his hand to my lips and kissed his knuckles.

Living with Travis and knowing he was there for me each day brought *wholeness* to my life, a kind I had never experienced before. Finally, I belonged to someone and he belonged to me. Despite his peculiarities and the differences in our worldviews, we fit together as well as any two people could, I thought.

For me, Travis became the missing piece in the jigsaw puzzle of my life.

Each weekday, I arrived home a little past 5:00 p.m. for my daily lovemaking session with Travis. This was our special time. We'd lock the front door and wouldn't let anything interrupt us, not the phone, not people knocking. As weeks passed, Travis seemed to become more comfortable with himself and our life together. When I introduced him to Fergal as "my boyfriend," Travis didn't even blush. He looked Fergal in the eye and shook Fergal's hand.

"I hope we'll be friends," he told Fergal.

Fergal gazed at me, then Travis. "If Andy likes you, mate, I'm sure I will, too."

On a Sunday night, after much coaxing on my part, Travis attended a Gay Rap Group session with me. While there, he rarely spoke unless someone asked him a question, and the same held true when we visited the Pastime Tavern after the meeting. He cracked peanuts or sipped from his beer glass, just listening to other guys talk. Afterward, while we drove home in my Vega, I stopped at a red light. Then I turned toward Travis.

"You certainly were quiet tonight. How come?"

Travis pulled a handful of hair from his forehead, tucked it behind an ear. "This is all new to me, appearing in public as your boyfriend, declaring myself as gay to people I don't know. It'll take me a while to adjust, I guess."

"Am I pushing you too fast? Am I making you uncomfortable?"

He shook his head. "On the contrary, you're far too easy on me." Then he placed a hand on the back of my neck and squeezed.

"That's why I love you, Andy."

Chapter Twenty-Three

ON A SATURDAY night in late October, we gathered in a circle about a campfire: Travis and I; Biff Schultz and his girlfriend, Carol; Fergal and his girl, Gina. Jerry Justus joined us as well; he was now a first-year student at Tallahassee Community College. We had pitched four tents among the dunes at St. George Island State Park.

The weather was unusually warm. We all wore shorts and T-shirts, excepting Biff, who strode about the campsite naked with his cock wobbling and his ass cheeks twitching. We passed a jug of cheap Chablis—the kind that burns the back of your throat on the first swallow—and each of us took swigs. Already, my brain had fuzzed and my limbs were relaxed.

How good it felt to escape the world of case law, statutes, and the rules of court procedure.

The terrain around me looked much as it had two hundred years before: pristine and unsullied by civilization. Above us, stars twinkled in the night sky; they looked like loose diamonds scattered across a jeweler's cloth. To the east, a fingernail moon rose. Waves smacked the shore, making slushy noises. A light breeze stirred an expanse of sea oats; they grew among the dunes, looking much like a wheat field.

Travis and I sat on a straw mat with our arms around each other's shoulders. Firelight reflected in Travis's blue-green eyes. Because he hadn't shaved in a few days, stubble blued his chin and cheeks.

My thoughts turned to a moment only a half hour before when Travis had tuned his guitar. We sang a duet, Travis and I, the same we'd performed in Biff's backyard so many months before: the Beatles' song, "Blackbird." I sang the melody, Travis the harmony, and our sweet sound resonated off nearby dunes.

While we sang, the fire's glow illuminated my friends' faces; the flames reflected in their eyes while they listened to the words we sang.

Our moment had arrived—Travis's and mine—and I think if Dr. Seuss had seen us just then he would have been proud of us.

I truly do.

About the Author

Jere' M. Fishback is a former journalist and trial lawyer. He lives on a barrier island on Florida's Gulf Coast.

Website: http://www.jeremfishback.com

Also by Jere' M. Fishback

Tyler Buckspan
Kevin Corrigan and Me

Recently Released from Jere' M. Fishback

Tyler Buckspan

Fifteen-year-old Tyler Buckspan lives with his mom and grandmother in 1960s Cassadaga, a Florida community where spiritual "mediums" ply their trade. The mediums—Tyler's grandmother among them—read palms and tarot cards, conduct séances, and speak with the dead. Tyler's a loner, a bookish boy with few interests, until his half-brother, Devin, nineteen and a convicted arsonist, comes to live in Tyler's home.

For years, Tyler has ignored his attraction to other boys. But with Devin in the house, Tyler can't deny his urges any longer. He falls hopelessly in love with his miscreant half-brother, and with the sport of basketball, once Devin teaches Tyler the finer points of the game. In a time when love between men was forbidden, even criminalized, can Tyler find the love he needs from another boy? And is Devin a person to be trusted? Is he truly clairvoyant, or simply a con artist playing Tyler and others for fools? What does Devin really know about a local murder? And can Tyler trust his own psychic twinges?

Also Available from NineStar Press

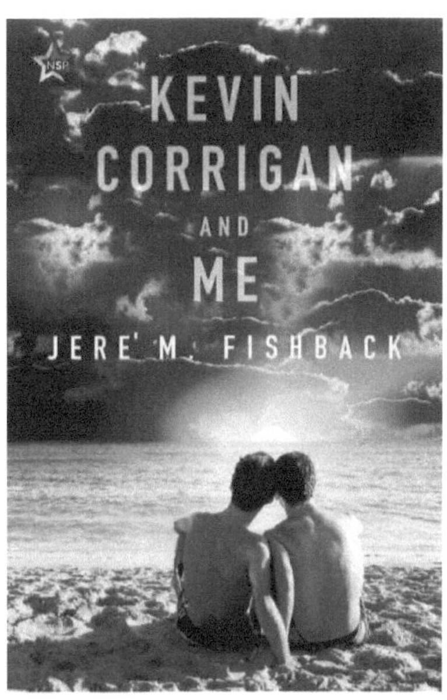

www.ninestarpress.com